I0557237

NOT ANGELS BUT ANGELS

Nino Hoti

This book is a work of fiction. Any references to historical events, real places, or real people are used fictitiously. Other names, characters, places, and events are products of the author's imagination, and any resemblance to actual events or places or people, living or dead, is entirely coincidental.

Copyright © 2024 by Nino Hoti

All rights reserved. Printed in the United States of America.

No part of this book may be reproduced in any manner whatsoever without written permission.

Cover design by Onur B.

MEADOW BROOK PUBLISHING
D-Mecca (Detroit)

For the Yugoslav Partisans

"I bomb atomically, Socrates' philosophies and hypotheses
Can't define how I be dropping these mockeries
Lyrically perform armed robbery
Flee with the lottery, possibly they spotted me—
Battle-scarred shogun, explosion when my pen hits tremendous
Ultraviolet shine blind forensics…"

— Inspectah Deck (Wu-Tang Clan), "Triumph"

"I dream of a language whose words, like fists, would fracture jaws."

— Emil Cioran, *The New Gods*

"O Allah, I do not worship You because I lust Heaven or fear Hell. I worship You because You deserve to be worshipped."

— Imam Ali

PART I

Paradise

BENNETT: Wouldn't it be wonderful if Communism were true?
JUDD: It is true.
BENNETT: What, "Heaven on Earth"?
JUDD: No. Earth on Earth.

— Julian Mitchell, *Another Country*

CHAPTER ONE

In the autumn of 2003, about six months after the inauguration of the Iraq War, I began my sophomore year at Magnolia Academy, an all-boys Catholic school located on a leafy campus in Poughkeepsie, New York. I didn't bother to look into the school's history until earlier that summer when I came across a book at the public library chronicling Magnolia's history.

Originally called St. Paul's, the school was later renamed Magnolia Academy. Legend has it that the school's first headmaster, Augustus Todd—a Georgia-bred Southern Baptist who, in his later years, had converted to Catholicism—renamed the school after having heard Billie Holiday's "Strange Fruit." The song's lyrics ("Scent of magnolia, sweet and fresh, then the sudden smell of burning flesh") reportedly affected him so deeply that he began to weep. Augustus Todd, it should be noted, was rumored to have once been a member of the Ku Klux Klan during its heyday in the mid-1920s. I imagine he chose to rename the school as a way to escape the guilt of his shameful past and, in the process, redeem himself.

A month before the start of school, the sophomores were assigned a chapel partner. Simon, a fifth-grader with tousled brown hair and a dopey face, was my chapel partner. I'd first met him during orientation week, which was held on campus in August. Simon wasted no time in adopting the role of Sancho Panza, following me around campus all week as if he were my personal page boy.

My class schedule that school year consisted of the following: geometry, history, American literature, biology, and theatre. I was most excited about my history class, since I'd spent much of the summer devouring history books, everything from the Byzantine Empire to the Ming dynasty. I even decided that I was going to become a medieval historian, specializing in the Crusades. Little did I know, however, that walking into that history class, aged fifteen and still unworldly, would change my life forever.

———————

I sat at the front of the class in a room of twenty boys, all of them dressed in school uniform: khaki pants, light blue shirt, red and gold tie, and navy blue blazer, with the school insignia (a lion standing atop the Christian cross) on the breast pocket. Most of the boys wore either dress shoes or boat shoes, while I wore a pair of casual slip-ons, since I never learned how to properly tie my shoelaces.

As we sat in our seats, waiting for the history teacher to arrive, in walked an olive-skinned boy with pleasant, cherubic features and almond-shaped eyes. The moment I saw him, my insides went into a kind of burning frenzy, as if heroin had been injected into my loins. I watched in hushed reverence as the boy, who had a keffiyeh wrapped around his head like a Moorish prince, walked past me, his body emanating a rich scent of cinnamon and clove, and took a seat in the back of the classroom. The wonderful scent hit me so hard that I momentarily experienced an intense feeling of ecstasy that, I imagine, only a select few mystics and saints have ever experienced.

While staring at the boy, he suddenly caught my gaze and shot me a playful scowl. I quickly looked away, sickened with fear, realizing that I was not only enamored with him but also terrified of him. I don't mean the kind of fear that one has of monsters and such; rather, it was the kind of fear that one has of the power of the universe.

The history teacher, Mr. Van Orton, a grossly slender man in his late twenties with platinum blond hair, entered the room, carrying a satchel. He wore black pants and a white linen dress shirt with the sleeves rolled up. Although I never had him as a teacher before, I immediately recognized him due to his striking hair, which made him stand out among the other teachers.

Van Orton put his satchel down on the floor near his desk, then went to the chalkboard and wrote the following: "Were the Dark Ages a time of ignorance for all civilizations?" He then turned to the class, chalk in hand. "Anybody have an answer?" he asked.

Nobody raised their hand for a while, until finally, the boy sitting next to me slowly raised his hand.

"Go ahead," Van Orton told him.

The boy, a bit nervous, cleared his throat. "Well, um…I—I think everybody was ignorant during that time, sir."

"You don't have to call me 'sir' like I'm Sidney Poitier. 'Mr. Van Orton' will do. But I'm afraid your answer isn't quite right. Still, good effort."

The olive-skinned boy, or rather "the prince," as I had nicknamed him, suddenly raised his hand. Van Orton nodded to him.

"The Dark Ages refers only to the time period from the fifth century to the tenth century in Europe," the prince said, in a honeyed voice. "And not everybody was as ignorant as the Europeans during the so-called 'Dark Ages.' It was during that time that the Islamic Golden Age began, which would later give birth to the Italian Renaissance and the Scientific Revolution."

"And what do you know about the Islamic Golden Age?" Van Orton asked, as if playfully challenging him.

"I know that Muslims during that time were making monumental contributions to the arts and sciences," the prince replied, his voice rising, "while most Europeans were still illiterate and had no understanding of basic fucking hygiene."

Some of the students gasped upon hearing the prince utter the obscenity, while an amused Van Orton gazed at him, intrigued. He then asked the prince, "What's your name?"

"Jeremiah," he replied.

"And your last name?"

"Kateb."

Van Orton looked curious. "Is 'Kateb' an Iranian surname, by any chance?"

"No—Algerian."

"Were you *born* in Algeria?"

Jeremiah nodded.

"I take it you can speak Arabic, then?" Van Orton said.

"Yeah, I grew up speaking Arabic and French. I learned English a bit later."

Van Orton chuckled in delight. "Well…that's certainly impressive. Don't tell me you can also read and write in all three languages, too."

Jeremiah grinned and replied, "I think you'd be surprised just how easily I can get through a Molière satire."

An entranced Van Orton stared at him as if analyzing him. This lasted for what felt like an uncomfortable amount of time. He eventually turned his attention to the rest of the class and, with his hands stuffed into his pants pockets, walked toward the front of the class. "Now, I'm sure every teacher in this school thinks that the subject *they* teach is the most important subject in the world," he told us. "I know your math teacher couldn't care less about history, just like I couldn't care less about math. Your science teacher believes that studying our galaxy is the greatest pleasure known to man, while your art teacher believes that art is the sole purpose of existence. Although, in your art teacher's defense, when the Allies entered Nazi Germany, they were far more concerned with saving European art than European Jews, so perhaps your art teacher has a point."

Van Orton paused and looked at the class with a soft smile, as if having heard a joke that was audible only to him. "I know that some of you," he continued, "or rather *most* of you, I should say, don't care in the least about history. You look at me and all you see is an overpaid babysitter with a college degree. And yet…you'll continue to attend my class, because I hold the golden key to your future. However, after I've given you your desired grade and you eventually leave this fine school, I'll be forced to relinquish my power over you. Meanwhile, you'll dive headfirst into the brutal world of capitalism, dragging yourselves naked across Wall Street. But until that day arrives, gentlemen, just remember that you belong to *me*." Van Orton took his hands out of his pockets, revealing a piece of chalk in one hand. He dropped the chalk onto the floor and pulverized it into the wooden floorboards in one swift stomp.

I recoiled, as did most of the other students, who looked at Van Orton in dumb amazement, probably wondering what the hell they'd gotten themselves into with this teacher.

"On a lighter note," Van Orton said, walking around the classroom, "Dr. Jeunet has given me permission to start a film studies club. You're all more than welcome to join the club, cinephile or not. We'll be meeting in the school auditorium every Thursday after school, where I'll screen a movie of my choosing. This week I'll be screening Stanley Kubrick's *2001: A Space Odyssey*. An oldie but a goodie."

Van Orton stopped next to Jeremiah and looked at him with a smirk. "Are you a cinephile at all, Mr. Kateb?"

"I think so," he replied. "And I like Kubrick a lot."

"Oh? Which other directors do you like?"

"Too many to name, but…Orson Welles, Ingmar Bergman, Paul Thomas Anderson, Spike Lee." Jeremiah paused briefly. "I like Charlie Chaplin, too."

Van Orton looked amazed. "It's good to know that your generation hasn't completely given up on silent cinema." He looked around the room. "Any other cinephiles among us?"

I hesitated before finally raising my hand.

"And what's your name?" Van Orton asked, walking toward me.

"Sean Quell," I said.

"Which films or directors do *you* like, Mr. Quell? Let's see if you can match Pauline Kael over there," Van Orton quipped, looking in Jeremiah's direction.

I tried to think of the most pretentious film director I knew. "I, uh…I like Jean-Luc Godard. His movies are really cool."

"Oh! I like Godard too," Van Orton said with a smile, which made me feel as if I'd won a victory over Jeremiah. "When discussing the impact of the French New Wave, Godard was quoted as saying, 'We barged into the cinema like cavemen into the Versailles of Louis XIV.' Beautifully stated."

"The *fifteenth*!" Jeremiah interjected.

Van Orton turned to him. "What's that, now?"

"Godard said Louis XV," Jeremiah corrected him, "not Louis XIV." He smiled and added, "You got the wrong Louis."

Van Orton, stupefied, looked at him for a moment. "It seems I did. How embarrassing for a history teacher." He turned around and, walking back to his desk, said to the class, "Please take out your textbooks, gentlemen, and turn to page five."

It seemed that my victory over Jeremiah was short-lived. All I could do was bite my thumb like a child and seethe. Then, after taking out my textbook and staring mindlessly at the cover for a while, I turned around so I could steal a glance at Jeremiah. I pretended to look out the windows behind him, and I saw the Sun as it broke through the autumn clouds, illuminating the room and creating a slanted halo over Jeremiah's head.

All the sophomores were required to attend chapel after lunch hour, accompanied by their chapel partners. Simon and I sat a few rows behind Jeremiah, who didn't appear to have a chapel partner. Father Hawkins, a rotund elderly man who must've been a Grand Inquisitor in a previous life, performed the introductory rites, assisted by a group of altar boys. When it came time for the altar boys to bow and kiss Father Hawkins' pudgy hand, I looked away in repulsion and, as I had done so many times before, examined the chapel, whose architecture captivated me.

The Gothic style chapel, which resembled a mini-cathedral, was located in a wooded area on campus and was surrounded by sycamore trees, each one drooping with green leaves. The inside of the chapel featured a frescoed ceiling depicting biblical scenes, as well as a Caravaggio painting depicting the crucifixion of Saint Peter that hung off to the side.

I stared at the Caravaggio painting, which I found strangely hypnotic, as if beckoning me to join Saint Peter on the inverted cross. Sitting in a chair near the edge of the altar was the school's long-time headmaster, Dr. Marc Jeunet, dressed smartly in a bowler hat and thick overcoat, with a monocle over his right eye. Jeunet, who stood under five feet and whose resemblance to Henri de Toulouse-Lautrec was uncanny, held an ivory-handled walking stick in his left hand as if it were a scepter.

Simon turned to me and whispered, "Do you like your classes this year?"

I was too engrossed in the Caravaggio painting to respond. Simon nudged me, and I finally turned to him. "What…? I mean—yeah, sure, I like my classes."

"Me too. I have music this year, and we get to play guitar. It's classical guitar, not electric, but it's still cool."

I nodded and turned my attention to Jeremiah, staring at the back of his head with the focus of a Tibetan monk, as if trying to read his thoughts.

"Do you want to come over to my house after school?" Simon asked me.

"Um…not today," I replied, still looking at Jeremiah. I turned back to Simon, who looked disappointed. I felt bad, so I told him, "If you want to get something to eat, we can go to Blondie's after school, OK?"

Simon's face lit up. "Yeah!"

Father Hawkins was at the pulpit, facing the congregation. Behind him hung a banner that read: "SPACE IS GOD, MATTER IS CHRIST, TIME IS THE HOLY GHOST." He appeared a little flustered, as if something unpleasant had happened to him just moments before reaching the pulpit. Then again, he always wore an expression of deep agitation.

"It was exactly two years ago," Father Hawkins began his sermon, "when the enemies of Christ carried out the shocking attacks on 9/11. I still weep when I think about that sad day—a day which has no equal, except when the vile Ottoman Turks conquered Constantinople in 1453. Both days haunt my dreams. We must never forget the days when Christianity was put in grave danger, for those are the days that truly define us as Christians. We must become like Saint Michael and defend Christendom at all costs, even if it means taking up arms against the mullahs, just as Saint Michael had done in the War in Heaven against Satan and his wretched army of fallen angels. But now it appears that Satan has moved his army to Iraq," Father Hawkins howled, becoming more animated, "where the long-awaited Tenth Crusade, which will undoubtedly be the bloodiest battle of all, has been launched!"

Jeunet, walking stick in hand, got up from his chair and walked toward Father Hawkins, who continued to howl like a rabid dog, his arms swinging wildly.

"With backing from our Christian brethren, the United Kingdom, we will expunge the vile infidels—the savages who disguise themselves as men of God, when in reality they worship Satan himself!"

Jeunet, forcing a smile, placed a gentle hand on Father Hawkins' shoulder and ushered him away from the pulpit, as if the old cleric had gone senile. Father Hawkins, now subdued, sat on a cushioned bench next to the altar boys, while Jeunet, standing at the pulpit with an unexpectedly solemn expression, looked at the congregation. He cleared his throat before speaking in a French accent so thick that one would think he was doing an impression of Inspector Clouseau.

"Although you boys attend one of the finest schools in New York, Magnolia Academy is by no means an unblemished school. We have our faults just like any other educational institution. In fact, during my first year as headmaster, some of the students at the school started a nasty rumor that I had met my Filipino wife of twenty years at a whorehouse in the Philippines. How *repugnant*! But such is the world we live in, smoldering with scorn and fury. The first thing we do now when we awake in the morning is ask ourselves, 'What new hell exists today?' If you listen closely, you can hear Nero playing the fiddle, while his beloved Rome burns. To be an honorable man in today's world is like herding sheep with your elbows. From Venice to Xanadu, the world is amiss and in desperate need of aid. But, then again, I have yet to visit the Virgin Islands."

Jeunet smiled faintly, although nobody else appeared amused, least of all Father Hawkins, who looked baffled.

"In any case," Jeunet continued, "we must move onward, strive to better ourselves, and, in the words of Abraham Lincoln, hope to once again be touched by the better angels of our nature." He paused for a moment. "That is, if the angels are indeed still with us. At this point, I have great doubts."

Jeunet suddenly walked away and exited the chapel, while Father Hawkins, looking even more baffled, shook his head in bemusement.

I had to put my hand over my mouth to keep myself from laughing.

CHAPTER TWO

Simon and I sat in a booth at Blondie's, a retro-themed diner that looked like a downsized version of the Jack Rabbit Slim's restaurant from *Pulp Fiction*, featuring a toy race track that ran the entire perimeter of the eating area, dining booths that were made to look like classic cars, and old pinball machines. Movie posters for B-movies and musical acts from the mid-twentieth century covered the walls.

The diner even had its own mascot, an anthropomorphic white duck named Wolfgang von Strudel, who donned the garb of a scholar. Figurines and illustrations of the anthropomorphic duck could be seen all over the diner, including on cups and napkins.

I readjusted myself in my seat, a 1949 Ford, while Simon, sitting across from me, munched on his fried food. I'd only ordered a Coke and fries, since I didn't have much of an appetite. Simon looked at me and grinned as if to say, "Thanks." He was a good kid, and smart for his age. I smiled back, then turned and stared at a poster on the wall of a young Elvis Presley in a pink suit.

"Can you believe he got away with wearing a pink suit in the Fifties?" I said.

Simon turned and looked at the Elvis poster, then turned back to me. "What's wrong with wearing a pink suit?" he asked, puzzled.

"Nothing, in my opinion," I replied. "But I can't imagine what the people back then thought about it. If I wore a pink suit *today*, I'd be afraid that people would stone me."

"Why would anybody do that?"

"I have no clue," I said, after a pause. "Anyway...tell me about your music class. You said you get to play guitar?"

"Yeah, every student gets his own guitar. But you have to sit down when you play it, which makes it easier to play. Our teacher wants us to learn how to play an étude by the end of the month."

I just looked at Simon.

"Do you know what an 'étude' is?" he asked me, as if he could tell that I had no idea what the word meant.

I shook my head.

"It's like a short instrumental," Simon explained to me. "But it's a simple instrumental, so it's not that hard to learn how to play."

"Very cool," I said nonchalantly, and took a sip of my drink.

The Ronettes' "Be My Baby" began to play on the jukebox, when suddenly, looking over Simon's shoulder, I saw Jeremiah enter the diner, with a girl at his side. They seemed to be walking in slow motion as they made their way to a booth. Jeremiah was still wearing his school uniform, while the girl, who had fair skin and dark shoulder-length hair, was donning a tight black tank top and shorts, denim jacket, low-cut sneakers, and Ray-Ban sunglasses.

A hodgepodge of emotions began to stir within me: surprise, wonder, jealousy, resentment, euphoria. I watched as the couple took their seats in a Checker taxicab. The girl took off her jacket and sunglasses, while Jeremiah, sitting across from her, looked over the menu. I tried not to stare at them, but I couldn't help it. They looked like the coolest couple imaginable, like a contemporary Bonnie and Clyde, minus the bank robberies. A waitress came over to their booth and took their order, then left. Moments later, the waitress returned with their drinks, a Coke for Jeremiah and a vanilla milkshake for the girl, who looked at the milkshake as if it were a holy relic, before sipping on it through a straw.

"Hey," Simon said to me, snapping me out of my daze.

"Huh…?" I said, looking at him.

"I'm going to go play on the pinball machines for a while." Simon made a pouty face and added, "Please don't eat my food, OK?"

I smiled faintly. "Don't worry, I won't."

Simon took a quick sip of his drink, then got up and went to go play on the pinball machines in the back of the diner, while I turned my attention back to the divine couple sitting in the Checker taxicab. Jeremiah and I suddenly locked eyes as if by design, and then, after a moment, I sheepishly looked away. I waited a full minute before looking again in the couple's direction, with a smiling Jeremiah graciously waving me over and his girl turning to look at me. I thought maybe my eyes were deceiving me, or that I was experiencing a psychotic delusion. But no, Jeremiah *really* was waving me over to his booth, with his girl now staring at me with a curious expression.

I swallowed hard and waited a moment, not wanting to seem too eager. Then, after taking a sip of my drink, I got up and walked slowly toward Jeremiah's booth. When I reached the booth, half-smiling, I looked straight at Jeremiah, ignoring his girl, though I could feel her glaring at me with disapproval for not paying adequate attention to her.

"You can sit next to Mallory," Jeremiah told me. "She doesn't bite… from what I can tell."

Mallory, smiling crookedly, looked at me and said, "Only on occasion."

I sat down next to her. She was a beautiful girl, a little older than Jeremiah and me, though just about the same height as us. I felt a little intimidated sitting next to her because of the aura she gave off. It was a don't-fuck-with-me-or-I'll-eat-you-alive kind of aura that pretty girls with balls of steel possess, the kind of aura that would've scared off most boys, but not Jeremiah. It would've taken a lot more than sheer audacity to scare off someone like him.

"What's your name?" Mallory asked me.

"Sean," Jeremiah interjected on my behalf, sneering at Mallory. "And he's got much better taste in movies than you."

"Are you still giving me shit because I like *Romeo + Juliet* with Leonardo DiCaprio? You like it too, asshole."

"Yeah, but not because I want to sleep with DiCaprio like you do." Jeremiah turned to me and said, "Do you like that movie?"

"I—um…yeah, I like it. The guns are cool. And the Shakespeare dialogue is kind of neat."

"See?" Jeremiah said to Mallory. "He likes it for legitimate reasons, unlike you."

Mallory rolled her eyes. "Anyway," she said, turning to me, "judging from your clothes, I take it you go to Magnolia with Jeremiah, huh?"

"Yeah. We're actually in the same, uh…history class together."

"Are you going to join the film studies club?" Jeremiah asked me. "Dumb question. I know you are."

"Oh—definitely," I replied. "Are you?"

Jeremiah nodded and said, "Yeah. I'm sure I'll see you in the auditorium this week for the Kubrick movie. It's a good one."

"Yeah," I said, smiling like an imbecile, "I've seen it before."

"So…what do you think of the teacher?"

"Mr. Van Orton?"

Jeremiah nodded.

"Well…um…he seems fine, I guess. I've never seen a teacher with hair like that before. It looks almost white."

"Doesn't he remind you of the main villain from *Blade Runner*?"

"Yeah, I can kinda see it," I said, and began to laugh, as did Jeremiah. What a great feeling it was to share a laugh with him. It was as if I'd gained favor with a royal prince who would surely bless me with his friendship.

"I gotta use the bathroom," Jeremiah said suddenly, getting up. "Hold down the fort while I'm gone."

He left, while Mallory, who seemed to be sitting a bit closer to me than before, took a sip of her milkshake, then moaned in delight with her eyes closed. "Goddamn," she said, opening her eyes and turning to me. "I can't get enough of these malted milkshakes."

"Looks like it."

"You want to try it?" she asked.

"No, thanks," I replied.

"Are you sure? It's better than your average milkshake, I swear."

"I'll take your word for it."

Mallory shrugged and took another sip of her milkshake, though with less enthusiasm this time. After a while, I asked her, "How old are you?"

She laughed and wiped her mouth. "I knew that was coming. I'm seventeen."

"Wow, really?"

"You didn't have to add the 'wow.' Anyway, is it really that shocking?"

"No," I said, "I just…didn't think a sophomore would be going out with a seventeen-year-old. You guys *are* dating, right?"

Mallory nodded and then winked at me. That simple wink held more power than anything I could've mustered.

"Do you have a driver's license?" I asked her.

"A junior license," she said.

"What's that?"

"It's what they give to teens before they get the real thing," Mallory explained to me. "And yes, I have a car. See? I'm a big girl now. I can even go potty by myself and everything."

She had a good sense of humor, I had to admit.

"How did…?" I started to ask, then stopped, as if I didn't trust myself to ask her a question that wouldn't make me seem pathetically infantile. But she already knew what I was going to ask.

"How did Jeremiah and I meet?" Mallory said with a smirk.

I nodded timidly.

"We met earlier this year at a bookstore in Arlington. I was surprised when he approached me, because I didn't think someone younger than me would have the guts to just walk up to me. I thought it was kind of endearing, though, and we started talking about books and politics, and we really hit it off."

"Politics?" I said, as if I'd never heard the word before. I realized a moment too late how dumb I sounded.

Mallory chuckled and replied, "Yes, *politics*. Didn't you notice the little pin on Jeremiah's blazer?"

I shook my head. Mallory chuckled again and took a sip of her milkshake. Just then, as if on cue, Jeremiah returned and sat back down. I looked carefully at his blazer and noticed a hammer and sickle pin on the lapel. I turned to Mallory, who looked at me as if to say, "Well, now do you see?"

"Why are you two exchanging looks?" Jeremiah asked playfully.

"Oh, I was just telling Sean about how we met," Mallory said, "and he was shocked when I told him that we discussed politics during our first meeting. Maybe 'shocked' isn't the right word, but…definitely surprised." She turned to me with a sly grin. "You probably didn't think girls like me talked politics, did you?"

I responded with a pathetic chuckle.

"It's cool if politics isn't your thing," Jeremiah told me in an empathetic tone that put me at ease. He even smiled, or maybe that was just my imagination. "Shit, man, until three years ago, it wasn't *my* thing either. Then I went back to Algeria for a visit, and I talked to some locals who were members of the Workers' Party. Now here I am, a devoted Trotskyite," he said with a laugh. "Also, having a mom who used to work as a pharmacist, but now works as a housekeeper—that'll turn you into a Commie for sure."

Jeremiah's comical expression suddenly changed to anger. I wanted to ask him why he had left his home country and decided to settle in America, but for fear of upsetting him further, I just kept my mouth shut.

After a long pause, during which the music on the jukebox had switched from the Ronettes to surf rock, Mallory looked at Jeremiah's headdress and asked, rather curiously, "Did the students say anything to you about your headgear?"

"It's called a 'keffiyeh,' my adorable Yankee wench," Jeremiah replied. (Mallory stuck her tongue out at him.) "Besides, why the hell would anyone say anything to me about it?"

"Come on. Someone like you wearing *that* in America. I know we're not living in the butt-crack South, but you don't know how people are going to react."

"This is my fifth year at Magnolia, so I'm pretty sure the students have gotten used to my fashion sense by now."

"I like the headdress," I blurted out.

Jeremiah smiled a little and mouthed "Thanks," while Mallory turned to me with a mixture of confusion and mockery. It looked like she was about to say something, but she simply chuckled and shook her head, as if she somehow knew how I felt about Jeremiah. They say women are more intuitive than men, so it was definitely a possibility, and a frightening one at that.

"How long have you been going to Magnolia?" Jeremiah asked me.

"Um…since I was seven," I said. After a pause, I added, "I'm surprised I hadn't seen you on campus before."

Jeremiah shrugged. "It's a big school, you know, so it makes sense."

"He got a scholarship," Mallory interjected, smiling.

Jeremiah glared at her as if to say, "Why would you tell him that?" He then looked at me and explained: "My mom really wanted me to go to Magnolia…but she couldn't afford it, so she sent some poems I'd written a while back to Dr. Jeunet, and basically, that's how I ended up getting a scholarship. It sounds more impressive than it actually is."

"Don't be modest," Mallory said. "You're like a goddamn Rhodes Scholar. Most guys get into Magnolia the old-fashioned way, by having rich parents." She then turned to me with a slight sneer. "Is that how *you* got into the school?"

Embarrassed, I said nothing.

"Who cares how he got into the school?" Jeremiah said, looking at Mallory. "Anyway, you live in a McMansion with your Rockefeller family, so leave the kid alone. And I think it was *your* ancestors who gave the Native Americans smallpox blankets, wasn't it?"

Mallory reached over and grabbed his chin as if to push him, but she instead kissed him on the lips and told him, "Don't forget, I'm your ride home." Then she gave him a playful slap on the cheek, which angered me as much as the kiss.

"Hey," Jeremiah said suddenly, looking over my shoulder, "I think your friend over there is wondering why you'd left the Ford."

I turned around and saw Simon, now back in our booth, staring at me with puppy dog eyes, as if I'd abandoned him.

"That's Simon," I said, turning back around. "He's my chapel partner."

"I'm so glad I was able to talk my way out of having a chapel partner."

"How did you do that?" I asked.

"You know I speak French," Jeremiah said with a smirk, "and so does Dr. Jeunet, naturally. It's easy to convince a Frenchman when you talk to him in his native tongue."

I hesitated. "Can you say something in French?"

"I'm not a performing monkey," Jeremiah shot back, his face solemn.

Taken aback, I remained silent. All of a sudden, Jeremiah let out a spirited laugh and said, "*C'est vraiment dégueulasse.*"

"What does that mean?" I asked.

"It's really disgusting," he replied, his face solemn again.

I didn't know if he was translating, or if he was speaking candidly to me. Some things are better left unknown.

CHAPTER THREE

I was behind the wheel of a Checker taxicab, driving aimlessly around Toontown, an area of New York reserved for cartoon characters, with Wolfgang von Strudel as its mayor. I swerved to avoid an oncoming motorbike driven by Bugs Bunny, who gave me the middle finger as he sped past me. Simon, sitting in the passenger seat and wielding an old RCA camcorder, was recording Jeremiah and Mallory having sex in the backseat of the cab.

I turned to watch the couple have sex, bewildered at what I was seeing. Mallory looked at me and said, "Keep your eyes on the road, faggot," uttering the homophobic slur with such venom that it made me wince in dismay—and I turned back around.

"Yeah! Give it to her! Hell, yeah!" Simon shouted, cheering on Jeremiah while continuing to record the couple having sex.

More than confused, I was now terrified and felt as if I were on the verge of a panic attack.

"Sean," I heard Jeremiah say. "Hey, paisan!"

I turned to Jeremiah, who had a big smile on his face as he penetrated Mallory. "Once I'm done with her," he said, "do you want some of this?"

"That white boy can't handle *you*," Mallory interjected with a shriek of laughter. Then she looked at me and said, "I told you to keep your goddamn eyes on the road, you pussy!"

I turned back around, dizzy and short of breath. I couldn't see straight anymore, although I could make out what looked like an oncoming semi-truck. I floored the accelerator, determined to collide with the massive ten-wheeler. I gripped the steering wheel and thrust my body forward, anticipating the imminent collision with glee. I could hear Simon laughing, Mallory moaning, and Jeremiah panting, all of which galvanized me even further and justified our impending doom. The semi-truck honked its horn once I'd gotten into its lane, but

I ignored it. Just as we were about to collide, I woke up in a cold sweat, clutching my blanket like a frightened toddler. Trembling, I lay in bed for a while, not yet ready to face the world.

Fear then gave way to joy when I realized that it was Thursday, the first day of film studies club, which was set to be held in the school auditorium after school, where Jeremiah was sure to make an appearance. *He had better*, I thought, *or else what's the point of going?*

———————

Remnants of the awful dream, with its vitriol and debauchery, lingered in the corner of my mind as I went about my day. I wondered how I'd come to know "Toontown," despite never having visited that world before, but I soon shrugged it off as dream logic, which has its own rationale, as if in a parallel universe. Nevertheless, when I saw Jeremiah for the first time that day in our history class, I was afraid to make eye contact with him because I thought, foolishly, that he may have had the same dream as me.

The dream loosened its grip on me during chapel, as I listened to Father Hawkins deliver another one of his frenzied sermons about "defending Christendom," and was eventually replaced by a recurring memory from when I was in the sixth grade. I was taking a Biblical Literature class, with Father Hawkins as the teacher. One day in class, Father Hawkins told us the story of Lucifer and the War in Heaven, which, to a young boy, sounded like the most remarkable story ever. I was intrigued by Lucifer and his fall from grace, as he seemed more "human," or rather relatable, than God, who was too immaculate for my taste. Enthralled by this defiant figure, who went by multiple names (Lucifer, Satan, the Devil), I raised my hand and probed Father Hawkins for answers about him.

ME: Why did God cast out Lucifer?

HAWKINS: Because Satan was consumed with envy.

ME: But he was God's favorite angel. He just wanted to be great like God.

HAWKINS: Nobody can be greater than God. Satan doomed himself with his arrogance.

ME: What if Lucifer apologized? Would he be allowed back into Heaven?

HAWKINS: Not possible.

ME: Why not?

HAWKINS: Because he committed the ultimate sin—the sin of envy.

ME: Is it really that bad to envy someone?

HAWKINS: Not just "someone," but God Himself.

ME: What if *I* envied God?

HAWKINS: Then God would hate you just as much as He hates Satan.

ME: I like the name "Lucifer" better than "Satan."

HAWKINS: "Satan" is now his proper name!

ME: What about "the Devil"?

I was suspended for three days for being "confrontational" (that was how Father Hawkins had described my behavior to the headmaster) and, as penance, was told to recite ten Our Fathers and five Hail Marys. I recited none. Because of me, or so I believed, Father Hawkins amped up his rhetoric about Satan, the fallen angels, and the War in Heaven in his subsequent sermons and referenced one or all three so often that it became something like a tic.

————————

I arrived at the school auditorium before most of the students, although I figured not many people would actually join the film studies club. Less than a dozen, I predicted. Ten minutes later, the auditorium was filled with over thirty students, mostly sophomores, but also some juniors and seniors. Jeremiah arrived and took a seat in the middle of the auditorium, about three rows in front of me. I assumed he didn't see me, or else he would've sat next to me. We weren't exactly friends, but our conversation at Blondie's a few days prior made me think that he liked me, or at the very least, tolerated me. I would've settled for either, just so long as he didn't find me utterly repulsive or weird.

Van Orton, who had arrived at the auditorium soon after Jeremiah, tinkered with the image projector. Jeremiah suddenly got up and went over to him, and the two started chatting. I wondered what they were talking about, other than the movie that we were going to watch. It was difficult to hear what they were saying, since they were all the way in the back of the auditorium, but I could hear them laughing. I thought maybe Jeremiah was brown-nosing the teacher, but he didn't seem like the type. In fact, there was little about Jeremiah that said "ass-kisser." Even his school uniform was irregular. While most of the students wore cream-colored khakis, Jeremiah's khaki pants were dark brown and wrapped in black linen cloth from the ankle to the knee, which made it seem as if he were wearing military-style puttee.

After Jeremiah had gone back to his seat, Van Orton walked to the front of the auditorium and addressed the crowd, which had ballooned to some fifty students, including elementary and middle school-aged students. I suddenly felt guilty for not having invited Simon.

"Thank you all for being here today!" Van Orton bellowed, sweeping his hand across the auditorium as if he were a Roman emperor addressing a Colosseum-sized room. "On our first day of film studies club, we're going to be watching one of the most important and influential movies ever made, a movie that even the Vatican considers among the greatest of all time—and you can't get a better endorsement than the Pope. The movie is *2001: A Space Odyssey*, directed by Stanley Kubrick and released in 1968. The groundbreaking film touches upon many themes, from human evolution to artificial intelligence, and it's every bit as relevant today as it was when it first came out thirty-five years ago. Also, although the film moves at a glacial pace and is well over two hours long, I believe that even those of you who suffer from ADHD will be able to enjoy it."

Van Orton bowed in jest, then walked to the back of the auditorium, where he dimmed the lights and started the movie.

During the lengthy "Dawn of Man" sequence that opens the movie, which features a tribe of ape-men living in prehistoric Africa, I began to think about my childhood and how, even at age ten, I knew that I was different from other kids: sensitive, solemn, passionate, obsessive—although "passionate" and "obsessive" mean the same thing to me, more or less.

Age ten proved to be a significant time for me, as that was the age I came to the realization that I was gay. I even remember the exact day that it happened. It was a Friday in the early winter of 1998, and my parents had tickets to go see an opera.

I wasn't allowed to stay home alone yet, so I had a regular babysitter, Chloe, a freshman at the Emma Goldman School, a girls' preparatory school where my mother used to teach art. Chloe was always nice to me, and I enjoyed spending time with her, especially since I didn't have many friends. My father took an immediate and perverse liking to Chloe, ogling her whenever she came over to our house. My mother somehow never noticed my father's creepy ogling, but I imagine if she had, she would've castrated him.

After my parents had left for the opera, Chloe ordered pizza and we watched music videos on MTV. At one point, I got up to use the bath-room during a commercial break, but just as I was about to leave the room, I suddenly saw a face on TV that I'd never seen before. The face belonged to a young man with dirty blond hair and piercing eyes. His face rattled me in the most wonderful way and, for the first time in my life, I felt a thirst for another human being.

I watched in awe as images of the young man flashed across the screen in what was a trailer for an upcoming documentary about the young man.

"Who's that guy?" I asked Chloe.

"The guy in the trailer?" she said.

I nodded.

"Oh...that's River Phoenix," Chloe told me. "He was an actor who died a few years ago."

"He's *dead*?" I said in shock, as if I'd known the late actor all my life.

Chloe gave me a puzzled look. "Yeah. Why, what's wrong?"

From that moment on, it was as if a whole new world had opened up to me, just as it did to Columbus when he first stepped foot in the Americas. But unlike Columbus, I longed for neither gold nor spices. I only wished to be in the presence of someone with a face as beautiful as the one I'd seen on television—and maybe more. Yes, yes, I wanted something *more*. I wanted to feel and smell this special someone, to love as they love, to cry as they cry, to breathe as they breathe, and then, after years of living like Siamese twins, to die as they die, in jubilation.

———————

Just after the introduction of the *Discovery One* spacecraft and the sentient supercomputer HAL 9000, Jeremiah, who hadn't so much as moved an inch during the movie, rose to his feet as if to stretch, then exited the auditorium. I waited a few moments before doing the same, curious as to where Jeremiah was going. The thought that he might simply be going to the bathroom entered my mind as I stood in the hallway outside the auditorium, but no matter. I wanted a chance to talk to him again, even if it was in the bathroom. I was determined to become friends with him sooner than later.

I walked down the long hallway and turned a corner, where I spotted Jeremiah conversing with Van Orton, both of them smiling. I hid behind a wall and watched as Van Orton placed a hand on Jeremiah's shoulder, then leaned forward and either whispered something into his ear or kissed him on the cheek. I was too far away to tell which, but it made my stomach churn just the same. I went back to the auditorium and tried watching the movie, but all I could think about was Jeremiah and Van Orton, conversing, smiling, hand on the shoulder, a whisper—or a kiss.

Jeremiah returned to the auditorium about half an hour later, as did Van Orton, who, after the movie's psychedelic conclusion, walked to the front of the auditorium and addressed the crowd once again. The lights were still dimmed, but Van Orton had a spotlight on him as if he were going to put on a performance for the crowd.

"How's that for an ending? You're not going to see an ending like that anymore, let me tell you. Nowadays, movies have to be spelled out for audiences."

"Yeah, but what does it mean?" a boy asked. "I didn't understand the ending. Actually...I didn't understand most of it."

"That's because you're so used to watching movies that don't demand too much from their viewers that anything even remotely abstract baffles you," Van Orton told him. "Tossing you the tiniest bit of knowledge is like dropping an atomic bomb. Is that it, young man?"

The boy didn't respond. I felt kind of bad for him because I could imagine how embarrassed he must've felt. I hadn't known Van Orton to be an asshole—until that moment.

"The ending with the 'Star Child' might represent a rebirth," Jeremiah interjected. "Maybe the rebirth of...humanity."

"Interesting take," Van Orton said. "A far better explanation than 'I didn't understand.' In any case, if this movie has taught you anything, gentlemen, I hope it's that great cinema has existed long before you were born. I'm sure that comes as a surprising revelation to some of you. Contrary to what you may have heard, the Stone Age did not end thirty years ago, and *The Matrix* is not the greatest movie ever made... or whatever drivel your generation has anointed as the best movie of all time."

"*Fight Club!*" a boy shouted.

"*The Lord of the Rings!*" another shouted.

"No—*Shrek!*" a third boy shouted, eliciting laughter.

Van Orton, however, didn't find any of this amusing. He just stood there, glaring at the sea of young hormonal boys, although it wasn't exactly a "sea" anymore, since about fifteen boys had left during the movie.

"The greatest movie ever made is any Quentin Tarantino movie," a boy declared, with such unbridled confidence that he could only be a senior. Van Orton gestured to him with the wave of a hand, as if shooing him away.

"It was only a matter of time before someone brought up Mr. Tarantino," he said, shaking his head. "Because of him, everything today is ironic and postmodern and 'meta'—and all of *you* are living proof of that. Congratulations, gentlemen, you've reached the Promised Land."

Some of the boys snickered and laughed, while Van Orton, grimacing, put his hands in his pockets and stared at the boys. I suddenly felt the need to make my presence known, if for no other reason than to let Jeremiah know that I was in attendance.

"What about Godard?" I said to Van Orton in a near shout. He scanned the auditorium for the voice, and I raised my hand to let him know that it was me. When he spotted me, his grimace morphed into a smirk.

"Mr. Quell, nice to see you here. Now, what *about* our old friend Godard?"

"Well...before Tarantino, there was Godard, who was the first, um... postmodern director, wasn't he?"

Van Orton thought for a moment. "Some might say that. But Godard's postmodernism is pure, whereas Tarantino's brand of postmodernism is smug to the point of nausea."

"Why do you say that?" I asked.

"Because I'm right," Van Orton said, after a pause. He then turned his attention to the other students. "Once again, thank you all for being here today. For our next meeting, I'll be sure to pick a movie that's more to your 'liking.' I believe I still have a copy of *Debbie Does Dallas* somewhere at home. Good day, gentlemen." He walked away in a huff and exited the auditorium, kicking the door on his way out, which startled some of the students.

Although I was still unsure of what exactly I'd seen in the hallway earlier between Jeremiah and Van Orton—a whisper, a kiss, an illusion—I became convinced, after Van Orton had revealed himself to be a staunch traditionalist, that Jeremiah would never align himself with someone like that. Granted, I didn't know Jeremiah that well, but I knew he was a self-professed "Commie" and not part of the old guard.

I watched as Jeremiah got up and started to walk out of the auditorium. On his way out, he suddenly turned to me with a half-smile and winked, as if toying with me. The wink paralyzed me, and I remained in my seat until everyone had left the auditorium. Sitting alone in the silent, dimmed room, I thought about how instant and delirious my infatuation with Jeremiah was, like Saint Paul's conversion while on his way to Damascus. I knew that wasn't normal, even for a teenage boy. But what did "normal" mean in relation to *love*, if one could even call it that? No, this was more like a fervent obsession, as proven by the fact that I was willing to worship this boy until my knees gave out, despite only knowing him for a mere four days.

CHAPTER FOUR

I remained in a blissful daze for a week following "the wink" in the auditorium, as if I were being raptured or abducted by benevolent extraterrestrials. When Jeremiah's girlfriend had winked at me during our first meeting at Blondie's, it felt like a sly threat, a far cry from the overwhelming embrace I'd felt from Jeremiah's wink, which, though lasting half a second, I kept replaying in my head over and over again.

During that entire week of drunken bliss, I scrutinized everything Jeremiah did, believing that his every gesture, even a tilt of the head or a brush of the brow, was as worthy of analysis as the Zapruder film. I even followed him around campus, though always at a distance, so as not to be detected. I saw the campus as a playground, with Jeremiah as its prominent swing. As pathetic as it sounds, I felt honored walking the same grounds as him, as if he were royalty.

Even though Jeremiah and I shared the same alchemy of flesh and blood, I still viewed him as being above me, both physically and intellectually. I felt small and, at times, ashamed compared to him. I imagined him as a child reading Molière in French, while at the same time I was reading *Green Eggs and Ham*. It's a strange feeling—to both admire and envy someone—but that was the paradox I'd found myself in, a paradox that I was unaware existed until the second week of school (after the "blissful daze" had ceased), when Jeunet dropped by Van Orton's classroom just as we were reading aloud from the textbook. The boy who was reading stopped suddenly when he noticed Jeunet standing in the open doorway, observing the class. All the students, as well as Van Orton—who was standing at the front of the room, textbook in hand—turned to Jeunet.

"Don't mind me, gentlemen," he said cheerfully, then entered the room and turned to Van Orton. "*Monsieur* Van Orton, I hope you don't mind my unexpected intrusion."

"Not at all. You're always welcome here, Dr. Jeunet. We're currently learning about Spain after the *Reconquista*, in particular the policies of Queen Isabella and King Ferdinand."

"Possibly the most disastrous meeting of two individuals since Brutus and Cassius," Jeunet quipped. "I'm only teasing. The Catholic Monarchs had their uses."

"Yes, very much so," Van Orton said, rather sarcastically. "We were just reading about the 'wonderful' Alhambra Decree that was issued by the Monarchs soon after the fall of Granada." He looked at the boy who had read last. "Mr. Thompson, please continue reading—loud enough for all to hear."

The boy, anxious, tried to find where he had left off, but he couldn't seem to find his place.

"It's the third paragraph at the bottom," Van Orton told him.

Jeremiah's voice suddenly bellowed from the back of the room: "I'll read! If that's all right with you." He was looking at Van Orton.

"Take it away, Mr. Kateb."

And with that, Jeremiah began to read: "'The Alhambra Decree, also known as the 'Edict of Expulsion,' was issued by the Catholic Monarchs of Spain, ordering the expulsion of Jews from Spanish territories in order to eliminate their influence on Spain's large *converso* population—that is, Jews who had converted to Catholicism as a result of religious persecution. Following the Edict of Expulsion, over 200,000 Jews converted to Catholicism to remain in Spain, and between 40,000 and 100,000 were expelled, migrating to the Ottoman Empire, North Africa, and Europe. The edict was issued in March of 1492, just months after the Moors were defeated in the Granada War, thus bringing an end to religious coexistence that had previously flourished in Muslim Spain. It wasn't until 1968 that the Alhambra Decree was formally revoked in Spain, following the Second Vatican Council.'"

Jeremiah stopped reading and looked at Van Orton. He paused for a brief moment, as if for dramatic effect, before speaking. "The defeat of the Moors was the worst thing to ever happen in Europe. If the Moors hadn't been defeated, then the Alhambra Decree wouldn't have been issued, the Spanish Inquisition wouldn't have been established, and Christopher Columbus wouldn't have been able to embark on his, let's say, 'genocidal' voyage." He turned to Jeunet, who was standing next to Van Orton. "*Êtes-vous d'accord, monsieur le directeur?*"

A faint smile formed across Jeunet's face. "*Oui, Monsieur Kateb,* I agree...somewhat. But don't forget that if the Moors hadn't been defeated in Granada, the Spanish Golden Age wouldn't have arisen. That means no El Greco, no Diego Velázquez, no Tomás Luis de Victoria, and most painful for me, no Miguel de Cervantes and his *Don Quixote.* I can do without the others, but not Cervantes."

"I can do without them *all,*" Jeremiah said bitterly. "As for the Spanish Golden Age...that had already taken place centuries earlier. It was called the Caliphate of Córdoba, when the Moors transformed Córdoba into the most advanced city in Europe and helped usher in the Jewish Golden Age. I like the 'second' Spanish Golden Age that you mentioned just fine, but Muslim Spain was the cultural and intellectual center of Europe for centuries, and they produced a lot more than just art. Don't you think al-Zahrawi, known as the 'father of modern surgery,' is more important than Cervantes and the other Spaniards?"

Jeunet and Van Orton exchanged looks of wonderment, and I suddenly felt a prickly thorn digging into my flesh as admiration merged with envy. It was as if a moral leprosy had developed inside me, and Jeremiah was the cause. Despite having consumed countless history books over the summer, I was left flabbergasted by Jeremiah's deep knowledge of history, and it became obvious that his intellect dwarfed mine. I'd already known this, albeit subconsciously, from the first day of school, but now it was undeniable.

"You know," Jeunet said, clutching his walking stick, "all this talk of Spain has me thinking about Pelagius of Córdoba, the child saint who was allegedly martyred by the Moors in the early tenth century." He turned to Van Orton. "Do you know the story?"

Van Orton shook his head.

Jeunet grinned. "It's a unique martyr story wrapped in medieval 'homoeroticism,' the kind of story that Father Hawkins would find both uplifting and abhorrent, I'm sure." He looked at the class. "According to legend, Pelagius is said to have been a Christian boy whose beauty was such that the Caliph of Córdoba fell in love with him and attempted to court the boy, who had been held hostage in the Caliph's palace since age ten. The Caliph offered Pelagius his freedom when the boy attained thirteen years of age, upon the condition that he convert to Islam. Pelagius, having remained a pious Christian, refused the Caliph's offer, as well as his sexual advances. Furious, the Caliph had the boy tortured for six hours and then dismembered."

There was silence.

"Is the story true?" Van Orton asked finally.

Jeunet shrugged and replied, "No way of knowing for certain. The story may just be a work of Spanish propaganda made to portray the Moors as barbarians and sexual deviants. In any case, we live in a world of half-truths, and only God knows the full truth." After a brief pause, he added, "Perhaps that's my takeaway from this fable: Nothing is ever as it seems." He suddenly looked at Jeremiah. "*Que pensez-vous de l'histoire, Monsieur Kateb?*"

"I think it's one hell of a story, *monsieur le directeur*," Jeremiah replied.

Jeunet smiled, then turned back to Van Orton. "Say, which film will you be screening at today's film studies club?"

"What do you recommend, Dr. Jeunet?"

"Something French would be nice. Not Godard, though. We wouldn't want our students to walk out of the auditorium with thoughts of Marxism." Jeunet chuckled.

"Too late," Van Orton told him, glancing at Jeremiah.

"What's that?"

"Nothing."

Jeunet paused. "Well, then…I'll let you get back to it, *Monsieur* Van Orton." He exited the classroom.

Van Orton looked at the class. "That was informative."

Some of the students laughed.

There weren't as many students at the film studies club this time as there were the previous week. I counted no more than twenty-five students, and most of them were sophomores, probably Van Orton's students. I brought Simon along with me, and he was excited that I'd even asked him to join me. Jeremiah was there, sitting in the middle of the auditorium as before.

Van Orton showed us a 1933 French featurette called *Zero for Conduct*, which, according to him, was banned in France until after the end of the Second World War because of its anarchist views. The film is set in a conservative boarding school and follows four rebellious boys who plot a revolt against their teachers. It was an odd choice for a movie, since after all, Van Orton himself was a conservative.

At the end of the movie, the rebellious boys wave a makeshift anarchist flag in their dorm and announce: "War is declared! Down with monitors and punishment! Long live rebellion! Hoist our flag on the school roof! We'll bombard them with rotten old books, dirty tin cans, smelly boots, and all the ammo piled up in the attic! We'll fight those old goats! Onward!" The boys then proceed to tear up their dorm in triumph, and the movie concludes with a slumbering teacher being crucified and the other faculty members being pelted with objects hurled from the school roof.

"For those of you who weren't here last week," Van Orton addressed the crowd of students after the movie had ended, "I screened *2001: A Space Odyssey*, a different kind of film compared to the one we've just seen, with the former focusing on the future and this one, although ahead of its time, focusing on the past. Of course, the only thing that makes *Zero for Conduct* a film of 'the past' is the fact that it was made in the 1930s. That being said, does anyone have any thoughts on the featurette we just watched?"

A boy raised his hand and said, "I'm curious—what's a 'featurette'?"

Van Orton sighed before responding: "A movie that's shorter than a feature film but longer than a short film. I'm sure you could've figured that out on your own had you given it just a little more thought. Anyone else have something to add?"

There was a long silence.

"Why did you pick this movie?" I suddenly asked, my voice a little shaky as if anticipating a berating response.

"I believe you were there when Dr. Jeunet recommended that I show a French film, weren't you, Mr. Quell?" Van Orton said.

"Yeah…but I don't think he meant *this* kind of movie."

"What's wrong with *Zero for Conduct*?"

I felt stupid for even saying anything. Some of the students turned to look at me, including Jeremiah, which made me want to crawl out of my skin. I thought about what to say next.

"I—I just meant…it's not a very conservative movie, so I don't think, uh, Dr. Jeunet would like it. Also…I—I'm surprised that *you* like it."

Van Orton smirked. "You take me for an 'old goat,' like the faculty members portrayed in the film, is that it?"

I remained silent.

"Speak up, Mr. Quell!" Van Orton howled. "You were the one who brought this up. Now explain yourself. Am I an 'old goat'? Am I deserving of being pelted with dirty tin cans and smelly boots? Tell me, what makes *me* a conservative?"

No longer able to tolerate the humiliation, I turned to Simon and said, "Let's go." I got up and headed toward the exit door, with Simon trailing behind me. Neither of us said anything until we'd exited the school building and stood in the main quadrangle, the site of the school's renowned bronze statue of Christopher Columbus, which depicted the Italian explorer standing over a naked Native woman.

"That teacher seems kind of mean," Simon said to me.

"He's an asshole," I replied. "Now I gotta fucking deal with him for the rest of the school year."

"I definitely wouldn't want to get on his bad side. None of my teachers are like that." After a pause, Simon added, "Sorry…that probably doesn't make you feel any better."

"Don't worry about me."

Simon looked at the Columbus statue. "Was this statue here when you started going here?"

"Yeah. It was commissioned by Dr. Jeunet when he first came to Magnolia."

"How do you know that?"

"I read it in a book about the school's history." I examined the statue. "Dr. Jeunet must be loaded if he can afford this fucking thing." I spat on the statue.

"Hey, you're going to get in trouble!"

I turned to Simon, indifferent. "How old are you?"

"Sean, you know I'm ten."

I paused. "Do you like boys or girls?"

"That's a weird question."

"Yeah, I know, but I'm just curious."

"Well, um…I like girls, I guess," Simon told me. "What about you?"

"Have you ever kissed a girl?"

Simon shook his head.

"Then how do you know that you like girls?"

"I—I don't know. I just do."

I paused. "I kissed a girl...once. Actually, *she* kissed me. It was during summer camp when I was eight or nine. One day, this girl who was a year older than me took me behind a cabin...and she stuck her tongue down my throat. Her breath smelled like Pepto-Bismol."

"Did you like it? The kiss, I mean."

"No. It was gross, and so was she."

I began circling the Columbus statue with my head hung low. Simon watched me for a long while, then followed my lead. We must've looked like two planets orbiting the Sun, or just a pair of drunks.

"I hope the first time I kiss a girl," Simon said to me, "she doesn't do what that one girl did to you...you know, stick her tongue down my throat."

"I'm sure your first kiss will be better than mine," I replied.

"So do you like girls now?"

I paused. "I like what likes *me*. Actually, I take that back. I like River Phoenix."

"Who's she?" Simon asked.

"She...was my first crush," I told him, smiling.

We stopped and looked at the Columbus statue. Simon suddenly turned to me. "That was the weirdest conversation I've ever had, but I liked it. Nobody talks to me like that, especially not my parents, so thanks."

"You don't have to thank me for talking to you. We're friends, so we should be able to talk about almost anything."

A beaming Simon nodded, then turned his attention back to the statue. "Why do you think Christopher Columbus is stepping on the Native lady?"

"Because he's a piece of shit."

I spat on the statue again. After a moment, a reluctant Simon did the same, then looked at me and smiled.

CHAPTER FIVE

I hadn't gone back to Blondie's since I'd seen Jeremiah and his girlfriend there, primarily because I was intimidated by the divine couple, especially Mallory, and I didn't want to risk seeing her again. However, I desperately wanted to talk to Jeremiah again, and since I was too anxious to approach him at school, I went back to the diner, half-expecting to see Jeremiah there, preferably without his girlfriend.

Simon had to stay after school for music practice, so I was at Blondie's by myself, which I preferred. Unfortunately, I didn't see Jeremiah at the diner, but I did see someone whom I hadn't seen or thought about in almost two years, a girl named Athena White, who, for a brief time, was my first and only girlfriend. Although I was quite certain that I was gay, I'd felt compelled to "test myself" when I'd turned thirteen by dating Athena, who lived in my neighborhood and was brought up in a Mormon household with strict parents, both attorneys, and three younger brothers, all Aryan blond. Athena and I never so much as kissed, although she did attempt to give me a handjob while we were at McDonald's one night, and she got upset when I couldn't get aroused.

I gawked at Athena as she played on the pinball machines with two of her girlfriends. She was wearing a white tennis skirt, turquoise cashmere sweater, and white sneakers—a fitting outfit for a young socialite. One of Athena's girlfriends noticed me staring at her, then tapped her on the shoulder and pointed in my direction. I looked away, and when I turned back, I saw Athena walking toward me with a bottled drink in her hand. She stopped when she got to my booth and looked at me, smiling.

"Sean?" she said.

I nodded, forcing a smile. I didn't know what to say.

"You *do* remember me, right?"

"Yeah, of course…Athena. It hasn't been *that* long."

"Two years, more or less." Athena stared at me for a moment, still smiling. "I'm here with some girlfriends from school. Does your mom still teach at Emma Goldman?"

I shook my head and said, "No, she quit teaching just over a year ago. Now she volunteers at an art museum."

"Which art museum?"

"It's the one at Vassar College."

"Oh," Athena said with a nod, then sat down across from me, realizing that I wasn't going to ask her to sit down. "Do you still live on Cypress Avenue?"

"Yeah, I haven't gone anywhere." I paused. "Where did you move to?"

"I live in Spackenkill now—the rich part of town where they call us 'cake-eaters.' Better a 'cake-eater' than a Communist, though."

Athena giggled and took a sip of her drink. She hadn't changed all that much since I'd last seen her; same preppy clothes, wavy bob haircut, and a brazen attitude that didn't seem to coincide with that of a Mormon girl living under the thumb of strict parents. But that was what attracted me to her in the first place.

"You know," I said, pausing for a moment, "I still haven't dated anyone besides you, even though we only 'dated' for less than three months."

"Don't worry, Sean, I'm sure you'll find Mr. Right soon enough." Athena grinned, while I just stared at her, dumbstruck. "What, you didn't think I noticed?"

"Noticed what?"

"That you play for the other team."

I didn't say anything.

"It's not like I told anybody," Athena said. "But yeah, every time I tried to kiss you or hold your hand, you'd totally reject me. And that one night at Burger King when I tried to—"

"McDonald's," I corrected her.

"Right. I don't think any guy would turn down a handjob, even at a dirty restaurant, unless he's gay—or a germaphobe. And you don't strike me as a germaphobe." Athena looked at me with a solemn expression. "That actually hurt me...when you kept rejecting me. You almost killed my self-esteem. That's not a nice thing to do to someone, especially girls, because we take that shit to our graves." Athena paused. "So did you even find me attractive?"

Ashamed, I said nothing for a while, then nodded.

"Don't feel bad, though," Athena told me. "I don't hate you or anything. But why did you even date me if you were...*you know*?"

"Because I wanted to make sure," I replied, after a pause. "And I got my answer. But I feel like a dick for using you as a guinea pig. Anyway, I'm sure you've dated plenty of other guys since me, so you should be used to guys being dicks. I'm sorry I was one of them."

Athena scoffed, smiling faintly. "By the way, were you surprised that my parents let me go out with you?"

"Yeah. I thought they kept you and your brothers locked up in chains."

"They didn't know that we were dating. They thought I was going out with my girlfriends to the mall or something. But now...they don't care what I do."

"What do you mean?"

Athena finished her drink and wiped her mouth with a napkin, then said to me, "The reason we moved was because my mom caught my dad cheating, and she was too embarrassed to continue living in that neighborhood. That's when my parents stopped caring about what I did. But I'm not complaining."

"I thought you guys would've moved somewhere farther, like Utah. Isn't that where all the Mormons live, or am I thinking of the Amish?"

Athena giggled. "It's the Mormons. But I don't believe in any of that bullshit. The last two bishops at our church were accused of child molestation, so you can imagine how I feel about the Mormon Church. I don't even think my parents believe in any of it anymore, but they still go along with it for the sake of tradition...or whatever."

I smiled.

"Why are you smiling?" Athena asked.

"I've never heard you talk like this before," I said. "Hearing you cuss is funny to me. It's like hearing a little kid swear for the first time."

"Oh, I can do a lot more than just cuss."

"I'm sure. You know what, though? I always knew there was an angsty side to you, because nice little Mormon girls don't just grab a guy's dick under the table at McDonald's and try to jerk him off."

Athena formed her hand into a gun, pointed it at me, and fired, then smiled. "Believe it or not, your mom caught me smoking one time when

I was at Emma Goldman. I had her for drawing class, so she knew who I was, and she caught me smoking out in the yard by the gym. But she was cool about it, though. She didn't narc on me to the headmistress. She just threw my cigarettes away and told me never to smoke again."

"And what, you haven't smoked since?"

"Not exactly," Athena said, and got up. "I should get back to my girlfriends."

"You wouldn't want them to think that we're flirting."

"They know you're not my type," Athena quipped, and started to walk away.

"Hey, wait!"

Athena stopped and turned to me, expecting me to say something, but I struggled to get the words out. "Sean, what is it?"

Finally, I said, "This might sound stupid, but...when you went to Emma Goldman, did you know a girl named Mallory?"

"Mallory *who*?"

"I don't know her last name, but she's two years older than us, fair-skinned, with dark hair down to her shoulders."

Athena shrugged and shook her head.

"She, um...also likes to wear sunglasses," I added.

"Are you fucking with me?"

"No, Athena. She's a real person, I promise. I just thought you might know her. Maybe she goes to your current school, whatever that is."

"Why are you interested in some girl, anyway? That's not even your thing."

I didn't respond.

Athena gave me a cheeky wink and walked away, while I remained seated and let my mind wander, thinking of ways to get Jeremiah to notice me. I could either keep coming to Blondie's in hopes that I run into him again, or I could continue attending the film studies club and simply sit next to him in the auditorium. But the latter meant that I'd have to put up with Van Orton's bullshit and possibly have him berate me again.

I eventually left Blondie's and began the twenty-minute walk to my house, still ruminating over how to get Jeremiah to notice me. Then I remembered Athena's flippant Communist remark. Jeremiah was evidently a follower of the sociopolitical ideology, so maybe I could get his attention by feigning interest in Communism. After some thought, I reasoned that the best, or rather *simplest*, way to do that was by having Jeremiah see me reading a Communist book. I stopped at the public library on my way home and searched the massive social science and humanities sections for just the "right book." Before I knew it, I'd spent over an hour skimming through books.

Marxism and Dialectical Materialism in the Postmodern World.

Asian Socialism: Utopian, Scientific, Practical.

Lenin's Bolsheviks.

I found most of the books too dense for my taste—until finally, I discovered a book about Communism's contributions to the arts called *Beyond Socialist Realism*, highlighting many of the best-known artists on the Left, including Pablo Picasso, Diego Rivera, Frida Kahlo, and Jean-Luc Godard. I read parts of the book at the library and was surprised to discover that hard-boiled author Dashiell Hammett and hip-hop artist Tupac Shakur were associated with the Communist Party. I took the book home and spent much of the day reading it, momentarily forgetting why I'd checked it out from the library to begin with, but I didn't forget for long.

CHAPTER SIX

I placed the book on the edge of my desk and waited for Jeremiah to arrive. He was always one of the last students to enter the classroom, which made me think that he purposely waited until everyone else had arrived before coming to class, believing himself to be *too cool for school*. He finally arrived and, just as he walked past my desk, I pretended to accidentally knock the book off my desk, which landed at his feet. He crouched down and grabbed the book, looking at the cover with intrigue.

Jeremiah rose to his feet, still looking at the book cover, while I anticipated his next move as if it were a matter of life and death. He suddenly looked at me and said, "Socialist realism?"

The combination of his cherubic features, almond-shaped eyes, and wonderful scent were almost too much for me to handle, especially with him looking directly into my eyes.

"It—it's about…Communist artists," I told him, my heart palpitating.

Jeremiah looked at the cover again, then handed me back the book. "Why are you interested in that, though?"

"Because I like art. And also because I want to learn more about Communism."

"Seriously?"

I nodded.

Jeremiah stared at me for a moment, almost like he was studying me, then asked, "Can you meet me in the library after chapel?"

My heart was beating so fast that I thought I was going to go into cardiac arrest. More than Jeremiah's delicate face, it was his alluring *scent*—that cinnamon and clove aroma that seemed to follow him everywhere, as if that were his natural scent—which affected me the most.

"Y—yes, yes," I replied, staring back at Jeremiah. "I can meet you in the library right after chapel."

"I'll be in the art history section on the second floor. Nobody will bother us there." Jeremiah went to his seat.

All I could think about for the entire class period was Jeremiah and how I was finally going to talk to him one-on-one in relative privacy. I didn't hear a word Van Orton said in class, even as he spoke a mere three feet from me, since I had my head in the clouds and was thinking about what I was going to say to Jeremiah. The one thing that alarmed me was the thought that he'd "unmask" me as a fraud and figure out that I had no genuine interest in Communism. But that wasn't entirely true, because, after having read *Beyond Socialist Realism* in just three days, I'd actually developed a slight interest in the ideology, to my surprise.

———————————

Father Hawkins denounced Satan from the pulpit, likening the malevolent figure to Saddam Hussein, who had gone into hiding following the invasion of Iraq. The cleric foamed at the mouth as he sermonized against Satan and "all his ilk," taking pauses in between, while the rest of us just looked at him in bewilderment. I turned to Jeremiah, who was sitting in the same pew as me, and I could see that he was trying not to laugh while listening to Father Hawkins.

Simon, sitting next to me, tapped me on the shoulder and whispered, "Do you want to come over today? You can listen to me play the guitar. I've gotten so much better."

"Not today," I told him. "But some other day, I promise."

"Are you sure?"

I nodded.

After concluding his sermon, Father Hawkins, still vexed, instructed us to recite the three pillars of Magnolia Academy: Tradition, Faith, and Discipline. "Now repeat after me," he said, "as I recite the Divine Praises, which were originally written for the purpose of making reparation for uttering profanity or blasphemy—and I know many of you have uttered heresies, even if you dare not admit it! Repeat after me, gentlemen, with voices loud enough for God to hear..."

Blessed be God.

Blessed be His Holy Name.

Blessed be Jesus Christ, true God and true Man.

Blessed be the Holy Spirit, the Paraclete.
Blessed be the great Mother of God, Mary most Holy.
Blessed be her Holy and Immaculate Conception.
Blessed be the name of Mary, Virgin and Mother.
Blessed be God in His angels and in His saints. Amen.

I tried to catch up to Jeremiah after chapel had ended, but there was such a flood of people pouring out of the chapel that I quickly lost sight of him. I went to the library and found Jeremiah sitting at a study table on the second floor, staring at a marble bust of a Spartan soldier that rested on an elevated plinth off to the side. I sat down at the table across from him and waited for him to notice me. However, after a few moments went by without any kind of acknowledgement of my presence, I started to feel awkward.

"You see that bust?" Jeremiah said suddenly, still gazing at the sculpture.

I looked at the sculpture and said, "Yeah."

"I don't know why the school would have a bust of a Spartan soldier, but it makes me think about the Battle of Leuctra." Jeremiah turned to me. "Have you ever heard of it?"

"No."

"The battle took place in the fourth century BC, just after the Corinthian War, and it pitted the Spartans against the much smaller Boeotians, who had a secret weapon—a military unit called the Sacred Band of Thebes." Jeremiah paused for a moment as if expecting me to chime in. When I didn't say anything, he went on: "The Sacred Band of Thebes was an elite force of three hundred men. Do you know what made them so 'sacred'? They were *lovers*."

I tensed up.

"Even though the Spartan army was bigger," Jeremiah continued, "it lacked the passionate camaraderie that the Sacred Band of Thebes shared. Imagine going to war against three hundred soldiers, each one determined to protect his lover on the battlefield."

I didn't understand why he would tell me this, and I was unsure of how to respond. Finally, I chuckled and said, "You sound like a professor."

"That's because I was quoting from an article that I'd read in a military history magazine," Jeremiah told me, smiling. "But it's legit."

"H—how do you know so much about…everything?"

"I read a lot. Anyway, I'm sure you know a lot of stuff too. Picking up a book or magazine isn't anything special."

"Yeah, but you seem to know a lot more than everyone else."

Jeremiah looked confused. "Who's 'everyone else'?"

"Like our classmates…including me."

"I doubt I'm smarter than you or anyone else." Jeremiah gestured to his headdress and said, "Don't let the keffiyeh fool you."

"So do you, um…wear a keffiyeh because it's part of your culture?"

"Actually, I wear it because I don't like baseball caps, and also because of Raekwon. He's a rapper from the Wu-Tang Clan who likes to wear headdresses. But when I first started wearing a keffiyeh in the seventh grade, the school asked me about it, and I just told them that it was 'part of my culture,' as you said. Only problem is, now they think I'm a jihadist."

I laughed, then abruptly stopped.

"It's fine," Jeremiah said. "You can laugh. I think it's funny too. And it's better they think that I'm a jihadist than what I actually am—a Commie nonbeliever."

"Nonbeliever?"

"I don't like the word 'atheist,' so I say 'nonbeliever.' It makes me sound less of an asshole, you know?"

"So, uh…is your family Muslim?"

"My mom is. Not devout or anything, but she respects the faith and tries to live righteously. I respect Islam, more than most religions, but I can't put faith above science."

I grinned.

"What?" Jeremiah said.

"Nothing," I replied. "I just…I like how your mind works. I've never met anyone like you before. I—I'm sorry if that sounds kind of weird."

"No, you're fine."

Jeremiah and I looked at each other as if we were having a staring contest. I couldn't believe that I was actually sitting opposite Jeremiah and having a serious conversation with him, without the presence of his girlfriend or anyone else. Just the two of us, as if we were on a date, which was what it felt like at certain moments, especially when he'd smile or gaze at me with those penetrating eyes of his that, I was certain, had the power to burn a hole through my skull.

"I saw you trying not to laugh during chapel," I told Jeremiah. "I've had that experience so many times. Father Hawkins is a trip."

"A *bad* trip. I can't believe some of the stuff that comes out of his mouth. He must've lost his shit after 9/11. I'd like to think that America was somewhat 'normal' before the attacks, but…I don't know. I'll tell you what I do know, though—I'm getting the fuck out of this country as soon as I turn eighteen."

I felt as if the rug had been pulled out from under me. I didn't want to imagine living apart from Jeremiah, even if it was years away. I'd grown attached to him so quickly in such a brief span of time that it seemed almost grotesque that he'd eventually move to a different part of the world, away from my prying eyes. I began to stammer for a moment, then blurted out, "But where would you *live*?"

"Kerala," Jeremiah replied, assuming I'd heard of the place, but I had no idea where Kerala was even located on a map. I made a face to say as much. "It's an Indian state in the southern part of the country with a population of over thirty million people. That's a bigger population than most European countries. The only thing is, if I'm going to move there, I first need to learn the official language of Kerala—Malayalam— and it's not an easy language to learn. I've been learning it for the past three years, and I've only learned about…fifteen percent of it so far."

"What's so special about this Kerala place?" I asked.

"It's the gold standard of a Communist utopia," Jeremiah said with a hint of a smile. "That's not a joke. Kerala has the highest life expectancy, literacy rate, and sex ratio in all of India, maybe the entire subcontinent—and it's purely Communist-run. You can get free heart surgery there, no matter how poor you are. Every house in Kerala has electricity, unlike many of the other states in India." He paused briefly. "But you know what's the most impressive thing about Kerala? It's the only place on Earth where Hindus, Muslims, Christians, and atheists can live side by side without cutting each other's throats. Kerala is even home to the oldest group of Jews in India, dating back to the time of Solomon. There's no patriarchy and no discrimination against gay or bisexual people there. Don't ask me how they did it, because I'm still baffled, but the Communists in Kerala have basically created a modern-day Muslim Spain. Pretty cool, huh?"

Jeremiah's words left my head spinning, and I simply stared at him for a while, then finally, I said, "How do you know all this?"

"When I went back to Algeria three years ago, some of the Workers' Party members told me about it."

"So is that why you became a Communist?"

"Well, *that*…and also because of my mom. I think I told you before that she used to work as a pharmacist. That was when we lived in Algeria. Then we immigrated to America in the spring of '98, and the only job my mom could find was the job she has now—as a house-keeper. What a humiliating downgrade that is. I didn't realize just how depressing it was for her until she took me to work with her one day, and I saw her scrubbing the kitchen floor with sweat pouring down her face. She was on all fours like a dog, and I remember feeling so fucking angry at the family whose house my mom had to clean. That's what my mom does for a living now—she cleans rich WASPs' houses, the same WASPs whose ancestors hopped aboard the *Mayflower* like roaches for a better life, but at whose expense?"

Jeremiah looked at me as if expecting me to provide an adequate answer, but I didn't know what to say, so I just nodded, thinking that would make me seem empathetic in a way.

"I guess you didn't really need to know all that," Jeremiah said.

"No," I quickly replied. "I mean—I'm glad you told me. I want to know more about you…"

I stopped suddenly when I realized how desperate I sounded. *You idiot!*

Jeremiah smirked. "Anyway, let's talk about *you* now. Why are you suddenly interested in Communism?"

I flinched at the question. "Oh, well, uh…I just randomly came across that socialist realism book at the public library and I—I thought it was interesting. I didn't realize just how many famous artists were Communists or socialists. The one that surprised me the most was Tupac Shakur, and also the funny actress from *I Love Lucy*. I forgot her name."

"Lucille Ball. Can you imagine if she'd told the press in the 1950s that she was a Commie? They probably would've tarred and feathered her."

"There were a bunch of names in that socialist realism book that I didn't recognize, but the ones that I did recognize surprised me."

"So that's why you're interested in Communism?" Jeremiah said, looking at me in a funny kind of way. "Because some famous artists are Commies?"

I couldn't tell if he was upset with me, or if he was simply curious about my sudden interest in Communism, but I thought in earnest before responding.

"I'm interested in Communism because of *you*," I confessed, with candid devotion. "That socialist realism book—I didn't just 'randomly' come across it at the public library. I spent over an hour at the library looking for the right book, something that would grab your attention. I tried to get your attention the past two days by reading the book at my desk, but when you didn't notice me, that's when I intentionally knocked the book off my desk in class today as you went by. Here's the surprising thing, though. I actually enjoyed reading the book, and my interest in Communism isn't bullshit anymore. I'm still not deep into politics or economics, and I don't exactly see myself as a Che Guevara type, but after reading that book, I'm definitely interested in learning more about Communism."

Jeremiah stared at me thoughtfully. To my surprise, I wasn't intimidated by his gaze like I normally would've been. I just stared back at him as if he were anyone else. The only thing about him that still had the ability to overwhelm me was his attractive scent, which always seemed to hit me with the force of a tsunami. But I welcomed the impact.

A gracious smile suddenly formed across Jeremiah's face as he said, "I have some things at my house that I want to show you. What are you doing after school today?" Before I could even respond, he added, "Mallory and I are going to the movies after school, but she can drop us off at my house afterward. And of course, you're coming to the movies with us. I *want* you to."

He said exactly what I'd been fantasizing that he'd say to me one day, but it was all wishful thinking on my part—until that day.

"I'm not doing anything after school," I told Jeremiah, my heart palpitating again.

"Mallory's picking me up from school, so you can meet me at the front of the school after your last class. By the way, your parents won't mind you coming over to my house, will they? I'm right by Poughkeepsie High School."

"That's not too far from my house. Anyway, my parents don't care if I go out, as long as I come home in one piece."

Jeremiah chuckled a bit, then got up and said, "I gotta get to my next class. But we'll have more to talk about later at my place."

I got to my feet. Jeremiah walked over to me, and for a moment, it looked like he was going to embrace me. But instead, he affectionately slapped me on the arm.

"What was that for?" I said, smiling.

"I was just thinking how cool it would be if we became the new Bolsheviks, like Lenin and Sverdlov."

"I don't even know who Sverdlov is, but if you say so."

Jeremiah smiled. Neither of us said anything for a while, then finally, Jeremiah asked me, "What did you mean when you said you were interested in Communism because of *me*?"

I paused. "Was that a weird thing to say or something?"

"No. I'm just wondering…why me?"

I hesitated for a moment, then said, "I just think you're really smart and cool, unlike most of the students at this school, and if *you* think there's something special about Communism…then there must be."

Jeremiah nodded and replied, "Sounds good, partisan."

CHAPTER SEVEN

I sat in the backseat of the beige Lexus sedan, which Mallory's parents must've bought her for her sweet sixteen, and tried to think of something to say. Jeremiah was sitting in the passenger seat, looking out the window, with his girlfriend behind the wheel. She was a good driver, although she had a habit of running yellow lights. I eventually gave up thinking of something to say, fearing that I'd say something stupid. I noticed a book lying on the floor near my feet. I picked it up and looked at the cover: *Kaddish and Other Poems*. I opened it and began to read.

"Where did you find that?" Jeremiah said suddenly.

I looked up and realized that he was talking to me. "I, uh...found it on the floor right here."

Jeremiah, rather annoyed, turned to Mallory. "My fucking Ginsberg?"

"What?" she said. "I...*read* it. Some of it, anyway."

"But why was it on the floor in the back of your car? I let you borrow it weeks ago, thinking that you were still reading it."

"Christ, get a grip. It's not like I pissed on it. Your book is fine, trust me. It must've fallen on the floor when I took a sharp turn or something. Please forgive me, Your Majesty. I'll never do it again."

Jeremiah shook his head, then turned to me. "I don't know if you're into poetry at all, but Allen Ginsberg is a good place to start. The main poem in the book, 'Kaddish,' is about Ginsberg's mom, who struggled with mental health problems and was sent to an asylum. Ironically, she was a Communist."

"Isn't that where all Communists end up," Mallory said, "in an asylum?"

Jeremiah scoffed and said to me, "As you can see, I'm dating Eva Braun. You can always count on a capitalist for a show of empathy. That's why conservatives are terrible at making good art. You can't make good art if you lack empathy."

"Hey, if I'm Eva Braun," Mallory said, "then what does that make you?"

"A dumbass," Jeremiah replied, and gave his girlfriend a peck on the cheek. "You're lucky my second head doesn't know how awful you really are." Jeremiah turned back to me. "You can borrow the Ginsberg book if you want, since Mallory doesn't have any use for it, apparently. Who knows, it might inspire you."

I smiled and said, "Thanks. I can't wait to start reading it. I mean, at home, not just in your girlfriend's car."

"You can't even say my name?" Mallory said, looking at me through the rear-view mirror. "We're on a first-name basis now, aren't we?"

I forced a chuckle and replied, "Sorry. I just don't know you like that."

"Well, until a few weeks ago, you didn't know Jeremiah either, but you don't call him 'the Algerian' or whatever. Why do I have to be 'the girlfriend,' like I'm a pariah?"

"Um…I don't know. Like I said, I'm sorry…"

Mallory suddenly burst out laughing. "I'm just playing with you. I wanted to see how you'd react. I'm curious, though, do you have a girlfriend?"

I wasn't expecting that question. Jeremiah, no longer facing me, remained silent, while his girlfriend continued to look at me through the rear-view mirror with what appeared to be a "Fuck you" smirk.

"No," I replied, "I don't have a girlfriend."

"Well…have you *ever* had a girlfriend?" Mallory asked.

"Yeah, two years ago," I said.

"What was his name?" Mallory laughed in embarrassment. "Oh, I'm sorry—Freudian slip there. What was *her* name, I meant?"

I knew that wasn't a slip of the tongue. She definitely meant to humiliate me, and I hated her for it. "Her name was Athena," I said with a sigh, which was my gutless way of telling her off.

"Oof, that sigh came with a threat. What was she like?"

"She was a lot like you, actually. I'm sure you two would've made great friends."

"Somehow I believe you," Mallory said. "So why haven't you had a girlfriend since? Are you afraid of girls?"

"I'm not afraid of girls. I just haven't met a new girl that I'd like to spend more than fifteen minutes with."

Mallory chuckled. "That's a subtle shot at me, isn't it?"

"You'd be surprised how few things are actually about you," Jeremiah said to his girlfriend.

"Hey, you keep looking out the window and fantasizing about Stalin."

"I fucking hate Stalin, and so does every Communist I know. Stalin is to Communism what Constantine the Great is to Christianity—a false prophet, a deceiver, the fucking Antichrist. They perverted both ideologies for their own gain, and now we're all paying the price for it. I swear, if I could go back in time, I wouldn't kill Hitler. I'd kill Stalin instead. Then go further back and kill Constantine in his sleep, just before he saw the Christian cross in his dream."

A shocked Mallory let out a shrill, braying laugh and said, "Jesus Christ! That's all it took to set you off? I'd hate to see what you'd do if I insulted one of your Commie heroes. You'd burn my fucking house down or something, wouldn't you?"

"No, I'd just throw a brick through your windshield and write 'capitalist pig' in red paint."

"So what do you think of Communism, Sean?" Mallory asked.

I was a bit taken aback by the question. "I don't know too much about it, but I'm trying to learn. The one thing I've recently learned is that Communism isn't just for the working class. It's also for artists and intellectuals."

"But that's the fucking problem," Jeremiah interjected, turning to look at me. "Communism should first and foremost attract the working class—custodians, truck drivers, miners, construction workers, farmers, housekeepers, plumbers. Instead, it mostly attracts artists and intellectuals, and that's a problem, because the blue-collar workers need Communism more than some professor or theatre major at Columbia. *I* don't need Communism, but you know who does? My mom and the custodian at Magnolia who cleans the fucking toilets."

"Then why are *you* a Communist?" Mallory asked him. It was a fair question that I wish I had asked him earlier at the library.

Jeremiah turned back around, then said in a wistful tone, "I'm a Communist because there's gotta be a better way to live, because I want to be able to wake up in the morning and actually feel good about myself. Communism isn't the endgame—it's a prelude. Karl Marx cast the first stone. Now we have to do the rest. I don't care if Communism isn't perfect. It may not even be the right system. But it's a *start*, a start to something better. Call it 'Communism,' call it 'socialism,' call it 'utopia,' whatever the fuck. But it's a start! Marx at least had the balls to say,

'Stop! Something is wrong. This isn't working.' Nobody before him had the fucking courage to say that."

"What about all the people who have died under Communism?" Mallory said. "What is it now, something like over a hundred million?"

Jeremiah shook his head in annoyance and let out a hollow laugh, then replied, "Have you ever heard of the Thirty Years' War? It was a bloody religious conflict that pitted Catholics against Protestants. They say an estimated eight million people died during that war, which took place in the seventeenth century. Adjusted to world population, that eight million would rise to well over a hundred million today. And that's just *one* conflict—because of religion. Now, imagine if I were to adjust the death tolls of other wars and famines and genocides, everything from the Crusades to the Atlantic slave trade to all the famines in British India. The death tolls would be outrageous. If a hundred million people have died under Communism, then millions more have died because of religion and capitalism. I know conservatives couldn't care less about the peasants who died in the Soviet Union and Maoist China, just like they don't give a shit about the million people who died in the Irish Potato Famine because of capitalism. I don't fall for that tricknology like I'm goddamn Forrest Gump."

Mallory parked her Lexus on the street outside an Art Deco movie theater that looked like it was built in the 1930s. She then turned to me and, smiling, said, "I hope you enjoyed Jeremiah's history lesson. Now you know what I have to put up with every time we hang out."

I looked out the window at the movie theater. "What is this place?"

"The Art Mill," Jeremiah said to me. "It's an art house theater that shows classic, foreign, and independent films. I go here all the time."

"He means whenever *I* drive him," Mallory told me, and stuck her tongue out at Jeremiah.

A man donning the uniform of what looked like a bellhop from an old Hollywood screwball comedy, including white gloves and a cap, manned the concession stand of the movie theater. He appeared to be the sole attendant in the large theater, besides perhaps the projectionist. The interior of the theater was grandiose, resembling an opera house more so than a movie theater, what with its ornate chandeliers and cantilevered stairway.

Jeremiah and I didn't get anything from the concession stand, but Mallory bought a bag of cotton candy and a drink.

"What do you think of this place?" Jeremiah asked me as we walked up the stairway to the top floor of the theater, with Mallory ahead of us.

"It's pretty amazing," I said. "But I feel like I should be wearing a tuxedo."

"Your school uniform is good enough," Jeremiah quipped.

We entered a 1,000-seat theater with a broad balcony and a grand stage. There appeared to be only a handful of people there, mostly older folks. Mallory began stuffing her face with cotton candy as soon as she sat down. I sat next to Jeremiah, who sat next to his girlfriend.

"Babe...did you really have to get cotton candy?" Jeremiah said to Mallory, glaring at her.

Hearing him call her "babe" was like nails on a chalkboard.

"What?" she said. "You said this was, like, a three-hour movie, so I deserve to treat myself a little."

Jeremiah shook his head. I turned to him and said, "I forgot to ask. What are we watching?"

"You'll see," he replied.

The lights dimmed and the movie began with a startling prologue—an old man slashes his own throat with a straight razor and gestures to his servants, who look on in terror. The title of the movie appeared on the screen, *Amadeus*, which tells the story of a rivalry between Mozart and an Italian composer named Salieri. I didn't think I'd enjoy a movie set in eighteenth-century Vienna, because I thought it was going to be boring. But while watching the movie, I put myself in Salieri's shoes, and I imagined that Jeremiah was Mozart, whom Salieri was immensely jealous of because of his musical prowess. At the end of the movie, when Mozart dies, I became teary-eyed, because to me it was as if Jeremiah had died.

Down the street from the movie theater was a Denny's, where we went to grab a bite to eat after the movie. Jeremiah and Mallory sat next to each other, while I sat across from them, gorging on country-fried steak and gravy-smothered mashed potatoes. Normally, I would've been too self-conscious to pig out in front of Jeremiah, but I hadn't eaten anything since lunch hour at school. I looked up from my plate and realized that both Jeremiah and Mallory were staring at me. I stopped eating and wiped my mouth with a napkin, feeling a little embarrassed.

"Has anybody ever told you that you eat like a death row inmate?" Mallory said to me with a grin.

"I don't usually eat like this."

"You don't have to explain anything," Jeremiah told me. "Eat away. Here, I'll join you..." He grabbed the burger from his plate and bit into it like a starving pit bull, then smiled.

Mallory, drinking a milkshake, looked at her boyfriend in disgust. "Thanks for reminding us that you're a carnivore."

I continued eating.

"What did you think of the movie?" Jeremiah asked me.

"It was really great," I said. "Way better than I expected. Now I feel like listening to some Mozart when I get home. I don't listen to classical music that much, but everything I heard in that movie sounded incredible."

"I knew you'd like it," Jeremiah said, then turned to Mallory. "What's the verdict, Ms. Eva Braun?"

"It was all right, I guess. Did Mozart really laugh like that, though?" Mallory imitated the composer's irritating laugh from the movie. "He sounded like a fucking hyena."

"I don't know if he really laughed like that, but that's not the point of the movie. It's about the creation of art and jealousy and obsession—all the things that make us human. I mean, humans aren't the only species that get jealous, but we're the only ones who can create art. That's the one thing that separates humans from other primates...art."

Mallory looked at me with a fatigued expression and pointed at her boyfriend as if to say, "This is what I have to deal with."

Jeremiah noticed and said to her, "What is it?"

"Nothing," she replied. "Please tell us more about how we're all primates and apes, because I know it gets your dick hard when you talk about that stuff. Go ahead."

"We *are* primates and apes. That's basic biology. But as long as you've got your Ray-Ban sunglasses and Gucci handbag, what the hell do you care, right?"

Mallory let out a deep sigh and, looking in my direction, said, "This is what happens when Jeremiah doesn't get his dick sucked for longer than a week—he starts talking like a philosopher."

I snorted a laugh, then quickly put my hand over my mouth, embarrassed at having laughed at something Mallory had said.

Jeremiah, half-smiling, looked at me and said, "She's not totally wrong." After a pause, he asked me, "Why didn't you show up at the film studies club yesterday?"

I was flattered that he'd even noticed that I wasn't there. "I just... didn't feel like going," I told him.

"Too bad. You missed a good movie—*Battleship Potemkin*, directed by Sergei Eisenstein. It's a Soviet silent film about a mutiny aboard a Russian battleship. The movie was almost banned in America because Hollywood elites were scared that it would turn Americans into Communists. I had to convince Mr. Van Orton to show the movie, since he's not a big fan of Soviet films—or Commies."

I felt nauseous just hearing Van Orton's name, especially coming out of Jeremiah's mouth.

"You don't like him, do you?" Jeremiah said suddenly.

"I don't know," I replied with a shrug.

"Come on. That's why you didn't show up at the film studies club yesterday, isn't it? You don't like him because he scolded you last week when he showed us that French movie."

I didn't say anything for a while, then finally, I told Jeremiah, "I don't think he is what you think he is."

Jeremiah, taken aback, studied my face. I must've had a strange look on my face, because Jeremiah's expression changed from confused to disturbed. After a few moments of uncomfortable silence, Jeremiah said to me, "First impressions are important...and I guess your first impression of Mr. Van Orton wasn't good. Personally, I think he's the best teacher at the school. Take it from me, Mr. Van Orton is someone worth befriending, so don't write him off yet."

I wasn't sure if Jeremiah still wanted me to come over to his house, but I hoped that I hadn't blown my opportunity because of the remark about Van Orton.

CHAPTER EIGHT

Mallory pulled up in front of a modest ranch house with a small, withered lawn and an old white Saturn parked in the driveway. My first thought upon seeing Jeremiah's house was, *How am I ever going to invite him over to my house?* I didn't want Jeremiah to know that I lived in a two-story suburban house and have him think that I was "bourgeois," which, according to my primitive understanding of Marxist philosophy, I apparently was.

"Don't forget the Ginsberg book," Jeremiah told me as he got out of the car.

I grabbed the book and exited the car, thrilled at the thought of stepping foot in Jeremiah's house for the first time.

Jeremiah looked at Mallory through the open passenger window and said, "Babe, I'll call you tomorrow morning. I love you."

"Love you too," she replied, then turned in my direction. "Sean, make sure you remember my name next time we meet. I'd appreciate it."

I forced a smile and nodded. Mallory drove off. It was about six o'clock and already getting dark.

"Come on," Jeremiah said to me. "It looks like my mom's home from work, so you'll get to meet her."

As soon as we entered the house, Jeremiah called out to his mother and mentioned that he had brought home a friend. His mother, a thin woman in her mid-forties, greeted me with a gentle smile and said, in a slight accent that hinted at her Algerian roots, "Hello, young man. It's nice to meet you."

She wore denim jeans and a cotton button-up shirt, with a red bandana wrapped around her head like Rosie the Riveter. I didn't know what I expected her to look like, but she was lovely.

"Pleased to meet you," I said, shaking her hand. "I'm Sean."

"We're in the same history class," Jeremiah told his mother. "Anyway, we're gonna go to my room now." He turned to me and said, "Let's go."

"Wait," his mother said. "What about dinner? I made *bourek* and *chorba frik*."

"We already ate," Jeremiah told her.

His mother looked at me and said, "I'll wrap some *bourek* for you to take home then. You'll like it. It's a flaky meat pie."

"Yes, Mom, we all know. It's *so* delicious. Come on, Sean."

I followed Jeremiah down a short, narrow hallway leading to his room, which was located next to the laundry room and was almost half the size of my own bedroom. The walls of Jeremiah's room were covered with posters of historical figures and artists, including Ho Chi Minh, Malcolm X, Frida Kahlo, and Orson Welles. There was a twenty-inch television set with a built-in VCR on the wooden floor and a bunch of videocassettes stacked next to it. There was also an old bookshelf in the corner of the room stuffed with books and CDs.

"Check this out," Jeremiah said to me, then walked over to a wall near his bed. I followed him. There were some pictures from magazines taped to the wall, including a grisly image showing the corpses of Mussolini and his cronies hanging upside down in a town square. Jeremiah pointed at the picture and, smiling, told me, "This is what Communists do to fascists. Did you know that the Soviets were responsible for over seventy-five percent of all Nazi German losses? They almost single-handedly defeated Nazi Germany. And they also liberated Auschwitz, which was the largest Nazi concentration and death camp. But they don't tell you that in school textbooks, because 'fuck Stalin.' I agree, fuck him...but the Russian Commies definitely did some great work."

"I know they launched the first artificial Earth satellite," I said.

Jeremiah nodded and replied, "Sputnik 1. They also launched the first human spaceflight. Besides defeating Nazi Germany, those were the Soviets' greatest accomplishments."

"But do you think those good things outweigh all the bad things they did?" I asked, curious.

"What do *you* think?"

I shrugged.

"Let me put it to you this way," Jeremiah said, cocking his head. "When people think about Vlad the Impaler, they don't think about the fact that he massacred tens of thousands of Turks and Bulgarians, or that he impaled pregnant women and children. Instead, they mostly think of him as the national hero of Romania."

"I think of him as the inspiration for Dracula."

Jeremiah chuckled. "That too." He pointed at a picture of a bespectacled young man sitting in a chair and gazing thoughtfully into the distance. "*That's* Sverdlov. He was a Jewish intellectual and one of the Old Bolsheviks who supported Vladimir Lenin. The piece of shit Stalin executed a lot of the Old Bolsheviks, extinguishing any hope of a 'Communist utopia' in Russia."

"Is that how Sverdlov died—he was executed?"

"No, actually...he died of the Spanish flu. But had he lived longer, I'm sure Stalin would've killed him."

I looked at the bookshelf in the corner of the room. "So that's your bookshelf?"

"Yeah, ain't it a beauty?" Jeremiah said sarcastically. We walked to the bookshelf. "I found it at a garage sale. It used to be stuffed with nothing but books, but I've been collecting a lot more music lately, so now I've got a bunch of albums, too. What do *you* listen to?"

"Um...I like Radiohead a lot."

"Shit, me too. Did you listen to their new album, *Hail to the Thief*? That was, like, the only thing I listened to all summer. Not really, but you know."

"I bought the album the day it came out," I told Jeremiah, "and I was so excited to listen to it. I really liked it, but I thought it was just a bit too long."

"Did you see them when they were on *Saturday Night Live*?"

I shook my head.

"This was three years ago," Jeremiah said. "Anyway, Radiohead performed two songs from *Kid A*. I videotaped it, so we can watch it if you want. It's fine if you don't want to. I've got plenty of movies that we can watch instead."

"No, I'm down for whatever."

Jeremiah grabbed a CD from the bookshelf and held it up for me to see. "This is Canibus, a rapper. Do you listen to hip-hop at all, or is that not your thing?"

"The only hip-hop I know is Tupac and popular rappers they play on the radio, like Eminem and stuff."

"You should listen to some underground rap. It's not like the mainstream shit on the radio. Immortal Technique, Jedi Mind Tricks, Ras Kass. I think you'd really like them. Here…"

Jeremiah handed me the Canibus album. "Thanks," I said.

"If you don't like that album, then hip-hop isn't for you. Don't worry, though, I won't think any less of you, I promise."

We both smiled.

"That's his newest album, by the way," Jeremiah told me. "*Rip the Jacker*. It came out this summer. I had a lot of fun listening to it over and over again."

I examined the books on the shelf, most of which were nonfiction: *The Autobiography of Malcolm X*, *A People's History of the United States*, *The Communist Manifesto*, *How Capitalism Underdeveloped Black America*. There were also quite a few poetry books, including ones by Walt Whitman and Christopher Marlowe, neither of whom I'd ever read, although I knew of them. There was a Penguin Classics edition of Karl Marx's *Das Kapital* that caught my eye. I grabbed it, then turned to Jeremiah, who gave me a look as if to say, "Are you fucking kidding me?"

"Is this your favorite book?" I asked.

"Not exactly," Jeremiah replied, and grabbed the book from my hand. "It's way too dense for you." He put the book back on the shelf and grabbed *The Communist Manifesto*. "You should start with this." He handed me the book. "It's basically a pamphlet, and most of what you need to know about Communism is in there. After you read that, then you can decide if you want to be a Commie."

"I do!" I cried, which took Jeremiah by surprise.

"You haven't even read the book yet."

"I don't need to read the book. I mean, I *will* read it, but I'm just saying…if being a Commie means being smart like you…then I've already decided."

Jeremiah appeared on the verge of laughter, then suddenly looked at me with great warmth. "OK, comrade. Welcome to the Party. But, you know, still read the book when you get the chance."

"I will, for sure."

As I juggled two books (Ginsberg and Marx) and the Canibus album in one hand, I noticed a book on the shelf featuring a surrealistic cover art of a winged horse and a figure donning a skull mask. The title read: *Behold a Pale Horse*. Intrigued, I went to reach for it, but Jeremiah, in a swift motion, swatted my hand away.

"No," he said, with a grave expression.

Unnerved, I stared at him, and he stared back, still wearing the same funereal expression.

"What's wrong?" I asked.

"That's the one book on my shelf I can't give you," Jeremiah replied.

"I wasn't going to take it home with me or anything. I just wanted to look at the cover art."

"You can look at it without touching it."

I forced a laugh. "Are you serious right now?"

Jeremiah didn't say anything.

"So…what exactly is that book?" I asked him.

"It's something Mr. Van Orton gave me," he said, after a brief pause.

"Mr. Van Orton gives you books?"

"He gives me lots of things—books, movies, music. He lives on campus at the Todd House, so I go over there sometimes, and we talk about history, music, shit like that."

The Todd House was a modernist glass house that was built in the 1950s and commissioned by Magnolia Academy's first headmaster, Augustus Todd. Located at the edge of campus in a rural setting—not too far from the chapel—the house was constructed as a retreat for the school's elite faculty, of which Van Orton was evidently a part.

"Why are you going over to Mr. Van Orton's place?" I asked Jeremiah, trying to wrap my head around the thought of a sophomore student and his teacher spending time alone together in a secluded house.

"Because he invites me over," he replied. "Mr. Van Orton told me that I'm the first student to ever step foot in the Todd House. Anyway, I like talking to him. I know he can seem a bit stern, especially at the film studies club, but once you get to know him, you realize that he's pretty cool and down to earth. If you got to know him better, I'm sure you'd like him."

"Yeah…sure."

There was a moment of silence. Jeremiah suddenly smiled and said, "All right, let's watch that Radiohead performance from *Saturday Night Live*."

He put on a videotape, and we sat down on the floor with our backs against the bed. I could feel Jeremiah's hand grazing my arm as we watched the video, which sent a surge of bliss through my body. Combined with his intoxicating scent and simply being in his presence, I felt like I was going to burst from excitement.

After the Radiohead performance ended, Jeremiah turned to me and said, "I'll tell my mom to take you home, because I don't want you walking home this late. Not now, though. We can still hang out longer."

"Thanks," I said.

"Where do you live, by the way?"

I hesitated. "I live in, uh…Woodlynne. It's a small neighborhood."

"Yeah, I know. My mom cleans houses there."

Fuck, I thought.

"Mallory lives close to Woodlynne," Jeremiah told me. After a pause, he added, "It's crazy how some people live in luxurious homes, and then just twenty or so minutes away, you see houses that look like they were hit by a tornado."

I cowered in shame and didn't say anything. Jeremiah looked at me, his face earnest, and said, "You know…I thought you would've asked me by now why my mom and I decided to leave Algeria and come to America. Did it ever cross your mind to ask me that?"

"Yeah, actually, it did cross my mind. But I didn't know if that was something I should be asking you, since it's kind of personal."

"Now that we're comrades, nothing's too personal between us. You can ask me anything."

"OK," I said. "So…why did you and your mom come to America?"

Jeremiah smiled sadly. "It wasn't something that we'd planned, that's for sure. I thought I was going to spend the rest of my life in Algeria. But then my dad passed away, and that's when my mom decided that she didn't want to live in Algeria anymore, since it reminded her too much of my dad."

"I'm really sorry to hear about your dad. How did he die, exactly?"

"He killed himself."

"Oh—I'm sorry," I said, regretting having asked about his father.

"It's fine. I mean, it was a long time ago, and I only remember him in fragments. He worked as a barber, and he was always ashamed that my mom, who was a pharmacist, made more money than him. One day, he came home from work and went to take a bath. My mom found him in the bathtub with his wrists cut open. He'd used a straight razor to do it. My mom threw it away, but I fished it out of the garbage can." Jeremiah suddenly got up, went to the bookshelf, grabbed a book, and sat back down next to me. The book was a French hardcover edition of *The Three Musketeers*. "My mom has no clue that I kept the razor," he said, and opened the book, revealing a square point straight razor tucked into the hollowed-out book, as if it were contraband.

"Jesus Christ," I muttered, noticing specks of dried blood on the razor. "How did you even get that through airport security?"

"This was before 9/11," Jeremiah reminded me.

I nodded as if to say, "Oh, right." Then I told him, "Your mom would freak out if she found the razor."

"I don't fucking doubt it. Anyway, the only reason I kept it was because I wanted something to remember my dad by. He told me that he was going to teach me how to shave when I got older. That obviously didn't happen." Jeremiah closed the book and looked at me for a moment. "Do you think I'm some kind of weirdo?"

"I think you're many things, but not a weirdo."

Jeremiah smiled, this time with joy, and we shared an intimate moment, looking into each other's eyes with the kind of affection that's usually reserved for characters in Harlequin novels. I couldn't think of anything worse than being stricken with blindness at the very moment when this magnificent boy, whose beauty I had been marveling with obsessive fervor, was showing genuine interest in me. Perhaps the only thing worse than losing my eyesight would've been if I'd suddenly found myself waking from a dream. That would've been the cruelest of blows.

"Do you like kung fu movies?" Jeremiah asked me, ending our intimate moment. Before I could respond, he got up and went to put on another videotape. "This is my favorite kung fu film," he told me. "It's called *The Mystery of Chess Boxing*. No Radiohead here. Just straight-up martial arts."

We didn't talk much during the badly dubbed film, although Jeremiah would occasionally make comments about the fighting scenes and how skillful the martial artists were. After the movie was over, Jeremiah's mother drove me home, but not before giving me some *bourek* wrapped in a dish towel to take home with me. The savory pie smelled of onions and meat.

CHAPTER NINE

I spent a week and a half reading the two books that Jeremiah had loaned me, starting with *The Communist Manifesto*, which, at a mere fifty or so pages, I read in one sitting. Then, to make sure I understood the text, I read it two more times. I didn't find anything controversial or shocking in the book, contrary to what biased Hollywood movies had me believe. In the book, Marx and co-author Friedrich Engels advocate for a progressive income tax, in which people with higher income pay a higher percentage of taxes than people with lower income, thus mitigating income inequality. They also advocate for free public education and the abolition of child labor, while stressing that class struggle has long been the central issue in the world.

The Ginsberg book, which is a little over a hundred pages, took me longer to read, but that was because I wanted to savor its raw beauty. The only poetry that I had read prior to the Ginsberg book were a few Shakespeare sonnets and portions of John Milton's *Paradise Lost*, though I found Ginsberg's poetry more engaging due to its simplistic form. The main poem, "Kaddish," about the poet's late mother, Naomi Ginsberg, affected me deeply, as I was moved by Ginsberg's devotion to his late mother, a Russian immigrant who suffered from paranoid schizophrenia and who spent much of her life in mental hospitals.

"Communist beauty," Ginsberg writes of his mother, who was a fervent Marxist, "sit here married in the summer among daisies, promised happiness at hand—holy mother, now you smile on your love."

After having read the poem and being touched by Naomi Ginsberg's troubled life, as well as her unrelenting commitment to Marxism, I made the decision to remain a loyal Communist for the rest of my life as a way to honor the late woman, of whose existence I was completely unaware just a week prior. But that's how my mind works—passionate and obsessive to a fault. I had gone from a charlatan, adopting Communism as a mere ploy to attract Jeremiah, to a committed

Commie quicker than it takes most people to pass a kidney stone. It's both funny and remarkable how life works out sometimes, like a vaude-villian play.

I was supposed to meet Jeremiah in the library after chapel to dis-cuss the books, but during lunch hour, one of the school secretaries, a woman with a worrying disposition, came down to the dining hall and told me that Father Hawkins wished to see me in his office after chapel.

"Why does he want to see me?" I asked.

"I don't know," the secretary said, tugging at the sleeves of her knit sweater as if she were cold, "but you just make sure to be there, OK?"

"Can I just go see him now? I have to see a friend later at the…" I stopped suddenly. "Never mind."

"*Immediately* after chapel," the secretary stressed, then walked away.

During chapel, I tried to signal to Jeremiah with my hands, but he was sitting at the far end of the pew and didn't so much as look in my direction. Simon, who was sitting next to me, noticed my pantomime and whispered to me, "What are you doing?"

"Nothing," I replied. "Listen, after chapel, I want you to go to the art history section on the second floor of the library. Jeremiah—that kid over there," I said, pointing at Jeremiah. "He'll be there. I want you to tell him that I can't meet him after chapel. You got that?"

Simon contorted his face in confusion. "Why don't you just tell him yourself after chapel?"

"Because there's always a fucking stampede after chapel."

"Do you have to go somewhere after chapel?"

"Yeah. I gotta see Father Hawkins."

"Why?" Simon asked.

"Who the hell knows?" I said. "Also, tell Jeremiah to meet me by the Columbus statue after school, OK?"

Simon nodded sadly. After a moment, he said, "We never hang out anymore. How come?"

"I—I don't know. I just like hanging out with people my own age."

"You mean like your new friend Jeremiah?"

"Yeah…him. But don't worry, we can still hang out. I know I

promised I'd come over, but I've been distracted lately, sorry. This week, though, we'll go watch the movie at the film studies club, whichever movie it is, then we'll go to your place after."

"I thought you didn't want to go to the film studies club anymore."

I sighed, then said, "I know, but I figure I'll give it another shot. Then when we go to your place, you can play your guitar for me."

"All right," Simon said, smiling.

Father Hawkins cut his sermon short and left the chapel early, as an exuberant Jeunet, who was standing off to the side of the altar, walked to the pulpit and addressed the congregation with passion, saying, "When I look out at the sea of faces before me, I see young men of great integrity and promise. Although you older gentlemen have entered the horror of horrors—that is, *puberty*—I have no doubt that you will emerge from your adolescent cocoons with the might of the Spanish Armada and avoid being trampled by life's wild horses. Just as birds sing and the Earth revolves around the Sun, you gentlemen are sure to succeed where the prideful Icarus had failed."

Most of the boys looked dazed and sleepy, not at all interested in what Jeunet had to say. I looked at Jeremiah, who appeared to be lost in thought, unconcerned with the outside world, then turned my attention back to the headmaster.

"I admit, gentlemen, that when I first spoke to you in this chapel, I was rather morose. That was because the night before the first day of school—an elongated night that mirrored an El Greco painting—I was suddenly struck with the harrowing realization that the boys in this school and all over the world are born with the same tragic flaw that resulted in Adam and Eve being kicked out of the Garden of Eden. I thought to myself, 'What's the point of it all?' But then, on my way here today, I glanced out the window of my car and saw a young boy, who appeared to be on the cusp of puberty, struggling in vain to free his skin from its polyester prison. I tell you, gentlemen, it was the most accurate image of youth in revolt that I had ever seen, and it occurred to me that you boys, who possess an imagination audacious enough to rival the Book of Revelation, will find a way to return to God's good graces. Mind you, I don't condone cynical anarchy, but I am in favor of self-discovery. The mind of a child is both a wonderful and terrifying labyrinth, and the transition from infancy to adolescence is undoubtedly the most disturbing overthrow of innocence known to man. But I have faith that you gentlemen, you men of God, will persevere and lead extraordinary lives with extraordinary passages. I only ask that you remain humble during your journey."

Jeunet paused for a moment to observe the congregation. "One more thing," he continued with a grin. "For you sophomores fortunate enough to be in one of Mr. Van Orton's history classes, at the end of the first semester, Mr. Van Orton will pick six of the best students from his classes to attend the annual Rais Frolic, where six students, as well as Mr. Van Orton and myself, will spend a weekend at my splendid country house in Old Westbury. I need not remind you gentlemen what an immense honor it is to be chosen to attend the weekend getaway, as it will do wonders for one's college application."

The Rais Frolic was a peculiar event that never made much sense to me. Every year, a new teacher was selected by Jeunet to attend the event with six of the teacher's "best students," meaning the six biggest suck-ups. To me, it seemed like nothing more than a weekend field trip for Jeunet's benefit, though how exactly it benefitted him remained unclear to me.

I knocked on the large wooden door and waited for a response.

"Come in!" Father Hawkins bellowed.

I entered the cleric's office, which looked like what one would imagine an office belonging to a high-ranking Marine officer to look like, though instead of military regalia, the wood-paneled walls were covered with Catholic paraphernalia, including a huge painting of Saint Jerome writing in his study that hung behind the cleric's desk.

"Well, don't just stand there," Father Hawkins said to me, sitting behind his desk. "Have a seat."

I sat across from him, curious to find out what it was that he wanted to talk to me about. I waited for him to say something, but he just glared at me as if I'd somehow offended him.

"Mr. Quell," he said finally, with a sigh.

"Father," I said jauntily.

"Don't get cute with me, young man. I still remember our little dialogue when you were in the sixth grade. Have you gotten over your Luciferian fixation yet? I hope so."

"So why did you ask to see me, Father?"

The cleric snorted indignantly. "Are you aware, Mr. Quell, that every student from grades nine through twelve is required to go to confession within the first week of school? And yet, despite having been in school for over a month, I have yet to see you in the confessional. So I must ask, is there a valid reason why you haven't gone to confession yet? Perhaps the wicked spirit of Martin Luther has gotten a hold of you and has led you astray. Is that it, boy? Tell me."

I put my hand over my mouth to keep myself from laughing, then said, "No, Father, I don't think Martin Luther knows the way to my heart." I chuckled.

"Yes, yes…get the giggles out. Need I remind you, Mr. Quell, that, although your parents pay a hefty tuition fee for you to attend this school, we can still kick you out? You're not immune to expulsion by any means. I say this because you seem to be a little too comfortable in this school, especially when speaking to *me*. But I assure you, Mr. Quell, run afoul of me again like you did in our Biblical Literature class years ago, and I will swiftly replace the honey in my pen with acid. Is that understood?"

"I—I believe so, Father."

The portly cleric readjusted himself in his seat. "Now…I ask again, why haven't you gone to confession yet, boy?"

"Well, Father, I, um, I…"

"The *truth*."

I wanted to tell him that I'd recently become a Communist and that I no longer believed in God, for no other reason than to spite him, but I knew he wouldn't take kindly to that and would've possibly used my being a Commie as justification to expel me.

"I've been going through some…'physical' changes, Father," I told him.

"W—w—what do you mean, exactly?"

"You know…hormonal. I'm a young man now, Father, and my body is going through some massive changes. You were a young man once, Father. I'm sure you know what I'm talking about."

Father Hawkins swallowed hard. "Y—yes, my son, I know all too well."

"Anyway, now that my body's been going through all these changes, I've been—how do I say this? I've been, uh…*experimenting* with myself. Often, in fact…again and again. In the privacy of my bedroom, of course. After all, I'm not some heathen."

Father Hawkins, his forehead perspiring, shook his head fervently and said, "Of course not, my son. You're no heathen. But w—why exactly is this preventing you from going to confession?"

I quickly looked away as if too embarrassed to speak.

"Go on, my son…speak."

"Oh, Father," I said, feigning embarrassment. "I don't know how else to say it except"—I turned to Father Hawkins—"I can't seem to stop 'experimenting' with myself. And if I were to go to confession now, I know I'd just experiment again the next day…so what would be the point of receiving absolution? I'd just keep experimenting again and again and again…"

Father Hawkins, distressed, held up his hands as if to stop me and said, "Yes, yes, my son, I see what you mean now."

"It *is* a sin to experiment with yourself, isn't it, Father?"

"Well, um…indeed, it is a sin. It's in fact a mortal sin…against the Sixth Commandment."

"And what's the Sixth Commandment again?"

"'Thou shalt not commit adultery.'"

I nodded and said, "Oh—right. That's a good one. Anyway, Father… now you understand why I didn't go to confession."

"Yes, my son, I certainly do understand." Father Hawkins wiped the sweat from his brow. "But—I still want you to go to confession…when-ever you're ready, of course."

"Oh, Father…with how often I've been experimenting, I don't know when I'll be ready to go to confession."

The cleric let out a groan of pleasure and placed a hand on his chest. He looked like he was about to faint. "Mr. Quell, I have to be perfectly honest with you. Before today, whenever I'd look at you, I'd feel a ter-rible pang in my heart as if stabbed by a lance that was hurled by God Almighty Himself. But now that you've unburdened yourself to me, I no longer feel that terrible pang in my heart when I look at you. Instead, as I look at you now, I'm simply filled with benevolence. What a strange feeling."

"I guess we've both benefitted from this talk, huh, Father?"

"Yes, my son, I would say so."

I smiled, while Father Hawkins, still trying to collect himself, wiped his face and mumbled something to himself. Then he said, "Before I dismiss you, Mr. Quell, I have one last thing to share with you, and this is perhaps the most important thing I have to say to you today."

"What is it, Father?"

"Are you familiar with Muhammad Ali, the retired athlete?"

I nodded.

"Well," Father Hawkins continued, "despite being a heretic who will never reach the gates of Heaven, there's an anecdote about Mr. Ali that I find useful. It is said that he keeps a matchbox in his pocket, and whenever his heart slips toward sin, he burns a matchstick and heats his palm to remind himself of the potential hellfire that awaits him if he succumbs to sin. Now, Mr. Ali needs not worry about that because, being a Muslim heretic, he's certain to suffer hellfire. But *you*, Mr. Quell, do not have to, so long as you repent and remain pure in the eyes of God. Do you think you can do that?"

"I'll do my best, Father."

"Please do—because I'd hate to see a Catholic suffer eternal damnation alongside the likes of Muhammad Ali."

I waited until I'd left Father Hawkins' office before bursting into laughter, eliciting strange looks from the puritanical staff.

CHAPTER TEN

My heart leapt when I saw Jeremiah standing by the Christopher Columbus statue. It was as if I were seeing him for the first time. But simply *seeing* him wasn't enough, however, because one had to also stand near him and inhale his amazing scent with slow breaths to fully understand what made him seem so mystical and how easy it was to fall under his spell.

"Did Simon talk to you?" I asked Jeremiah as I approached him. "I mean, I'm sure he did, otherwise you wouldn't be here."

Jeremiah glanced at me and said, "He came to see me at the library. I guess that means our rebel base has been jeopardized. Gotta find a new base."

"Oh, right," I said with a half-smile, not sure if he was being serious.

"We talked for a bit, Simon and I. He's a nice kid…but I got the feeling that he resents you a little."

"I don't blame him. But I'm gonna make it up to him. Anyway, sorry I forgot to bring you your books, but I did read them."

Jeremiah waved it off and told me, "Forget it. Keep the books for as long as you want. Are you hungry, by the way?"

"Uh…yeah."

"Let's go to Blondie's. I'm meeting Mallory there. You can tell me about the books on the way there." Jeremiah looked at the Columbus statue with disgust. "I don't want to have to look at this thing for a second longer." He turned back to me and said, "Come on, Kemosabe."

He walked away, while I stood there and grinned like an idiot, awestruck at how effortlessly cool Jeremiah was. I caught up to him, and we walked side by side to Blondie's, our hands a mere two inches away from touching.

"I read *The Communist Manifesto* three times," I told Jeremiah, thinking that he'd be proud of me. "I thought the book was going to be crazy or something, since almost every movie I've seen that has

Communists in it makes it seem like Communism is all about people doing some evil shit, but I didn't find anything bad in the book. It was just Karl Marx and the other guy explaining how capitalism exploits people and takes away people's human rights."

"It does more than that. It also kills the environment and commodifies human beings. Not to mention it makes war and genocide inevitable."

"What about…Pol Pot?"

Jeremiah shrugged and said, "I don't know. All I know about him is that he was an amazing cricket player."

"I'm being serious. What do you say when people bring him up and all the horrible things he did?"

"Pete Seeger once said that he still calls himself a Communist, because Communism is no more what Russia made of it than Christianity is what the churches make of it—and he's goddamn right. Mind you, that's Pete Seeger talking, a dude with a Grammy Lifetime Achievement Award and an induction into the Rock and Roll Hall of Fame. It makes my dick hard knowing a Commie received those accolades."

I chuckled. "Come on, you're not answering my question. How do you justify Pol Pot, just as an example?"

"How do European Christians justify the Congo Free State and the Bosnian genocide? How do Shintoists and Buddhists justify the Rape of Nanjing? We can go on and on. And that's mostly the twentieth century. You don't even want me to go back to the St. Bartholomew's Day massacre, because that shit will make your blood curdle. As for Pol Pot, the guy was a Khmer nationalist and an anti-intellectual who turned into a totalitarian dictator. I swear, that motherfucker had to be the only anti-intellectual Communist in the world. That makes about as much sense as being a Jewish Nazi. Anyway, not every Commie can be as 'cultured' as Che Guevara."

"Do you like him—Che Guevara, I mean?"

"Sure," Jeremiah said. "I read his *Motorcycle Diaries*. The guy had a real hunger to explore the world. He studied medicine, cared about humanity, and he hated to see people being exploited. The only people who don't like Che Guevara are Uncle Toms from Florida who are still upset that Fidel Castro took away their families' slaves and plantations. Anti-Castro Cubans want to be white so badly that I bet they'd drop to their knees if the Yankees told them to."

I laughed and said, "You can be pretty funny sometimes. Do you think that's why Mallory likes you?"

"Actually, I know exactly why she likes me." Jeremiah looked at me with a smile and said, "She likes the way I smell, apparently."

Of course she does, I thought, as if I couldn't dislike Mallory any more than I already did.

We sat at a small table by the counter at Blondie's, since all the booths were taken. I nibbled on some cheese fries, while Jeremiah chewed on a greasy burger, wiping his mouth with a napkin after each bite. I kept hoping that Mallory wouldn't show up at the diner, then Jeremiah and I could spend the day together alone, but knowing what a heel his girl-friend was, I knew that wasn't likely to happen.

"What did you think of the Ginsberg book?" Jeremiah asked me.

"It was great," I said. "That book made me more sympathetic toward Communism than the Marx book, to be honest."

"So do you still want to be a Communist?"

"Definitely. After reading that poem about Ginsberg's mom and all the painful shit she had to go through, I'm more committed to Communism than ever before. I know that probably sounds like a poor excuse to be a Commie, but I guess I'm just weird like that."

Jeremiah took a bite of his burger, then muttered something, but I was too distracted by his gleaming lips to hear what it was. Only after he'd wiped his mouth did I realize that he was talking to me.

"What...?" I said.

"I'm going to tell you a dirty little secret about me. Even if I knew with absolute certainty that Communism was wrong, I'd still be a Commie. On the surface, that sounds pretty stupid, but you have to keep in mind that human beings are social creatures who thrive on collectivism, which is one reason why I believe, in the end, Communism will prevail. My belief in Communism is no different than the way Christians believe in God, or the way baseball nuts believe in the New York Yankees. To me, Communism is a team you root for. And we all need a team to root for, because it makes life just a little more fun and worthwhile."

I sat there in stunned silence, digesting Jeremiah's words. I was in wonder at how his mind worked, and I couldn't imagine what it would be like to spend the rest of my life with Jeremiah by my side—as a brother, a friend, a lover, even a neighbor. *What a luxury it would be to wake up in the same household, or simply live on the same street, as Jeremiah*, I thought. For the life of me, I couldn't imagine it! I seriously wondered if Jeremiah's own mother realized just how special, how intelligent, how unbelievably beautiful her son was. It was impossible that Mallory and I were the only ones enamored with him. Van Orton surely had an eye on him. How many others were there? If there had been a way to keep Jeremiah locked up inside my rib cage to myself, I would've done so at once.

"There you are," I heard a familiar voice say. It was Mallory, donning high-waisted pleated pants and a cashmere turtleneck with the sleeves pulled up. Standing next to Jeremiah, she leaned down to kiss him, then sat down next to him, ignoring me.

"Hey, Mallory," I said reluctantly.

She looked at me as if surprised and replied, "Oh—hi. You actually remembered my name. I knew you had it in you."

I expected her to respond with a smart-ass comment, as that was her nature. I didn't know how Jeremiah could tolerate being around her for an entire day, multiple times a week. *She either cast a potent spell on him*, I thought, *or she gave the world's greatest blowjobs.*

"So what do you want to do?" Mallory asked Jeremiah, who glanced at me, then turned to his girlfriend.

"Let's go to your place," he said. "Your parents and brother are away for the week, right?"

"Yeah."

Jeremiah looked at me. "Are you cool with that?"

"Y—you mean going to Mallory's place?" I said.

Jeremiah nodded.

"Shit," I said, hesitant. "My parents expect me home for dinner tonight."

Mallory let out a derisive laugh, prompting Jeremiah to glare at her. He then turned to me and said, "You live in Woodlynne, right?"

"Uh-huh."

"Well, Mallory lives about five minutes away from there...so you can come with us to her place and still be home on time for dinner. She can even drive you home."

I thought about it for a while. "All right," I said finally.

Jeremiah smiled, then bit into his burger, his eyes fixed on me. Mallory looked at his plate and said, "You didn't order any fries, just a goddamn burger?"

"I ate the fries," Jeremiah told her.

"Asshole."

Jeremiah looked at me and asked, "By the way, did you listen to the Canibus album I gave you? I forgot to ask earlier."

"Yeah," I said with a nod. "It was fucking heavy, man. Some of the lyrics went totally over my head. I felt like I needed a dictionary just to keep up because of all the scientific references he was making. I'm still listening to it. My favorite line is when he says 'I'm the first rapper to speak over beats dogmatically—'"

"'—Mixed with Elizabethan drama and tragedy,'" Jeremiah finished the rhyme. "I like that one too."

Mallory rolled her eyes and said, "Jesus Christ, you guys are such fucking nerds." She got up. "When you two are done rapping, I'll be in my car, OK?"

"I'll order some fries for you," Jeremiah said, taking his girlfriend by the hand.

"Thanks, babe," she said, then held up Jeremiah's hand and licked his index finger, smiling. She then walked away.

Jeremiah turned to me and shrugged, then went back to eating his burger. "Oh—yeah," he said suddenly, and wiped his mouth. "Did you hear when Dr. Jeunet was talking about the annual Rais Frolic?"

"Yeah," I replied. "Do you know why it's called the 'Rais Frolic'?"

"I don't know, but the word 'Rais' is an Arabic title meaning 'leader.' Anyway, how lucky for us that Mr. Van Orton got selected to be the teacher this year. I think you and me have a good shot of getting picked for the Rais Frolic."

"*You*, definitely—since Mr. Van Orton likes you so much. But I don't know about me. And besides, I don't think I want to spend an entire weekend at Dr. Jeunet's country house…no matter what it would do for my college application." I thought for a moment. "But I guess if we *both* got to go, then that'd be cool."

A smiling Jeremiah nodded and said, "Exactly. It'd be like a little vacation. And I can talk to Mr. Van Orton about picking both of us, but I don't know if he'll do it."

I kind of shrugged. Then, suddenly remembering something, I looked at Jeremiah and said, "Isn't it weird, though, that the Rais Frolic still takes place, even though a student died during it?"

Jeremiah, confused, stared at me, then said, "What?"

"This one student, Chandler Faust, he went to Dr. Jeunet's country house for the Rais Frolic and killed himself in the house. It happened in the Eighties."

"I've never heard about that before in my life. Where did you hear about it?"

"I read about it over the summer. I found this book about the school's history at the public library, and they talked about how this kid, Chandler, hung himself in Dr. Jeunet's country house. I mean, it was kind of a big deal when it happened, they said, but I don't think anybody talks about it anymore—probably because they don't want to be reminded of a dead kid." I paused. "But you know what's creepy, though? When the forensic team inspected Chandler's dead body, they found the word 'Chronovisor' written on his forearm under his sweater. They said he probably wrote it himself."

Jeremiah gave me a sardonic look. "Are you joking?"

"No, I swear. It's all true."

"Where did you actually find this book?"

"At the Adriance Memorial Library," I said. "I wasn't allowed to check it out of the library, though…so I had to read it there."

Jeremiah nodded a little and told me, "I'll probably swing by the library tomorrow and see if I can find the book." He finished his burger. "What's that book called?"

"Just *Magnolia Academy*, I think. There were several authors, but I can't remember any of their names. It was kind of an old book with a battered cover."

We both got up.

"I gotta get some fries for Mallory," Jeremiah said to me, digging into his pants pocket for money. "By the way…what does 'Chronovisor' mean?"

"I don't know," I said with a shrug. "I figured if anybody knew, it'd be a brainiac like you."

Jeremiah smiled and gave me the middle finger.

CHAPTER ELEVEN

Mallory unlocked the door to her upper-middle-class home and opened it, letting herself in first, then Jeremiah, who had the dishonor of holding his girlfriend's fries in a paper cone bearing an image of Blondie's mascot, Wolfgang von Strudel. I walked into the pristine house and noticed that it bore a striking resemblance to my own house, especially with regard to its nautical-themed décor and blonde wood flooring.

I wondered how Jeremiah felt about going over to Mallory's lavish home, knowing that his own house wasn't nearly as posh. It didn't appear to bother him, however, as he walked about the house as if he owned the place. Mallory snatched the paper cone fries from Jeremiah's hand, then walked up an opulent spiral staircase, which was topped by an enormous skylight.

Jeremiah walked over to me and, with a wry smile, said, "So how does this place compare to yours?"

"You mean the house?" I replied, playing dumb.

Jeremiah nodded.

"It's...about the same," I told him. "Maybe a little too similar. What do her parents do for a living, anyway?"

"Her dad's an investment banker, and her mom doesn't do shit except look pretty and make reservations at restaurants. How perfectly god-damned delightful capitalism is. Adam Smith would be fucking proud."

I looked at Jeremiah and asked, in earnest, "Do you love Mallory?"

He chuckled and patted me on the back. "That's not the right question, comrade. It doesn't matter anyway. I think about Kerala more than I think about Mallory. She doesn't even know what I plan to do after I graduate from Magnolia. Then again, she doesn't care."

"Then why are you with her?"

Jeremiah paused. "You'll find out soon."

We went into the spacious living room and watched TV. Mallory joined us moments later, having changed into a pair of leggings shorts and an oversized sweatshirt.

"What happened to your fries?" Jeremiah asked his girlfriend as she sat on the couch beside him, then rested his hand on her thigh. (I sat in a Rococo armchair across from them.)

"I'm saving it for later," she replied. "What are you guys watching, anyway?"

The Exorcist was playing on TV. Mallory watched in disgust as the possessed Linda Blair masturbates with a crucifix, then buries her mother's face into her crotch.

"That's so gross," she said, looking away. "Change the channel, you weirdo."

Jeremiah changed the channel to PBS, which was airing a documentary about 9/11. "Christ, how many documentaries are they going to make about 9/11?"

"How unpatriotic of you," Mallory said with feigned outrage. "Don't you know that three thousand people died that day?"

"And do you want to know how many Palestinians have died since 1948?" Jeremiah replied bitterly. "It's a lot more than three thousand, I promise."

"Please don't give me another history lecture, or else I'm gonna do what the possessed girl did in that movie."

Jeremiah smirked and said to his girlfriend, "I wouldn't mind that at all. You've probably done it before, you dirty cow."

Mallory sneered. "It's 'pig,' asshole, not 'cow.' If you're going to talk dirty to me, then do it right."

"How about I call you a 'sow'?" Jeremiah said.

"How about I do this…?" Mallory replied, grabbing her boyfriend's crotch. "Don't think I won't suck you off in front of your Freddie Mercury friend over there. Plus, I'm sure he'd love to hear you moan." She looked at me and said, "You should hear the way Jeremiah moans. He sounds like a wounded animal. But maybe that's because you boys are still only fifteen."

"If you were a year older," I said to her, "you'd be a pedophile."

Mallory laughed. "Is that your way of trying to hurt me for calling you 'Freddie Mercury'?"

"What did you mean by that, anyway?" Jeremiah asked her with a scowl.

"Oh, come on," she said. "You don't see the way he looks at you? He's practically begging you to go down on him. I swear, boys can be so damn blind sometimes. How did your kind produce someone like Albert Einstein...or Vincent van Gogh?"

"Not sure," Jeremiah replied, "but I know that if Van Gogh had been a woman, he would've just cut off his bangs—instead of his ear."

Mallory giggled, then grabbed her boyfriend by the shirt, pulling him toward her, and said, "Come here, funny boy."

They started making out. It almost seemed like they were doing it to provoke me, or rather, Mallory was, as she was spiteful that way.

I turned to the TV and watched as the first hijacked plane crashed into the North Tower of the World Trade Center. I'd seen those images so many times before that I'd become desensitized to them. I eventually turned back to the couple, whom I no longer considered "divine," and forced myself to watch them make out. Jeremiah took off his school blazer, while Mallory began to unzip his pants, then stopped suddenly and looked at me as if expecting me to protest.

"What's the matter?" Jeremiah said to her.

She smiled and turned back to him, then proceeded to unzip his pants and go down on him in a way that suggested proficiency in the sexual act. To avoid seeing this, I turned to the TV again and, preferring carnage to sex, watched as the second hijacked plane crashed into the South Tower of the World Trade Center.

I tried not to pay attention to what was happening on the couch across from me, but Mallory was making loud slurping noises, prompting me to once again turn my attention back to the couple. Jeremiah and I suddenly made eye contact. He grabbed Mallory by the hair and lifted her head, as if to show me what his cock looked like. As I stared at his dick in a trance-like state, I realized that that was the first time I'd ever seen another boy's dick in real life—and how blessed I was that it was Jeremiah's.

Mallory resumed sucking Jeremiah off, and I began to wonder if I was experiencing a fever dream, or if I was actually seeing this. After having watched the surreal scene for longer than was necessary, during which Jeremiah's face had contorted in such a way that it almost frightened me, I finally looked away. Yet, despite facing away from the couple, I could somehow still see Mallory performing fellatio on Jeremiah, whose face remained contorted as if in agony. That was the closest I'd ever come to having an out-of-body experience, as I imagine that's what the phenomenon must feel like.

Jeremiah began to moan (his girlfriend was right—he moaned like a wounded animal), and I was tempted to leave the room, as this was getting to be too much for me. Then suddenly, I heard Jeremiah cry out, "I'm coming!" I turned to him as if compelled to do so and watched as he shook with exhilaration upon reaching orgasm, staining Mallory's sweatshirt in the process. He fell back on the couch, panting like a winded dog, and zipped up his pants.

Mallory, realizing that Jeremiah had ejaculated all over her sweatshirt, flew into a rage and squealed, "Jesus Christ, you came on my fucking Versace!" She then slapped her boyfriend on the chest and pulled her shorts back up.

"I'm sorry, babe…" Jeremiah said, holding back laughter.

"Yeah, I'm sorry too, dick."

Mallory took off her sweatshirt, revealing a cropped tank top underneath. She bundled her sweatshirt into a ball and stormed out of the room, while Jeremiah laughed. Soon, I began to laugh too. Our laughter eventually subsided until there was total silence. Jeremiah sat up, looking at me with mild curiosity, then said, "Have you ever gotten a blowjob?"

"No," I told him, after a brief pause. "I—I, um, I'm actually still a virgin."

"So you haven't done anything yet, then…?"

I shook my head.

"Do you *want* to lose your virginity?" Jeremiah asked me.

I almost laughed at the question. Maybe it was the way he emphasized the word "want." I told him, "Yes, I want to lose my virginity, like, when I'm ready."

"Maybe to a girl like Mallory?"

I paused. "No, not to someone like her. I mean, she is pretty, but she's also your girlfriend."

"What if she wasn't my girlfriend? Would you fuck her?"

I forced a chuckle, while Jeremiah, who was gazing at me like he was trying to figure me out, waited for me to give him an adequate response.

"No," I finally replied, "I wouldn't sleep with Mallory."

"But you do want to fuck *someone*, right?"

I nodded.

"Just not Mallory," he said, "or, really…any other girl."

"Yeah," I told him.

Jeremiah looked at me as if to say, "Now I know what you are." But I didn't care. I wanted him to know everything—that I'd been obsessed with him since I first laid eyes on him and yearned for him to such a degree as to render the word "yearn" obsolete, and that I wished I'd been the one to give him head, instead of his girlfriend. But despite wanting him to know all that, I didn't have the courage to tell him, because I was afraid of how he'd react. It's not easy telling someone whom you've known for just over a month that you venerate them and that being in their presence is like being high on opium. Such confessions are only voiced inward.

"Is there something you want to tell me?" Jeremiah said to me nonchalantly.

"What do you mean?" I replied.

"You just have that look on your face…like you want to tell me something."

I shook my head. Jeremiah scoffed, then looked down and picked lint from his pants, as if he no longer wished to speak to me—or even acknowledge me.

"There is something I want to ask you…again," I said. "But I want a *real* answer this time."

Jeremiah looked at me, curious.

"Do you love Mallory?" I asked him gently.

He snorted a bit, then said, "I love her about as much as she loves me, which is to say…not very much."

"But then—*why* stay with her?"

"You're a big boy, Sean. I'm sure you've heard of 'relationships of convenience' before. I need a safety net just like everyone else. How does that one song by the Smiths go…? 'I am human and I need to be loved, just like everybody else does.' That's the kind of relationship Mallory and I have. It sounds depressing, I know, and it *is*—but there was once a time when I genuinely loved her. She usually breaks up with guys after dating them for only a few weeks, she told me, but that I was 'special.' I think she just likes me because I'm an 'exotic' Brown kid and

not just some white boy who plays lacrosse and drinks Mountain Dew."
Jeremiah shrugged and added, "But it is what it is. And the fact that I
apparently smell pretty good doesn't hurt."

I looked at him with a grin.

"What?" he said.

"I just can't believe you listen to the Smiths." I chuckled. "I wasn't
expecting you to quote Morrissey."

"What, you think hip-hop and Radiohead are the only music I listen
to, asshole?" Jeremiah said playfully. "I'm full of surprises, you know."

"I bet you are, *comrade*."

Jeremiah's face suddenly turned sour. "Don't call me 'comrade' like
it's a fucking joke or something, because it's not. Leon Trotsky got his
head cracked open with an ice ax, you know, so don't make light of this
beautiful thing we share."

I recoiled a bit. "Oh...sorry. I didn't mean anything by it."

After glaring at me for a moment, Jeremiah's face softened with
indifference. "Fuck it," he said, shaking his head, then got up and put
his blazer back on, as if nothing had happened.

I wasn't sure if he was upset with me or not, so I asked him, trying to
sound as nonchalant as possible, "Are we still cool?"

"Sure," he replied. "I'm not *that* sensitive."

"By the way," I said, getting up, "tell your mom thanks for the *bourek*.
It was delicious. Is that, like, a popular cuisine in Algeria?"

"I think it's popular in a lot of places, especially the Balkans. I knew
you'd like it. Anyway, you want Mallory to drive you home?"

"No, that's OK. I'd rather just walk home."

"Are you sure?" Jeremiah said.

I nodded, then stretched my back. "Oh!" I said suddenly, remembering something. "When your mom drove me home that one night,
she played John Denver in the car."

Jeremiah rolled his eyes in bemusement and said, "Fucking always
with that John Denver."

CHAPTER TWELVE

My parents and I sat at the dining table eating dinner, which consisted of mashed potatoes, roasted chicken, and Caesar salad, all cooked and prepared by our maid, Stana, a Yugoslav woman in her late thirties with pale skin and dark hair. Stana ate dinner in the kitchen by herself, while the rest of us ate in the dining room, only a couple of feet away. Even though Stana had worked for us for almost three years, it never seemed to occur to my parents to ask her if she wanted to join us at the dining table.

"Should I, um…ask Stana if she wants to eat with us?" I asked suddenly.

My parents looked at me as if I'd just taken a shit at the table.

"Why would you want to do that?" my father replied.

"I just think she might want to eat with us, instead of eating by herself all the time."

My father, who always wore a morning suit as if he were the Monopoly Man, thought for a moment, then said, "I think she'll be all right."

I looked at my mother, who was the more empathetic of my parents, hoping that she'd have a different take. "It's fine, sweetie," she told me.

Disheartened, I dropped the subject. It had never bothered me before that Stana ate in the kitchen by herself—that is, until I met Jeremiah's mother. Now I felt guilty by association, which was a strange new feeling for me.

"So what did you do today?" my father asked me.

"Um…not much," I said. "I just went to Blondie's with a friend, then we went to his house and watched some TV. That's about it."

"You mean that Simon boy?" my mother interjected. "I hope you're nice to him."

"It was actually another friend."

My mother looked at me. "Which friend is this?"

"You don't know him," I said. "He's, uh…in my history class."

"Yes—and? What's his name?"

"Jeremiah."

"Like the miserable prophet," my father quipped.

My mother shot him a glance and said, "It's the 'weeping' prophet, for goodness' sake, not the 'miserable' prophet." She turned back to me. "So…what's he like?"

"Jeremiah?"

My mother nodded.

"He's…*incredible*," I told her. "Easily the smartest kid in our class. I mean, normally that wouldn't mean anything, since I think most of the kids at the school are idiots. But Jeremiah is not like the other kids. He speaks three different languages, and he knows almost as much about history as our teacher."

"He sounds like quite a boy. Why don't you invite him over to our place? I'd love to meet this polyglot friend of yours."

I shrugged and said, "Maybe."

After a moment of silence, my father suddenly turned to me and said, "Your mom tells me that you're reading—what was it…*The Communist Manifesto*? Why in God's holy name are you reading that trash?"

I shot my mother a scolding look.

"She came across it in your room while cleaning *your* mess," my father told me. "Anyway, what's with the pinko book?"

"It's just a book," I said. "And I know Mom doesn't clean my room, ever—not with Stana here."

"Stick to the subject. Why are you reading that book?"

"Because I like to learn. I'm going to become a historian, and Communism is a big part of history, you know."

My father thought for a moment, then said to me, "Didn't you say something about wanting to become a 'medieval' historian? Communism isn't medieval history, even if the ideology itself is *medieval*."

"It doesn't matter," I replied, "because I want to learn everything, medieval or not. What's the big deal?"

"Ask Stana what the big deal is. She came to America from a Communist country. Believe me, she didn't come here because her native country was a glorious 'utopia.'"

"Dad, how would you know why Stana came here? You don't even talk to her, except when you boss her around."

"I do *not* boss her around," my father growled, then turned to my mother. "Are you hearing this? Our son thinks I'm Mussolini, apparently. How terrific."

"If you were Mussolini, Dad, your corpse would be hanging upside down in a town square."

My father glared at my mother and said, "That's *your* son talking, OK?"

"Oh, give it a rest," she replied, "and stop turning everything into a federal case. It's not a crime to read a book. Just be glad he's not building explosives in his room. You know, most parents don't even know where their children are half the time, and here you are worried about a book our son's reading."

"I'd rather he read the fucking Koran than *The Communist Manifesto*, although the thought of him reading either one gives me an aneurysm."

"And I'd prefer it if he read both so he doesn't turn into a closed-minded Neanderthal who doesn't know anything about the world."

My father let out an exasperated sigh, then glared at me for a moment. "Why can't you just jerk off to Victoria's Secret catalogs like all the other boys? Leave the Communism shit for when you go to college and turn gay."

"You ignoramus," my mother muttered. She then grabbed a breadstick, tore it in half, and threw it at my father's head. I laughed hysterically.

"Great example you're setting for our son. And why did you even tell me about the Commie book in the first place?"

My mother rolled her eyes and said, "Because I just wanted to give you an *aneurysm*. Have I succeeded?"

My father waved her off.

I finished the last piece of chicken on my plate, then wiped my mouth with a napkin. "I'm done." I got to my feet.

"Did I excuse you?" my father said.

I looked at my mother, who nodded sympathetically. I turned to my father and, on the spur of the moment, gave him a Fascist salute, then exited the dining room.

Stana was sitting on a stool at the kitchen counter, eating mashed potatoes and salad. I went over and stood across from her. She looked at me and smiled. It was a genuine smile, the kind that mothers give to their kids when they're proud of them.

"There's still some more chicken left," I said to Stana. "And plenty of bread."

"It's OK...I have enough food," she replied, speaking with a trickling accent.

"The food was really good tonight, especially the mashed potatoes. Whenever Mom makes mashed potatoes, they taste like cement."

Stana covered her mouth with a napkin, trying not to laugh.

"You can laugh," I said, "because it's true. You're a much better cook than my mom. I'm sure she'd agree."

"Thank you, Sean."

I watched Stana eat, noticing the veins on her bony hands bulging as if they were about to break through the skin. I'd never noticed her hands before; they looked like the hands of a manual laborer. I imagined her cleaning up other people's shit with those hands—*my* shit.

"Hey, Stana...you're from the Balkans, right?"

She nodded.

"Have you ever had *bourek*?"

"Yes," Stana said, smiling. "Everyone from the Balkans has had *bourek*."

"I tried it for the first time recently, and it was really good."

"Well, I can make you some."

I shook my head and said, "No, no. You don't have to make me anything. I was just...you know...wondering if you knew about *bourek*." I paused for a moment. "I know I don't usually ask you these kinds of questions, but...when you were a little girl—in the Balkans, I mean—what did you want to be?"

Stana looked at me, puzzled.

"I mean, like...what did you want to become? Did you want to become a teacher or, um...I don't know...a doctor?"

Stana nodded as if she now understood what I was getting at.

"The reason I'm asking is because...I know this isn't what you wanted to do with your life. Nobody dreams about becoming a maid, you know?"

"Yes, Sean...that is true. I didn't dream of this. But, you know, life is 'funny' sometimes."

"Funny?"

"I, um…don't know how to say it exactly," Stana said. "I don't mean life is ha-ha funny. I mean it's *uncertain*. Yes, that's the word. Uncertain."

"But what did you want to become when you were a little girl? Didn't you have any dreams or goals?"

Stana pushed her plate aside and folded her arms, resting her elbows on the counter. "When I was a little girl many years ago—"

"You're not that old, Stana."

She chuckled. "Thank you. But…when I was a little girl in Yugoslavia, I used to love art, and I would draw all the time. And if I didn't have any paper to draw on, then I'd draw on napkins."

"Really?"

Stana nodded, beaming. She looked happier than I'd ever seen her before, and it made me happy in return seeing her looking so delighted, even hopeful.

"So you wanted to become an artist?" I said.

"Well…yes and no. Yes, because drawing made me very happy. And no, because it wasn't a realistic goal for someone like me."

"Why not?"

"For many reasons, but mostly because of where I lived."

"Oh…you mean Yugoslavia?"

Stana shook her head slightly and said, "No. I'm talking about the village where I lived. It wasn't a place where people could dream to become anything they wanted…and I knew that even as a little girl. But I accept God's plan for me, so I don't get sad about things like that."

"Do you think God's plan, though, was for you to come to America and work as a maid?"

"I don't really know, to be honest. But I believe in Him."

I paused. "Stana, what if there is no God?"

"There has to be."

"But what if there isn't? What if you're meant for something bigger than just…*this*? Don't you ever think about when you were a little girl and how happy you were when you were drawing? And I know it made you happy, because you were smiling when you told me about how you used to draw all the time. Don't you want to go back to that feeling?"

Stana smiled sadly, then reached across the counter and patted my hand. "I don't think that I can explain this to you in a way that will make sense to you. But just know that I'm content with my life, even though I'm not making a living as an 'artist' and instead work as a maid."

"OK," I said, after a pause. "I believe you."

Stana stared hard at me. "Wait there for just a moment," she said suddenly, then got up and went to the cabinets, where she grabbed something, and then sat back down at the kitchen counter. "I'm going to draw you," she told me, holding a dinner napkin and a ballpoint pen. "This will be my first drawing in many years, so you'll have to forgive me if it doesn't come out looking like a masterpiece."

I chuckled and said, "Don't worry, I'm sure it'll look good. By the way, how did you learn to speak English so well? Your accent is less noticeable than my French headmaster's. His accent is thick as hell."

Stana spoke while drawing me, occasionally glancing at me to study my face. "In the small village where I lived, there was only one family who had a television, and some of the kids would go to the family's house after school to watch American movies. I remember watching the movie *Rosemary's Baby*—the one about the Satanic cult. Oh, that movie scared me so much! That's how I learned to speak English. They also taught us some English and Russian in high school, because they said those were the 'languages of the future.' I guess now English is the language of the future, because after the Soviet Union collapsed, they stopped teaching Russian in schools. I even learned how to read in English by going through an old language dictionary that had words in both English and Montenegrin. That's the language I grew up speak-ing in Yugoslavia, and the country where I was born is now called Montenegro, since 'Yugoslavia' doesn't exist anymore. How strange to be born in a country that no longer exists. But there's still Montenegro."

"What does 'Montenegro' mean?" I asked Stana.

"It means 'Black Mountain,'" she replied. "I haven't been back there since the wars began, so it's been a while now."

"Are you ever going to go back there?"

"One day, I hope."

I tried to remain still while Stana drew me, but I had to itch my nose, so I itched it quickly, eliciting laughter from Stana, which then caused me to start laughing.

"Sorry," I said.

"No—it's fine. You're a good model."

There was a moment of serene silence, except for the sound of Stana's pen moving across the napkin as she shaded my hair. I couldn't help but look at her hands again. *How can they be so bony and frail,* I wondered, *and yet so rough?* I imagined she did some farm work while living in the Balkans, because there was no way her hands could be so rugged from simply doing domestic work. But then I started to wonder if *all* domestic workers had hands like Stana's. And if so, why weren't those hands wrapped around the throats of rich people?

"Stana," I said suddenly, in a curious voice.

"Yes?" she replied.

"Did you come to America because Yugoslavia was a Communist country?"

"Actually...I came to America because Yugoslavia *stopped* being a Communist country."

Stana's response took me by surprise. "What do you mean by that?" I asked.

"It's a long story," Stana said, "but once upon a time, Yugoslavs were able to sit down with one another and share a meal. Now they can't stand the sight of each other. But for a while, it was quite nice."

"Did you also work as a maid when you lived in Yugoslavia?"

"Oh, no. I owned a little convenience store with an Albanian friend. Then the wars started, and we had to sell it. But I didn't start working as a maid until I came to America."

Just as I was about to say something, my father's voice suddenly bellowed from the dining room: "Stana! More wine!"

Stana hurriedly finished the drawing, then handed it to me and said, "I hope you like it. It's from the heart." She smiled and went to fetch the wine, while I remained seated and examined her portrait of me. It was small but precise. She even managed to get my snub nose and hooded eyes just right.

CHAPTER THIRTEEN

In a casual diner somewhere in Los Angeles, a man is telling his friend about a nightmare he had in which he saw a terrifying figure lurking behind the very same diner that the two men are currently having breakfast.

And I'm scared like I can't tell ya, the man says to his friend, who agrees to investigate the matter by going with him behind the diner and seeing if there really is a "terrifying figure" lurking behind the diner. *I hope that I never see that face ever outside of a dream.*

The two men exit the diner and walk behind the restaurant to a narrow sidewalk that leads into a back alley. As the men reach the corner of the alley, a disheveled creature suddenly emerges from behind the corner, startling the man whose nightmare has now become a reality, killing him on the spot.

Simon gripped my hand at the jump scare and buried his face into my shoulder. "It's just a movie," I assured him, "even if it is weird as hell."

Jeremiah, who was sitting next to me on my left, grazed the side of my thigh with his pinky finger. At first, I thought he had done so unintentionally, but then he began to lightly rub my thigh repeatedly, again with his pinky finger, then with both his pinky and ring fingers, until eventually his entire hand was on my thigh. I looked at Jeremiah, who simply smiled.

As I turned my attention back to the movie (*Mulholland Drive*—another unusual selection from Van Orton), I felt Jeremiah's hand moving toward my crotch. For a brief moment, I thought about stopping him for fear of being seen by Simon, whose reaction I couldn't predict. But then I realized that I didn't much care what Simon thought, since he was just a kid.

I inhaled sharply as I felt Jeremiah's hand on my crotch, which he began to caress; at first slowly, then more vigorously, as if attempting to summon a genie from its magic lamp. I turned to Simon, whose eyes were fixed on the screen, then quickly scanned the sparsely-filled auditorium, noticing Van Orton standing off to the side, watching the movie. Jeremiah continued to caress my crotch, slowing down when I'd achieved an erection, then cupped the tip of my penis with just his fingers and started jerking me off through my pants.

Jeremiah and I turned to each other and, suddenly realizing how absurd we must've looked, I began to laugh. Simon glanced at me, then went back to watching the movie.

"No!" I whispered to Jeremiah, trying to suppress my laughter, then gently pushed his hand away.

"What's wrong?" he said.

"Not in here. It's creepy."

"Creepy?"

"I mean…this movie is weird. And there are *people* here."

Jeremiah made a pleading face, his round lips protruding, and I had to restrain myself from kissing him. It suddenly felt as if we were a long-time couple who had no inhibitions about messing around in public. The fact that Jeremiah had a girlfriend seemed irrelevant, at least at the moment. I couldn't believe that I'd become so comfortable with him that his hand on my dick could actually elicit laughter from me, rather than send me into a state of ecstasy.

"Do you want to come over?" Jeremiah asked, leaning toward me. "We can watch the rest of the movie at my place. I have it on VHS."

"Today?" I said.

"Yeah. My mom's working late, so it'll just be the two of us. And I have some shit I want to talk to you about, but not here."

I looked at Simon, who appeared engrossed in the movie, then turned back to Jeremiah. "I promised Simon I'd come over to his house after the movie today."

"Well…I guess he can come with us," Jeremiah said, "but that'd be kind of weird with him there, you know. Can you just hang out with him some other day?"

I thought for a moment, then turned to Simon and told him, "Hey, I can't come over today. I'm sorry, but I gotta do something with Jeremiah. I'll try to come over tomorrow, OK?"

I was expecting Simon to protest, but he just stared at me with a look of sadness, as if he'd heard the most devastating news of his young life. I felt like a prick, but the honest truth was that getting closer to Jeremiah was much higher on the totem pole for me than spending time with my fifth-grade chapel partner, with whom I had very little in common.

"Are you all right?" I asked Simon, but he didn't respond. "Like I said, I'll probably come over tomorrow. If not tomorrow, then for sure next week, I swear."

"Sean, you always say that," he finally responded, "but you never do."

"I'm sorry."

"Why are you like this?"

The simple question hit me like a blow to the head, and instead of saying something stupid in response, I decided not to say anything at all. In fact, I wasn't even sure how to respond to such a question.

I suddenly felt a hand on my shoulder. I turned and saw Jeremiah standing over me. "Come on," he said with a nod. "Let's not miss the bus."

I didn't know what he was talking about, but if he said there was a bus, then there must've been a bus. I looked at Simon, who gave me the cold shoulder. I then got up and left the auditorium with Jeremiah.

We sat in the back of a transit bus, away from the other commuters, of which there were a dozen or so. Jeremiah flashed me a smile and quipped, "We got the Rosa Parks seats."

"Very funny," I said.

"I try."

"Do you always take the bus home?"

"Pretty much, unless Mallory picks me up from school."

"Not to sound like a dumbass, but I almost forgot that there was a bus stop near the school."

Jeremiah shrugged a little and said, "Well, I'm sure most rich students forget."

I wasn't sure if that was a dig at me, but it sounded like it. I wondered if Jeremiah resented me because I came from an affluent background. I could only imagine what he'd say if he came to my house and saw my father in his Monopoly Man suit, then realized that we had a full-time maid working for us.

"I've been meaning to ask you," I said to Jeremiah. "How come I never see you at lunch?"

"Because I don't eat lunch in the dining hall."

"Oh. So where do you go to eat lunch, then?"

"Mr. Van Orton's room," Jeremiah told me. "He lets me eat lunch with him in his room. I like it better than eating in the noisy-ass dining hall. And we listen to records while we eat and talk about movies and books, just like we do when I go see him at the Todd House."

I felt my heart sink when he told me that, because I'd started to believe that Van Orton had somehow become less relevant in Jeremiah's life and that I'd soon replace Van Orton as Jeremiah's new "royal favorite," seeing as how Jeremiah and I had been spending a lot more time together as of late. But that didn't seem to be the case at all. Funny how I was initially concerned with Mallory, whom I disliked from the very beginning, only to realize that I had a more challenging adversary in Van Orton.

"How often do you go see Mr. Van Orton at his place?" I asked Jeremiah, both curious and afraid of the answer. *Please tell me it's no more than once a week.*

"Shit," he said, looking as if I'd asked him to solve a difficult math problem. "It depends, I guess. Sometimes I go over there three times a week, sometimes less…usually more."

I tried to hide my unease. I didn't even want to think what went on in the Todd House with just the two of them there. I'd never been inside the Todd House, since no students and few faculty members were allowed to go inside, though I'd seen the exterior of the house on a few occasions, and it always gave me the creeps. Perhaps that was because it was located in a secluded area, which gave it an air of mystery, like the Monolith in *2001: A Space Odyssey*. Why did the house—any house— need to be there in the first place? That was a question I'd occasionally ask myself when unconvinced that the house was constructed as a "retreat" for the school's elite faculty.

"Oh—I still have to talk to Mr. Van Orton about the Rais Frolic," Jeremiah said to me. "I'll talk to him about it next time I see him, I promise."

I nodded weakly.

"Is, uh, something wrong?" Jeremiah asked.

"No," I replied, looking directly at him, and for a moment, we stared into each other's eyes like combatants. I didn't know what prompted this awkward stare down (Jeremiah had positioned his body so that he was facing me), as neither of us harbored any ill will toward the other, or so it seemed. I lowered my gaze and, to my shock, noticed that the hammer and sickle pin that I'd been accustomed to seeing on the lapel of Jeremiah's blazer was no longer there.

Jeremiah, realizing that I was staring at the lapel of his blazer, grinned at me and said, "The dragon has come."

"What...?"

"Not a George Jackson fan, I take it. He was a Black Panther Party member and Communist activist who discovered Marx and Lenin while in prison. When he tried to escape from prison, he pulled a pistol on one of the guards and said, 'The dragon has come,' just before shooting him in the face. That's my kind of Commie, but that breed of Commie is all but gone today, and so is my lapel pin."

Taken aback, I remained silent for a while, staring at Jeremiah and feeling oddly betrayed. What's more, I felt a tinge of malice toward him, which was a first for me.

"Aren't you still a Communist?" I said bitterly.

"Sure. I can be a Commie while also being other things. It's not a 'one size fits all' type of thing, you know." Jeremiah chuckled.

I could feel myself getting wound up, as if readying for a fight. "What does that even mean, 'other things'?" I sneered.

"Don't worry, it'll make a lot more sense after I talk to Mr. Van Orton," Jeremiah told me.

The enmity that I was feeling suddenly morphed into bewilderment.

"W—what does Mr. Van Orton have to do with...*anything*?" I said. "Is he, like, telling you shit now?"

"He tells me shit, I tell *you* shit, we all tell shit to each other. That's how the world works." Jeremiah then added, "I wonder if our primate relatives have to deal with the same shit as we do."

After a pause, I asked him, "Why do you bring up the 'primate' thing?"

"You mean now?" he said.

"Just in general."

"I guess to remind people that we're not exceptional. We need to be reminded of that *often*."

"So you don't think anybody's exceptional?" I said.

"I mean, there are some exceptional people, sure, but as a whole... nah."

I paused. "I think *you're* pretty exceptional." I kind of winced after saying that because of how corny it sounded and hoped that Jeremiah wouldn't notice. But when I saw the Machiavellian smirk on his face, I knew a snappy wisecrack was imminent.

"You goddamn fairy," he quipped, and pinched my cheek. "Keep that energy when we get to my place."

My hands became clammy, thinking about what Jeremiah and I were going to do when we got to his place. I imagined us having clumsy sex, our bodies contorted like swastikas—or victims of a car crash. I was nervous about doing it wrong and not being able to satisfy him, which would be humiliating. I was still a virgin, so what did I know about sex, other than what I'd seen in porn magazines and on the Internet?

CHAPTER FOURTEEN

Jeremiah ordered in Chinese food, consisting of orange chicken, spring rolls, and egg drop soup. I insisted that I pay for our meal, since I owed him. When he asked me what I owed him for, I replied, "Everything." We grabbed Vanilla Cokes from the refrigerator and ate in the living room as we watched *Mulholland Drive*.

For a while, while watching the movie, I had forgotten that the reason Jeremiah invited me to his house (besides having "some shit" to talk to me about, which I figured was just a ploy to get me to come over) was so he could fuck me. That is, until he placed his hand on my thigh, just like he had done earlier in the auditorium. I turned to him, and he must've sensed that I was looking at him, because he suddenly chuckled—then moved his hand away.

On TV, a bungling hitman kills three innocent people in an attempt to retrieve a mysterious black book. I couldn't make heads or tails of the mystifying film.

"This movie makes no sense," I told Jeremiah. "It's one weird scene after another." I took a bite of my food. "But I like it. I should've known you'd own it."

"What can I say? I have superb taste in movies, comrade."

"So am I allowed to call *you* 'comrade,' or are you going to get pissy again?"

Jeremiah shrugged and said, "You can call me a 'dildo,' for all I care. Just don't call me a 'Reaganite,' because that would hurt my feelings."

I looked at him, astonished at how, in a mere three days' time, he had conspicuously altered his way of thinking. Unless he had undergone some kind of experimental aversion therapy akin to the kind that the protagonist in *A Clockwork Orange* undergoes, it seemed unlikely that Jeremiah's personality could've changed so drastically in such a brief span of time. Then again, I'd developed a deep, almost maniacal, attachment to him in a fraction of that time, so it wasn't beyond the realms of possibility.

"How have you never seen this movie before?" Jeremiah said to me, eating egg drop soup, which he had saved for last. "I saw it at the Art Mill when it first came out."

"And you actually understood it?" I replied.

"Not at first...but now that I've seen it a bunch of times, I get what David Lynch is saying."

"Oh, yeah? What's that?"

"He's basically saying, 'This is what America will become in the near future.' And it did—right after 9/11. That 'creature' behind the diner, that's America right now."

I chuckled incredulously. "Come on, are you saying a filmmaker predicted 9/11? For real?"

"When you say it like that, it makes me sound like a mental patient."

"And what about the scene with the hitman and the black book?" I said, teasing him. "What does that scene predict, exactly?"

"My dick in your fucking mouth!" Jeremiah growled in mock anger.

I started laughing so hard that I nearly choked on a spring roll and had to spit it out, while Jeremiah, slightly annoyed at my clowning, gave me a playful slap on the cheek and told me, "Stop playing with me. I invite you to my place and order us in Chinese food to celebrate the Handover of Hong Kong, and this is how you treat me? I should've left you in the auditorium with your child bride."

I laughed even harder, knowing that everything he had said was in jest, and then wiped my mouth with a napkin as I tried to suppress my laughter, to no avail.

"Speaking of 'mysterious' black books," Jeremiah said, before pausing to take a sip of his drink, "that book about Magnolia Academy that you mentioned to me—it doesn't exist."

I stopped laughing almost immediately. "W—wait...what?"

"I went to the Adriance Memorial Library two days ago and talked to one of the librarians there, and she told me that not only do they not carry the book but, according to the Internet, there's never been a book written about Magnolia Academy."

Nonplussed, I stared at Jeremiah for a moment, then said, "How's that possible? I definitely remember coming across the book at the library and reading it...*in* the library."

"When was this?"

"Over the summer. I went on a crazy history binge, since I'm a history geek, and I swear I remember finding the book in the local history section of the library. I literally held the damn book in my hands," I said, holding out my hands to mimic holding a book.

"Maybe you just dreamt it. Or maybe, instead of a history binge, you went on a drug binge like River Phoenix just before he collapsed." Jeremiah laughed, but I kept a straight face. "Sorry," he said, waving it off. "I'm just being a dick. But seriously, I think you probably read some history book that mentioned Magnolia and thought it was about the school, you know?"

It was possible, I reasoned, that I had read some history book that just happened to mention Magnolia—perhaps a book about Poughkeepsie's history, of which Magnolia was a part. And yet, when recalling the book's cover art, which featured a black-and-white photograph of the school's main quadrangle, including its prominent Christopher Columbus statue, the idea that I had read a book that wasn't specifically about Magnolia Academy seemed unlikely, if not far-fetched. It just didn't make any sense, especially since I distinctly remembered pulling the book off the shelf and looking at the cover, with its Columbus statue and multiple authors, whose names, unfortunately, I couldn't recall. Furthermore, I had a vivid recollection of reading about the school's headmasters, from Augustus Todd to its most recent headmaster, Jeunet, as well as the tragedy that occurred in the Eighties during the annual Rais Frolic. I couldn't possibly have dreamt or imagined something like that.

Jeremiah waved his hand in front of my face and said, "Hey...are you still with me, Sean?"

I snapped out of my reverie and said, matter-of-factly, "Chronovisor."

"Uh...come again?"

"Remember? I told you about that boy who died during the Rais Frolic back in the Eighties. His name was Chandler—Chandler Faust, remember? I didn't make that up."

"Yeah, I remember, but...there's no Chandler Faust."

I paused. "How would you know that?"

"Because I looked him up in the school records," Jeremiah said, "and there wasn't a single 'Chandler Faust' in there. I even asked the head secretary at the office if there were any yearbooks with the name

'Chandler Faust,' and after a quick search on the computer, she told me that there'd never been a student at the school with that name. If you don't believe me, you can go and ask her yourself."

All of a sudden, I felt mildly nauseous. "Ah...Christ," I groaned, rubbing my stomach like a pregnant woman. "Maybe I *am* on drugs." I leaned back on the couch. "And if I'm not on drugs, then I should think about getting on them, because my brain must be fried if I'm making up people and shit."

Jeremiah chuckled and told me, "You're perfectly normal." He grabbed my food and drink and put them on the coffee table next to his. "But you have a wild imagination like me. And that's not a bad thing. Remember what Dr. Jeunet said during chapel that one time—about how teenage boys 'possess an imagination audacious enough to rival the Book of Revelation'? That's you and me in a nutshell."

"Yeah, well...that's just a poetic way of saying we're fucked up in the head," I said, which made Jeremiah laugh. "By the way," I added, after a pause, "are you a River Phoenix fan?"

"Let me guess, your dick got hard when you heard me say his name."

I chuckled. "I mean, I *am* a huge fan of his. I've seen all his movies—*Stand by Me, Running on Empty, My Own Private Idaho*. That one, shit. I went to every video store in town trying to find it on videotape."

"I have it," Jeremiah said.

"*My Own Private Idaho*?"

Jeremiah nodded.

"Maybe we should watch that instead of *Mulholland Drive*," I said. "This movie is messing with my head, and I don't mean in a good way."

"I'm pretty sure that's what it's supposed to do. Anyway, forget movies." Jeremiah grabbed the remote control and paused the movie. "We can watch movies later. You don't have to be home early today, do you? No dinner with the family tonight or anything?"

I shook my head and said, "Not tonight."

"Good."

Without the movie playing, the room was now silent, which made me a little tense, since I knew what would come next. Jeremiah and I stared into each other's eyes—not as combatants but as admirers. He placed a gentle hand on my inner thigh, and the warmth of his hand sent a jolt of electricity to my leg, causing it to twitch. I smiled sheepishly and mouthed "Sorry." However, now that I think about it, I might've said the word out loud, but I can't be sure.

"It's the anticipation, isn't it?" Jeremiah said to me.

"Yeah," I replied. "I think."

"I'll be gentle."

Jeremiah moved his hand toward my crotch, and then, once his hand was on my crotch, he began to caress it ever so gently. I looked down and stared at Jeremiah's crotch, as if thinking that I could give him an erection simply by staring at his crotch. Jeremiah noticed that I was staring at his junk.

"You can grab it," he told me with a hint of a smirk.

There was a part of me that just wanted to get it over and done with, as the anticipation was building to an almost unbearable pitch. However, there was another part of me—a part that I tried to muffle—that was looking for a way out. Why? Because the thought of not being able to climax while having sex with Jeremiah terrified me. I'd be branded a fraud, a "cock-teaser." But there was no way of going back now.

I put my hand on Jeremiah's crotch, surprised, and also aroused, to discover that he already had an erection. As I stared at his junk, mouth agape, I imagined what it would be like to have him in my mouth. Jeremiah Kateb, the Algerian boy whose cherubic features and almond-shaped eyes could pierce through bone and marrow, in *my* mouth. The same boy who, if one stood next to for longer than two seconds and inhaled the rich scent of cinnamon and clove that emanated from him, would experience a high so potent as to be convinced that one had attained spiritual enlightenment. Just a month ago, I would've done anything, short of setting an orphanage ablaze, to merely shake hands with Jeremiah. Now I was about to do a hell of a lot more than just shake his hand.

"Go ahead," Jeremiah told me. "Pull it out."

I slowly unzipped his pants and pulled his cock out. It was thicker than I remembered, and the head was deep red, which I thought was unusual for a brown cock. I felt my dick getting hard as I held Jeremiah's cock in my hand, rubbing the head with my thumb.

"I can't believe you're a virgin," Jeremiah said. "You've honestly never been with anyone before, not even some random guy?"

I shook my head.

"Shit," Jeremiah said with a chuckle. "I'm not even gay, and I've been with three dudes. I only count the first one, though. The other two were just an obligation."

"So…you're bi?"

"Yeah. That's what I tell myself, anyway."

I stared at Jeremiah's cock as if in a trance, just like when I first saw his dick at Mallory's house. I bit my lower lip, excited at the thought of sucking him off.

"Do you know why girls like going down on guys?" Jeremiah suddenly asked me, his tone almost reflective. (I just looked at him.) "More to the point, why some girls enjoy being dominated by guys during sex? Because it feels good to let go and allow someone else to take the wheel. You want *me* to take the wheel, don't you?" He grabbed me by the throat with the same hand that he'd caressed my dick just moments ago. "Tell me the truth…do you want me to be gentle?"

I shook my head.

"Then what do you want?" Jeremiah asked.

"I…want you to fuck my face," I told him. "That's what I want. Please, just fuck my face." I suddenly felt my chest tighten and began trembling, as if I were having a panic attack.

"It's OK," Jeremiah assured me, releasing his grip on my throat. "I shook like a leaf during my first time too."

"Just please," I said to him, still trembling, "hurt me."

"I will, Sean," he replied, then swiftly grabbed the back of my head and, pushing my head down, shoved his cock in my mouth. I had to breathe through my nose just to get air. "This is what you wanted, isn't it? You faggot!"

I groaned with pleasure, my hands gripping his thighs. After a while, Jeremiah grabbed me by the hair and lifted my head, forcing me to make eye contact with him.

"You're in love with me, aren't you?" Jeremiah said, pulling my hair. "Tell me you fucking love me."

"I fucking…*worship* you!"

He kissed me with an open mouth, licking my face like a slobbering dog, then, once again, shoved his cock in my mouth. Just as I began to gag, he forcefully pushed me off of him.

I looked at him like a frightened child and said, "What's wrong?"

"Take off your pants," he demanded.

I hesitated. "What if your mom comes home, though?"

"She won't be home for a while," Jeremiah said, and pulled his pants down. "Now take off your pants so I can fuck your tight asshole."

I took off my pants, my erect cock protruding like a spear. Jeremiah looked at my dick and, smiling, said, "You're uncut." Then he grabbed my dick and gave it a squeeze. "Damn."

"What?" I said, worried that he didn't like the way my cock looked.

"You're rock hard."

"Thanks."

Jeremiah chuckled, then said, "Turn around and bend over. I wanna see that ass."

I did as I was told. Next thing I knew, Jeremiah was licking my asshole.

"Oh, fuck, Jeremiah," I moaned. "That feels so good!"

He slapped me hard on the ass and said, "Shut the fuck up, queer." I almost laughed because of how belligerent he sounded, like he was playing a character. He then stuck his cock in my ass, causing me to groan in pain. But as he began penetrating me, my painful groans soon turned into moans of pleasure. "Do you want me to come inside your ass?" he asked.

"I want you to fucking own me," I told him.

"You worthless Yankee shit!" Jeremiah howled, fucking me harder. "Born with a goddamn silver spoon in your mouth!" He began to moan, again, like a wounded animal. "I'm gonna fucking come!"

I buried my face in the couch as Jeremiah came inside me, moaning uncontrollably. When he finally pulled his cock out of my ass, I could feel tiny drops of semen oozing out of my asshole. I put my pants back on, then lay on the couch with my back to Jeremiah. I could hear him panting softly—and then, total silence.

CHAPTER FIFTEEN

We sat on the floor and watched *My Own Private Idaho* on a VHS tape that Jeremiah told me he had swiped from a mom-and-pop store years ago, as we waited for his mother to come home from work so she could drive me home. I was having a hard time focusing on the movie, though, since I was suffering from a severe case of blue balls as a result of not having ejaculated earlier. I considered going to the bathroom to masturbate, but the idea seemed tasteless and, what's more, a bit vulgar.

I looked around Jeremiah's bedroom, trying to take my mind off my penis, when suddenly I noticed an empty space on the wall where, I was sure, a poster of Ho Chi Minh had once hung. I stared at the empty space, wondering why Jeremiah had decided to take down the poster. But then I thought about our conversation from earlier regarding the supposed "Magnolia Academy" book and former Magnolia student "Chandler Faust," and I wondered if I'd simply *imagined* the Ho Chi Minh poster. After all, I'd supposedly only seen it once, so how could I even be sure that there had once hung a poster of Ho Chi Minh on the wall?

As I wrestled with my blurred thoughts, hoping to come to a satisfying conclusion, I turned to Jeremiah, whose eyes were glued to the TV. I finally gathered up the courage to ask him, "What happened to Ho Chi Minh?" But he ignored me and continued watching the movie. I suddenly got a sick feeling in my stomach. "Jeremiah, what happened to the Ho Chi Minh poster?"

He looked at me with a desolate gaze and replied, "Ho Chi Minh? I'm surprised you even remember. He's, uh…somewhere in the room. Must be busy fighting the imperialists."

"I'm serious. Why did you take down the poster?"

"I always take down posters. Then I put up new ones. What's got you so spooked, anyway? You look tense."

I paused. "Be honest, do you still consider yourself a Communist?"

"I already told you, yes. And besides, what if I said no? Are you going to have me shipped to the gulags or something?"

The sick feeling in my stomach became more intense as it dawned on me that the Jeremiah I'd spoken to just a few days ago was not the same Jeremiah that I was speaking to now. How that was even possible was still unclear to me, but that was the undeniable truth.

I looked at the bookshelf for a moment and remembered the book with the surrealistic cover art that Jeremiah was afraid I'd pull from the shelf. I turned back to Jeremiah and said, "Are you, by any chance, still reading that book that Mr. Van Orton gave you? Because, um…I think I'd like to read it."

"A lot of people want to, or *should*, read that book. But it's not that simple. You might get a chance to read it, though, after I talk to Mr. Van Orton."

There it was again. "After I talk to Mr. Van Orton," as if Van Orton were an overlord, from whom Jeremiah required constant approval. Although I'd become more tolerant of Van Orton over the past week or so, mainly as a result of our lack of interaction, I was still very much suspicious of him, considering Jeremiah seemed oddly devoted to him. The "Magnolia Academy" book that I'd believed to have read over the summer may not have existed, but the mysterious book that Van Orton had given Jeremiah certainly did, and I was determined to get my hands on it, because I was sure, or rather willing to believe, that the book was influencing Jeremiah in some way. His abrupt change in identity, from an ardent Commie to a lapsed Commie, was all the confirmation I needed to support the assertion that Jeremiah had been brainwashed by the enigmatic book.

"So are you still reading the book?" I asked Jeremiah again.

"It's called *Behold a Pale Horse*," he told me. "I finished reading it earlier this week, and I gave it back to Mr. Van Orton."

How convenient, I thought, *that he finishes reading the book around the same time that he decides to have a radical change in personality.* I've never much believed in coincidences, and I didn't think this was a coincidence, either. But the one question that kept nagging at me was, why did Jeremiah—who was evidently no longer a fervent Communist— snap at me when I'd playfully called him "comrade" just a few days prior? What was there to even get upset about?

"I *want* to read that book," I said to Jeremiah.

He smiled. "You don't even know what it's about. The only thing you know about the book is that it's got a bizarre cover art."

"I also know that Mr. Van Orton gave it to you—and that it's changed you in a lot of ways."

"The hell does that mean?"

I instinctively tugged at my crotch. "The lapel pin, the poster…giving me a handjob in the auditorium."

"Not quite," Jeremiah said.

"Close enough. And what would Mallory say if she knew that we'd fucked?"

Jeremiah shook his head. "No. *You* got fucked. Besides, you already know Mallory's kinky. What do you think she does when she's not with me—hangs out at the 'malt shop'?"

"That doesn't bother you?"

"What, that she's probably messing around with some horny douchebags behind my back? No, it doesn't bother me, because the love is gone."

Still suffering from blue balls, I tugged at my crotch again, this time with greater force, as if trying to tame my penis.

"Are you trying to flirt with me now?" Jeremiah quipped. "What's going on down there?"

"Nothing."

"You looked like you were about to…tear your dick off. What's wrong?"

I sighed in concession, then said, "Blue balls, all right?"

"Aw, poor baby." Jeremiah put his hand on my crotch. "That's my fault for being selfish." He began to caress my crotch with vigor. "I've gotta finish what I started, right?"

I wanted to talk to him about more pressing topics, but his hand on my crotch felt so good that there was no way I was going to tell him to stop.

"Hard already?" Jeremiah said, as if amazed. He unzipped my pants and, instead of pulling my dick out, rubbed his face on my crotch and licked my dick through my underwear, which made me moan.

"Jeremiah, fuck…wait, wait."

He lifted his head and, removing his keffiyeh, said, "What's the matter?"

I was so taken aback to see him without his headdress on for the first time that I froze. His hair was dark and short, and he donned a slicked-back haircut that reminded me of the silent actor Rudolph Valentino, who, based on photographs of him that I'd seen in a movie book, had a similar hairstyle.

"Sean, is something wrong?" Jeremiah asked.

"Uh...I just wanted to ask you," I said, trying not to stare at his slick hair. "You know when you kinda snapped at me for calling you 'comrade' at Mallory's place? Remember, you got pissy about it."

He chuckled. "Christ, *that's* what you're thinking about right now?"

"I just want to know...why did you snap at me?"

"You know why. I thought you were making light of something beautiful that we shared. I shouldn't have snapped at you, though. I was just being insecure, but it quickly passed."

"That's what worries me," I said. "How quickly it passed."

Jeremiah shrugged, then pulled my underwear down. "In the immortal words of Radiohead, 'For a minute there, I lost myself.' That's all that happened—I lost myself."

He began performing fellatio on me, and instead of pushing the matter any further, I leaned my head back and moaned in pleasure as Jeremiah sucked me off.

"Fuck," I moaned. "I'm gonna come..."

Jeremiah started jerking me off while simultaneously sucking my dick, and I immediately climaxed. He swallowed my semen, then continued to lick the tip of my penis, before finally lifting his head and wiping his mouth with the back of his hand. Smiling, he kissed me on the mouth, then said, "I swallowed your fucking soul, didn't I?"

A bit fuddled, I pulled my underwear back on and zipped up my pants. Then, as if suddenly possessed by an avenging spirit, I grabbed Jeremiah by the shirt, pulled him toward me, and stuck my tongue down his throat. I looked at him and said, "I'm so glad it was you, because I don't want anybody else to have me. I mean that." I gently bit his lower lip. "I really do worship you. You're the only one I want." I kissed him. "I swear to fucking Christ...I love you."

He laughed ruefully. (Not exactly the reaction I was expecting.) Then he told me, "We may be living in a new century, but queers don't live happily ever after. You know that. We can't even get married—not that I'd 'want' to get married…to anyone." After a moment, he added, "I know you're afraid that people at school might find out that you're gay. I'm damn sure you and I aren't the only queers at that Orwellian school. But we're both smart enough to keep our mouths shut. In Kerala, though, you don't have to be scared. You can be yourself."

"Sounds nice," I said.

"Yeah…except I'm not so sure if I want to go to Kerala anymore. But for *you*, it's an ideal destination, so think about it."

Just when I thought Jeremiah was finally coming back to his senses, he once again uttered something that would've been atypical of him weeks ago, further proving that his previous identity was swiftly eroding and being replaced by an entirely new identity.

"How can you not be sure about Kerala?" I asked, confounded. "You were so excited when you first told me about it, and you even mentioned it to me when we were at Mallory's place. And didn't you tell me that you're learning the language?"

"Not anymore," Jeremiah said. "I've been too distracted with other things. You know how it is, gotta focus on schoolwork and shit. By the way, do your parents know that you're gay?"

His question gave me mental whiplash, as it seemed like he was trying to change the subject for fear that I'd interrogate him further.

"My parents don't know," I told him. "What about you? Does your mom know that you're, you know, bi?"

"I seriously doubt it. How do you think your parents would react if you told them that you were a homo?"

I thought it was odd how he'd suddenly gone from saying "gay" to "homo," as if trying to offend me. However, no homophobic slur had yet to provoke me, even when uttered by someone whom I disliked, with the exception of Mallory, whose presence alone was enough to irk me. But that was because I saw her as an obstacle who I hoped would become less of a deterrent as Jeremiah and I developed a stronger bond, believing, perhaps foolishly, that he'd ultimately choose me over Mallory.

"I don't know how my mom would react," I said to Jeremiah, "but I'm sure my dad already thinks I'm half-a-fag, so he wouldn't be too surprised, just disappointed."

He grinned. "Were you surprised when I put my hand on your dick in the auditorium? You got hard quick, let me tell you."

"Yeah. So much for being *discreet* about our sexuality. You're lucky not that many people showed up today. What made you do that, anyway?"

"Because I knew you wanted me to, so I obliged. You see what a nice guy I am?"

As I gazed at Jeremiah in silence, minus the sound of *My Own Private Idaho* playing in the background, I began to wonder exactly what kind of person he was. Yes, he was intelligent beyond his years, as well as charming, funny, and, in the strictest sense, "achingly beautiful." But he wasn't a saint, as I had originally painted him. Nor was he an evildoer, or a sociopath. He was something of an oddity, a lost soul—or, more accurately, two steps removed from a fallen angel. If given the option between worshipping Jesus Christ or the thieves crucified next to him, I imagined Jeremiah would've chosen the latter, because the former would've seemed too convenient for someone like him. The fact that I was initially worried about Jeremiah finding out that I was gay, fearing that he might be repulsed by me, now seemed ridiculous, considering that he himself was queer.

We watched the rest of the movie without saying another word to each other (I don't believe Jeremiah even glanced at me), until his mother finally came home from work and I suggested that we exchange phone numbers. If we'd exchanged numbers during the first weeks of school, when my obsession with Jeremiah was at its peak, I would've been over the moon. But now, having had Jeremiah inside me, exchanging numbers with him didn't seem like that huge of a triumph.

———————

I was expecting Jeremiah's mother to play John Denver in the car while driving me home, like she'd done before, but she instead turned on the radio to a jazz station.

"Do you like this music?" she asked me, after a while.

"Um…sure," I replied, turning to her.

"I used to listen to a lot of jazz when we lived in Algeria, Jeremiah and me. Then when we came to America, I discovered John Denver and fell in love with his music. But sometimes I need a break from him."

Jeremiah's mother laughed softly, and I felt obligated to laugh as well. I found it endearing that she said "we" instead of "I," which made me realize just how close she was to her son.

"W—would it be OK," I said, "if I asked you about, um…Jeremiah's dad?" I was surprised at myself for even bringing it up, because normally I wouldn't have had the nerve to bring up such a delicate topic with someone I hardly knew, especially an adult. But I wanted to know more about Jeremiah's family.

"Sure it's OK," his mother replied. "What would you like to know?"

"Well…did Jeremiah and his dad get along?"

"Oh, certainly. They loved each other. His father would take him to the cinema, museums, to watch football games—or 'soccer,' as they like to call it here in America. They were practically inseparable. Oh, yes, they most certainly got along. You should've seen how happy Jeremiah was, always smiling and laughing. And then, tragically, his father passed away, and…Jeremiah became a sullen boy, almost overnight."

I felt like a scoundrel for even thinking about this, but while Jeremiah's mother was telling me about her son and late husband, I thought how absurd it was that less than an hour ago Jeremiah had fucked me and later sucked me off, and now here I was talking to his mother, who was unaware of what had transpired earlier in her own house. "Mrs. Kateb, your son's hard cock was in my ass while you were slaving away at a thankless job," I imagined telling her. "Then he sucked my dick and swallowed my cum like a good little boy." What kind of piece of shit would even think of such a thing during an intimate conversation, unless I really was a loathsome scoundrel?

"Does Jeremiah talk about his dad a lot?" I asked her.

She let out a confused scoff, as if I'd asked her a totally unexpected question. "He doesn't exactly *talk* about his father to me that much, but when I look at his face, I can tell he thinks about him, although he'd never admit it to me."

I paused. "Does he ever, like, talk to you about Mr. Van Orton?"

"Who?"

I shook my head as if to say, "Never mind," then looked away. I turned back to her after a moment and said, "What about Kerala?"

"I've…never even heard that name before. I'm sorry."

I nodded a little, then looked at her hands on the steering wheel. They were bony and frail, like Stana's, but less rugged.

It's true, I thought, *all domestic workers have hands like Stana's.*

I arrived home after dark. I went to my room and lay on the bed for a while—then hopped on the computer. I typed in Van Orton's name, followed by "history teacher," curious to see what would show up. But the only thing that appeared was Magnolia Academy's faculty page from their official website.

Milo Van Orton, History Department, Columbia University (1997).

Then I typed in "Magnolia Academy books," but nothing popped up. I tried "A history of Magnolia Academy," but again, nothing surfaced. And then, just to prove to myself that I was half-sane, I typed in "Chandler Faust," which took me to an ancestry website: "Chandler Damien Faust, born and died in El Paso, Texas (1896-1923)." Now I was beginning to think that I really had gone insane, considering there had never been any books published about Magnolia Academy, and that the only "Chandler Faust" (probably a cattle herder) died eighty years ago.

I suddenly got a headache, so I went to the bathroom to take some aspirin, then went back to my room and listened to the Canibus album that Jeremiah had loaned me. I must've fallen asleep soon after.

CHAPTER SIXTEEN

The next morning, I woke up in tears, having dreamt that I'd lured Jeremiah into the woods and bashed his face in with a rock. I kept hurling obscenities at him and calling him a "traitor," as I bashed his face in repeatedly—until he was no longer recognizable. I felt great vindication while committing the violent act, but after I'd killed him and his body went into postmortem spasm, with his arms raised upward, I began to cry as the realization of what I had done suddenly hit me. I knelt beside Jeremiah's lifeless body, awkwardly posed in rigor mortis, and begged him to forgive me, with tears streaming down my face. When I awoke from the nightmare, the tears were still flowing, as I believed that I'd actually killed Jeremiah. I struggled to block the nightmare from my mind as I went to school that morning, half-expecting the nightmare to turn into a reality.

I rushed into Van Orton's classroom and, to my immense relief, saw Jeremiah sitting at his desk in the back of the room. It was rather unusual to see him in class so early, but I was just happy to see him alive and well. We made eye contact, and he gave me a slight nod. It took me a moment to realize that he wasn't wearing a keffiyeh, which felt unnatural, like seeing a male lion without its mane.

"Mr. Quell," I suddenly heard Van Orton say.

I turned around and looked at him, sitting behind his desk and waving me over. I went over to him and said, "Yes?"

"What are you *doing* here?" he asked, as if I had no right to be in his classroom.

I stared at him with a befuddled expression, not knowing how to respond, other than to tell him, "This is my second period class."

"What I mean is," he said, "why aren't you at Dr. Jeunet's office?"

"Uh…what do you mean, sir?"

The troubled tone of his voice must've put fear in me, because I wouldn't have called him "sir" otherwise.

"Go see Dr. Jeunet," he told me, his tone less distraught, even a little upbeat. "He's waiting for you." Then he winked at me.

A wink from Van Orton was too strange for me to even contemplate, so I immediately left the room and went to see Jeunet.

I couldn't remember the last time I'd set foot in Jeunet's office, but it must've been at least three years ago. His office looked similar to Father Hawkins' wood-paneled office, though slightly bigger and devoid of any Catholic paraphernalia. Jeunet was standing with his back to me when I entered his office, seemingly looking at an oil portrait of Augustus Todd that hung behind his desk. Todd was portrayed as he looked in his later years, with a dour face and sunken eyes that followed you around the room.

"Have a seat, *Monsieur* Quell," Jeunet said with his back to me.

I can't remember if I'd knocked on the door before entering his office, but he was certainly aware of my presence. I sat down and waited for him to tell me why he had called for me.

Jeunet finally turned around and looked at me, bearing a soft smile. "I apologize, *Monsieur* Quell, if my secretary forgot to come fetch you during your first period. But now that you're here, I'll come straight to the point. Father Hawkins, who, if given the opportunity, would himself throw you into the Colosseum to be devoured by lions, wishes to have you expelled from school at once for the 'contemptible' crime of being a homosexual. How *benevolent*."

I reacted in shock and started to say something, but Jeunet, still smiling, quickly held up a hand as if to stop me from overreacting. "I assure you, *Monsieur* Quell, the 'esteemed' cleric does not have the power to expel you. Only I do. So do not fret."

The fact that Jeunet was smiling did nothing to put me at ease. On the contrary, it made me feel more anxious.

"Why does Father Hawkins think I'm gay?" I asked.

"Well," Jeunet said, sitting down at his desk, "because your former chapel partner, Simon Calloway, apparently saw you yesterday in the auditorium receiving sexual pleasure from a student whom he claimed he'd never seen before."

I had so many thoughts rushing through my mind. *Why did Simon squeal on me? He knew the student was Jeremiah, so why not tell them? Did Simon just want to get me in trouble and not Jeremiah? When did he tell Father Hawkins about this? Did he tell Dr. Jeunet too, or did the cleric tell him?* Then a funny thing happened. I simply stopped caring about the "whys" and "whens." I figured Simon was being a spiteful little bastard for all the times I'd reneged on my empty promises to him and wanted to hurt me in retaliation. Good for him, because I would've done the same damn thing.

"Did you say 'former' chapel partner?" I finally replied, as if that were the most shocking thing Jeunet had told me.

"Yes, well…Simon would rather remain alone than have you for a chapel partner, it seems. But never mind that melodrama. He's just a child. But you, *Monsieur* Quell…"

Jeunet stopped suddenly and stared at me with a curious expression, though still—*still!*—smiling, like he knew something about me that I didn't. But what? *Just tell me!*

"Before we proceed," Jeunet continued, speaking in a tone so gentle and languorous that it seemed as if he were trying to lull me to sleep, "I want you to know that you will not be expelled. You will, however, be suspended for a week for appearance's sake, just to get the old goat off my back…and *yours*. Now, you're probably wondering why I've decided to reduce your, let's call it 'sentence,' from expulsion to a mere week. Isn't that right?"

I nodded.

Jeunet's smile widened. "Because you show great potential, *Monsieur* Quell. You may be surprised to learn that I still remember when you were in the sixth grade and Father Hawkins asked me to suspend you for being—what was it, 'confrontational'? You know, when the cleric told me about your 'Luciferian' dialogue with him, I had to try my damnedest not to laugh."

He began to laugh, then covered his mouth with the back of his hand to muffle the laughter.

"So, then, you don't care that I'm gay?" I said.

"Frankly, I don't care if you hammered the first nail into Jesus Christ. The truth is, I admire you. That's why I'm being candid with you right now." Jeunet paused. "Think back for a moment to when I suspended you all those years ago and Father Hawkins asked you to recite however many Our Fathers and Hail Marys as part of your penance. Tell me the truth, did you recite any prayers at all?"

I remained silent for a moment, then shook my head and said, "No, I didn't."

"Good boy," Jeunet replied.

I couldn't tell if he was being sincere, or if he'd been deceiving me this whole time, but his plastered smile was off-putting to me. No one smiles that much, especially adult men, unless they have something to hide, or they're suffering from insanity. What's more, Jeunet, who looked like a caricature of a greedy capitalist from a humor magazine, what with his bowler hat and a monocle over his right eye, was difficult to gauge. How was I to interpret his words and motives when I had trouble convincing myself that I was even talking to a real person and not a cartoon?

"I thought the school didn't tolerate, you know…homosexuality," I said to Jeunet, who, no longer smiling, scoffed and shook his head.

"The school doesn't, but I don't represent the school, despite being its headmaster." I gave Jeunet a funny look, prompting him to say, "Do you recall what I said earlier about 'appearance's sake'? Every speech and lecture I've ever given at this school since being sworn in as headmaster over twenty years ago has been for appearance's sake. But here's the real 'kicker,' as the Yankees say: Every headmaster in Magnolia Academy's history, from the Honorable Augustus Todd to me has refused to bless himself with holy water or make the sign of the cross upon entering the grounds of this school." After a brief pause, Jeunet added, "I could say more, but I'd rather not overwhelm you and cause you any unnecessary alarm. You'll know more before the year's end, I promise…if not sooner."

Not sure how to respond, I stared at Jeunet, bewildered and a little uncomfortable. I didn't know if anything Jeunet had told me was even remotely true, or if my mind was just playing tricks on me and I was hearing something entirely different from what was actually being said.

"Would you like to ask me something?" Jeunet said.

I hesitated for a while. Finally, I asked, "When does my, uh…suspension begin?"

"Today," Jeunet replied, "the moment you leave my office. Then you may return to school next week. I'm not going to inform your parents of your suspension, so if you want to feign going to school, that's fine by me. Just don't come to campus, or else Father Hawkins might see you and give me grief about the way I've decided to discipline you. As you can imagine, the old goat is no fan of yours."

"But *you* like me?" I said.

"More than you know, *Monsieur* Quell. Believe it or not, I've been keeping a close eye on you since you were in the sixth grade, waiting for you to come of age and blossom."

Our conversation had taken such a bizarre turn that I wasn't sure anymore if I was speaking to the *real* Jeunet, or an impostor. It was hard to believe that the school's headmaster, with whom I'd spoken to perhaps two times in the past, was being so direct with me. But things took an even stranger turn when Jeunet suddenly rose to his feet, walking stick in hand, and began circling the office while speaking to me in that gentle and languorous tone of his.

"In his works on political philosophy, Aristotle states that people are born into a condition which makes them susceptible to being slaves, that slavery is both expedient and right. His words, dating back to the fourth century BC, would be used to justify slavery in Europe and other parts of the world for the next two thousand years. That may sound abhorrent to our modern ears, but the ancient Greeks knew a thing or two about the ways of the world...and of the heart. Take pederasty, for example. Both the ancient Greeks and Romans were known to have dabbled in man-boy love, from Aristotle, who tutored and penetrated the young Alexander the Great, to Julius Caesar, who was known to his soldiers as 'every man's woman and every woman's man.' Even in feudal Japan, samurai warriors would often take young boys to battle with them and make love to them before a major battle. Walt Whitman, America's preeminent poet, was a great lover of boys, as was another American poet, Allen Ginsberg, who was a member of NAMBLA—the North American Man/Boy Love Association. If those accomplished men saw no harm in embracing pederasty, then who are *we* to protest?"

Jeunet stopped to examine a miniature statue of a semi-nude teenage boy sitting in a chair reading a scroll, which sat atop a plinth. "I love this piece," he said, admiring the statue. "It shows a young Aristotle studying a scroll with a look of boredom. He's bored because, after all, what can a scroll teach a young man of Aristotle's intellect? I hope every boy in Magnolia aspires to be like Aristotle." He turned to me. "That's why the school introduced the Rais Frolic—to nurture future Aristotles and Julius Caesars and Walt Whitmans."

I took a moment to process everything that Jeunet had told me, wondering if he was simply testing me—but testing me for what? I had no idea. Then, with some trepidation, I said, "Can I ask you about Chandler Faust?"

Jeunet reacted as if I'd broken some terrible news to him, his face displaying great sadness. "*Monsieur* Faust…" He proceeded to say something in French that I didn't understand.

"So he *existed*?" I said, pleasantly surprised. "Chandler Faust?"

Jeunet closed his eyes for a moment, muttering to himself in French, then opened his eyes and gazed at me with a mixture of poignancy and warmth. "Before we continue, I need to ask you something: Do you feel the same way about Lucifer today as you did all those years ago when you were in Father Hawkins' Biblical Literature class?"

"W—what do you mean?"

"When you hear the names Lucifer, Satan, fallen angel, the Devil… what emotions do they stir in you? Are you disgusted by those names? Do they, perhaps, provoke curiosity?"

Those seemed like loaded questions, but I answered truthfully: "I find Lucifer interesting—you know, as a character…especially the War in Heaven story."

Jeunet, smiling, snorted a bit and said, "Yes, 'character.' But, then again, maybe more than a character. Let's say he's every bit as real as you and me. Would you still find yourself interested in this defiant figure we call 'Lucifer,' or would you tremble in terror and run away?"

I suddenly let out a ridiculous laugh—perhaps as a defense mechanism, or as an expression of the absurdity of our conversation—reminiscent of Mozart's irritating laugh from *Amadeus*. But when I saw Jeunet, his smile having faded, look at me in earnest, I knew he was expecting a sincere response, as this was no laughing matter to him.

"No," I said, "I wouldn't tremble in terror and run away if Lucifer was real."

"Are you sure?"

I nodded.

"And if Satan were real," Jeunet said, "what exactly would you say to him?"

"I'd ask him, 'Why did you change your name to Satan?'"

I laughed at my own silly joke, although Jeunet kept a straight face. I cleared my throat and said, "In all seriousness, though, if I could ask Lucifer anything, I'd probably ask him"—I thought for a moment—"I guess I'd ask him, 'If you could do it all over again, would you still have rebelled against God?'"

A pleased smile formed across Jeunet's face. "Now then, *Monsieur* Quell, earlier you asked me about Chandler Faust. Tell me, where did you hear that name?"

"Well…I first heard it—I mean, *saw* it—in a book from the library. But…I can't remember which book. To be honest, I—I'm not even sure if it exists, as dumb as that sounds."

Jeunet chuckled to himself and shook his head, then told me, "No, *Monsieur* Quell, it's not dumb at all." He then waved me over and said, "I'd like you to come and take a look at this picture here."

I got up and walked over to him. Above the Aristotle statue hung a framed black-and-white photograph of a chieftain donning ornately embroidered attire, including a feathered helmet, with a ceremonial blade at his side. The chieftain, who appears to be of Southeast Asian descent, stands atop a megalith surrounded by a few dozen armed warriors. I didn't understand why Jeunet wanted me to look at the picture, so I turned to him and asked, "Is the picture special?"

"Not in particular," Jeunet replied. "But you asked me about *Monsieur* Faust, and I imagine you'd also want to ask me why the young man had purportedly taken his own life during the 1983 Rais Frolic." He looked at me and added, "Or perhaps you didn't get that far into this nonexistent book of yours."

There it was! I wasn't insane after all! Jeunet himself had not only uttered Chandler Faust's name (*multiple* times) but had also referenced the boy's suicide from the Eighties, just like I'd read in the book. Granted, I still didn't know the title of the book or its authors, but Jeunet's confession, as it were, of Chandler's "purported" suicide was proof of the book's existence. But the one thing that still puzzled me was why the school's head secretary had told Jeremiah that there'd never been a student at Magnolia with the name Chandler Faust.

"Yes," I told Jeunet, "I *did* get that far. There was also something in the book about a place or thing called 'Chronovisor.' Do you know what that is? What does it mean?"

Jeunet, half-smiling, pointed at the black-and-white photograph and said, "This picture was taken by me during my visit to Nias, an island located just off the western coast of Indonesia. The island possesses some of the finest architecture in the region, and its inhabitants—who, at the time this picture was taken, had a penchant for headhunting, having developed a culture of war—have a fondness for three things above all else: gold, pigs, and slaves. Sadly, the only thing Niasans hold dear today is cheap tourism."

Jeunet had strangely evaded my inquiry about the meaning of "Chronovisor." What's more, he was speaking to me as if I hadn't already looked at and examined the photograph. Nevertheless, I kept quiet and listened as he went on about the picture, which, apparently, meant so much to him.

"Despite being repulsed by the grisly practice of headhunting, I was quite taken with Nias society and its people, who referred to themselves as 'pigs of the gods,' believing that their gods—who came out of chaos to create the world—had the right to do with them as they pleased. Niasans made regular sacrifices of pigs in order to satisfy the gods. My stay in Nias lasted for three months, spending much of my time 'tutoring' some of the young boys on the island, with whom I could do as I pleased, for I'd convinced the elder Niasans that I was a god. However, after having 'tutored' one of the chieftain's young sons a little too much, I was chased off the island by the chieftain and his soldiers. I was lucky to make it out of there with my head still intact."

I stared at Jeunet, flabbergasted, unsure of what to believe anymore. He then chuckled and said, "*Monsieur* Quell, the reason I'm prattling on like this is because you asked me about Chandler Faust and the meaning of 'Chronovisor.' Well...this picture that you see hanging in my office was taken in the year 1915, and as I've told you earlier, I was the one who took the picture. I'm currently in my late fifties, so the math doesn't quite add up, now does it?" Jeunet smiled. "If I attempted to explain the reasoning behind the 'math,' I'm afraid you would end up on the floor, flopping like a fish out of water, so I won't go any further for your sake." He put his arm around me and walked me to the door. "Just know that I have great affection for you, *Monsieur* Quell, not only as a student but as a human being. We'll be seeing a lot more of each other, I promise. And I'll make sure that Mr. Van Orton has you in mind when picking students to attend the Rais Frolic, because you, my dear Ganymede, deserve to attend."

Jeunet placed his hands on my shoulders and gazed at me like a proud father, while I stood there looking back at him, disoriented, thinking of something to ask him that would help me make sense of this most unusual conversation. Finally, after he'd lowered his hands, I said, in a low tone, "Can you tell me why Chandler Faust killed himself…and why the school's head secretary doesn't know he existed?"

Jeunet gave me an affectionate pat on the shoulder and said, "Never mind the staff. They're simply doing their job. But just between you and me, everyone at Magnolia, with the exception of Mr. Van Orton and myself, is full of shit. As for *Monsieur* Faust, this supposed book of yours left out an important detail, which is that there has been an unfortunate passing of a student at Magnolia Academy every twenty years since its inception—in 1943, 1963, and 1983. This year, I anticipate another tragedy."

"Why do you say that?" I asked.

Jeunet opened the door, then said, "Because the Light-Bringer, like the gods of the Niasans, demands an offering. Now go on home and tell your parents there was an early dismissal."

I hesitated.

"Don't look so spooked," Jeunet said to me with a faint smile. "I assure you, there's nothing to be afraid of." Just as I stepped out the door, Jeunet added, "You know, the fact that you haven't thought to ask me about how the Rais Frolic got its name surprises me."

I remembered my conversation with Jeremiah about the Rais Frolic from a while ago, when we were at Blondie's, so I said, "It has something to do with being a leader…doesn't it?"

Jeunet bellowed a laugh, then grabbed the door, as if he were eager to shut it in my face. I waited for him to shut the door, but then, suddenly, he told me, "Make sure to look up a fellow by the name of Gilles de Rais when you get the chance."

He closed the door.

PART II

Fall

"I calculate planet alignment like Mayan astronomy,
discovering atrocities worse than Aristotle subjecting children to
sodomy…"

— Immortal Technique, "The Prophecy"

CHAPTER SEVENTEEN

Every day for a week, I woke up at six o'clock in the morning, brushed my teeth and took a shower, ate breakfast, packed my lunch, and—feigning going to school—headed to the Adriance Memorial Library, where I'd pluck an abundance of books from the shelves, find an isolated spot, and stay there for six to seven hours, reading and daydreaming. At around noon, I'd eat my lunch, which remained consistent throughout the entire week: turkey sandwich, sliced apples, Twinkies, and a bottle of Yoo-hoo. While eating, I'd think about Jeremiah, Simon, Van Orton, Communism, Stana, and most of all, the bizarre conversation that I'd had with Jeunet in his office, which I tried in vain to disregard as just a figment of my overactive imagination.

For the sake of brevity, I will chronicle my faux "week of suspension" in epistolary form, starting with the day I left Jeunet's office.

October 20, 2003

I took the bus to the library, my head spinning from the ludicrous conversation I'd just had with Jeunet, as if a renowned headmaster of a prestigious private school would even divulge such information (or whatever it was that he spewed) to a student. I could maybe, through some mental gymnastics, imagine Jeunet telling a student all the stuff that he'd told me as a scare tactic, or even a morbid prank. Deep down, however, I knew a traditionalist like Jeunet didn't have the gall to do something so unorthodox. I presumed the most anarchic thing Jeunet ever did in his life was return a videotape to Blockbuster without bothering to rewind it. In any case, I was determined to research the name that the headmaster had provided me: Gilles de Rais.

I approached the librarian, a jovial elderly woman who had been working there as far back as I could remember. She was working at her usual spot, the reference desk, with a young assistant at her side, inspecting books for any irregularities. "Come again, dear?" she said to me, continuing her work as we spoke.

"Someone named 'Gilles de Rais,'" I told her. "I don't know if he's famous or not, or what he did, but I was wondering if the library had any books on him. I think he's French."

She thought for a moment. "Well…I've never heard that name before, but I'd have to check if we have any books on him. I seriously doubt it, however, as I'd remember a name like that. But if you say he's French, you can go to the history section and look for books about French historical figures. There might be something there on him. Or, you know what?" She turned to her assistant. "Follett, if you could, search the name—" She looked at me and said, "'Gilles de Rais,' was it…?" (I nodded.) She turned back to her assistant. "Right, so search 'Gilles de Rais, French history' on the computer and see what comes up." The librarian, still inspecting books, smiled at me and said, "These computers sure are a time-saver, aren't they? I just hope they don't put me out of work any time soon."

I forced a smile, then glanced at the assistant, who was still searching on the computer. If I had gone straight home after leaving Jeunet's office, I could've looked up Gilles de Rais myself, since I had my own computer. However, besides seeing if there were any books on Gilles de Rais, there was another reason why I wanted to go to the library, and that was to ask the librarian about the enigmatic Magnolia Academy book, which I was now certain existed.

"Here we are," the assistant said suddenly, looking at the computer. "So, the library doesn't carry any books on Gilles de Rais, unfortunately. But we do have one book that mentions him. It's a military history book called *Wars of the Middle Ages* by Harry Styman, conveniently located in the military history section."

"Do you need help finding it?" the librarian asked me.

"No," I said. "I've been to the military history section plenty of times before, so I'm sure I can find it on my own. But I want to ask you about something else. This might be a long shot, but do you remember when I came in here over the summer and asked you if I could check out a book about Magnolia Academy?"

The librarian looked like she was about to say something in the affirmative, then suddenly shook her head in panicked confusion, as if she had no idea what I was talking about. The way her facial expression had changed so swiftly, from initial agreement to sheer bewilderment, made me a bit uneasy.

"When I asked you if I could check out the book," I said, "you told me that the book wasn't allowed to leave the library because it was a loan. Do you remember that at all?"

The librarian, fumbling with a book and avoiding eye contact, replied, "I—I don't—no...I don't recall that. Are you sure it was, um... at t—this library?"

"Yeah, because I remember asking you about the book, and when you told me that it wasn't allowed to leave the library, I ended up reading it right here in the library. I mean, I know it was a while ago, and the library has hundreds of patrons, but I just thought you might remember. I guess not."

The librarian, conflicted, turned to her assistant and said, "Follett, we don't carry any books on Magnolia Academy, do we? Because I can't remember..."

"I'm not sure," she replied, "but I can check." She did a quick search on the computer, then turned to the librarian and said, "No, it doesn't look like we have anything on Magnolia Academy."

The librarian looked at me and shrugged as if to say, "That's the end of that."

She seemed more at ease now, and even smiled a little, reassuming her role as the congenial librarian. But I was still suspicious of how she reacted when I mentioned the Magnolia Academy book, like she wanted to tell me something, then suddenly recoiled.

I went to the military history section and, under "Styman," found a paperback copy of *Wars of the Middle Ages*, creased and torn. I sat down at a study table and flipped the book to the index, where there was only one mention of Gilles de Rais, on page 237. Thinking it was just going to be a passing reference, I flipped to the page and found a paragraph-length profile of the man known as "Gilles de Rais," as well as a portrait of him, showing a brooding, dark-haired man in a suit of armor sans helmet, with a sword at his side and a battle ax in hand. After staring at the portrait for a moment, I read the following:

"Gilles de Rais (1405-1440) was a French knight and suspected occultist of Breton descent who was a member of the House of Montmorency, one of the oldest and most distinguished noble families in France. Rais served as a commander in the French army and fought alongside Joan of Arc against the English during the destructive Hundred Years' War, for which he was appointed Marshal of France, having taken part in the momentous Siege of Orléans. Today, however, Rais is more widely known as a confessed serial killer of children, as well as a child rapist and necrophile, with victims numbering in the hundreds. After his retirement from military life, Rais purportedly dabbled in Satanism and depleted his enormous wealth in occult experiments, seeking individuals who knew alchemy and evocation, or 'demon summoning,' to aid him in his experiments, to little result. Rais confessed to having raped, tortured, and killed between 100 and 200 children, although some sources say the number of victims could be as high as 600, predominantly boys, who ranged in age from six to eighteen. Upon discovery of his atrocious crimes, Rais was excommunicated by the Catholic Church and charged with murder, sodomy, and blasphemy. Condemned to death, Rais was hung and his body cut to pieces, then burned, in October 1440. Some historians and occultists today believe that Rais was himself a victim of the Inquisition, with the latter believing that, rather than a murderer, Rais was in fact a witch and a martyr to an unknown pagan religion."

I stared catatonically at the page, trying to make sense of what I'd just read, then suddenly realized that my left hand was quivering. I put my other hand over it to stop the trembling. After a while, I got up and put the book back on the shelf, then left the library in a sickly daze.

I walked home and spent the rest of the day in my bedroom, only leaving to get food and to take a piss. I went to sleep early that day.

October 21, 2003

I told my mother that, instead of having her drive me to school like she usually did, I'd take the bus. Fortunately, she didn't question me about it. After leaving the house early in the morning, I went to a nearby Dunkin' Donuts and stayed there for an hour, since the library didn't open until nine a.m.

Before heading to the library, I used a payphone outside the restaurant to call Jeremiah, but nobody answered, and I figured it was because he was already on his way to school and his mother was at work. I wondered if he knew that I was suspended. *He saw me leaving our history class the other day, but did he notice that I didn't come back?* I would've noticed if *he* had left the class and hadn't returned. Then again, Jeremiah constantly occupied my mind, whereas I was certain that he didn't think about me with as much fervor.

I avoided the librarian for fear of making her feel awkward after our last encounter, which I tried to put out of my mind. I grabbed a bunch of books off the shelves, ranging from art history to biblical and film studies to biology. I'd always had a hunger for knowledge, ever since I was a little kid, so I figured I'd make the best of my suspension (and also suppress thoughts of Gilles de Rais) by reading as many different books as I could, no matter the subject.

October 22, 2003

I left the house earlier that morning so I could call Jeremiah from the payphone outside the Dunkin' Donuts. I didn't want to call him from my house because I didn't want to risk my mother overhearing our conversation.

"Holy shit, it's you!" Jeremiah said, when he heard my voice. "I thought your parents took away your phone privileges or something."

The fact that he sounded excited to hear from me put a smile on my face. "No, nothing like that," I told him. "I am calling you from a payphone, though."

"So I guess your parents didn't take the suspension too well, huh?"

I paused. "You know about the suspension?" Jeremiah didn't respond, so I repeated myself.

"Mr. Van Orton told me," he finally replied. "Is it just for a week?"

I didn't bother to respond because I figured he already knew the answer. There was a long silence. I thought about telling him about my conversation with Jeunet, but I figured he knew about that, too. *What else does he know?* I wondered. He and Van Orton seemed close, and the latter was evidently chums with Jeunet, so it was likely that Jeremiah already knew about "Chronovisor" and Chandler Faust, as well as the truth behind the Rais Frolic. In fact, I presumed he knew more than I did—although I was still skeptical about what Jeunet had told me, as it all seemed too outlandish to be true.

"What are you doing right now?" Jeremiah asked me.

"I'm outside a Dunkin' Donuts," I said in a monotone drawl, "talking to *you*." After a brief pause, I asked him, "Do you think about that day at your house…when we fucked?"

"It wasn't *that* long ago," Jeremiah said with a scoffing laugh.

"Do you want to do that again?"

"Sure."

He said "sure" in such a flippant way, as if I'd asked him if he wanted to go grab a burger, which annoyed me a little.

"Anyway," I said, trying to hide my annoyance, "I'm going to the library now. That's what I do, instead of staying home. But at least I'm catching up on a lot of reading."

"Do you go to the Adriance Memorial Library?"

"Yeah."

"I'll come see you on Friday," Jeremiah told me.

"You mean at the library?"

"Uh-huh. I don't mind ditching school to hang out with you."

I smiled softly. "I miss you, you know."

Jeremiah cackled.

"I'm being serious," I said. "I'm so used to seeing you every day at school that it feels kind of weird when I don't see you on school days, like something's broken, you know?"

"Yeah," Jeremiah said, "I do know. It feels like you're going through a breakup…without actually going through a breakup."

"Something like that." I paused. "Do you miss *me* at all?"

"I miss you…sucking my dick, for sure."

"Asshole," I said playfully.

I could hear Jeremiah laughing hysterically. I was going to ask him about Mallory, but then

I thought, *Fuck her.*

Later that day, in the library, I was flipping through an art history book, when I came across a startling painting depicting the martyrdom of Saint Sebastian. The young saint was shown bound to a tree, half-naked, with an arrow protruding from his abdomen and his head slanted, looking as if moaning in pleasure, not pain. As I stared at the painting, intrigued by its paradoxical nature, the figure of Saint Sebastian unexpectedly took the form of—Jeremiah! Rather than being shocked, I was aroused. I discreetly took the book with me into the restroom, entered a stall, and masturbated to the painting. I climaxed almost immediately, my body shaking with delight.

October 23, 2003

I spent the entire day at the library skimming through Communist books, from Marx's *Das Kapital* to Guevara's *The Motorcycle Diaries*. The former, though dense, makes valid arguments that the motivating force behind capitalism, as well as all class-based systems, is the exploitation of labor, and that capitalists will readily replace human workers with machines if it is deemed cost-effective. It's unfortunate that many people think of Marx as a political figure, because he seemed too compassionate and open-minded for politics, or rather that was the impression I got from *Das Kapital*.

Guevara's book, which reads like a coming-of-age story about self-discovery—tracing the Argentine's early travels as a medical student who is transformed after witnessing social injustices perpetrated against marginalized groups—was much easier to digest. I was surprised at how easy it was to fall in love with Guevara, who, despite having been born into an upper-class family, had developed an affinity for the poor at a young age and could empathize with their pain. He excelled in sports and chess during his adolescence and read the works of William Faulkner, Albert Camus, Friedrich Nietzsche, Jack London, and Sigmund Freud. He reminded me a little of myself, though he reminded me a lot more of Jeremiah. It wasn't until I read Guevara's book that I felt proud and honored to call myself a Communist.

I also read, in its entirety, Mao's so-called "Little Red Book," which consists of hundreds of quotations by the former Chinese leader, thematically organized into thirty-three chapters, with titles like "Classes and Class Struggle," "The People's Army," "Serving the People," and "Unity." I particularly liked the later chapters entitled "Criticism and Self-Criticism" and "Culture and Art," which encourage Communists to be open to criticism, rather than fear it, and also to create art that reflects the working class, scolding artists who neglect certain audiences just because they may be uneducated.

Conscientious practice of self-criticism is still another hallmark distinguishing our Party from all other political parties. As we say, dust will accumulate if a room is not cleaned regularly, our faces will get dirty if they are not washed regularly. Our comrades' minds and our Party's work may also collect dust, and also need sweeping and washing.

What we demand is the unity of politics and art, the unity of content and form, the unity of revolutionary political content and the highest possible perfection of artistic form. Works of art which lack artistic quality have no force, however progressive they are politically. Therefore, we oppose both works of art with a wrong political viewpoint and the tendency toward the "poster and slogan style," which is correct in political viewpoint but lacking in artistic power.

— Chairman Mao, "Little Red Book"

CHAPTER EIGHTEEN

On October 24, 2003—the last day of what I refer to as my "mock suspension"—Jeremiah met me outside the library, both of us dressed in school uniform, even though we had no intention of going to school that day. I was so excited to see Jeremiah again that I hugged him, which seemed to catch him by surprise, as if no one had ever shown him affection before.

"What was that for?" he asked, hands behind his back, like he was hiding something from me, something that he didn't want me to see until he was ready to reveal it.

"Because I fucking miss you," I replied, smiling.

"Shit, you really *are* gay, huh?"

"Would you rather I spit in your face?"

"No—but later you can spit on my dick if you want," Jeremiah said.

He said it with a straight face, so I wasn't sure if he was joking or not. But it turned me on nonetheless, as I briefly imagined spitting on his dick before going down on him. I wanted him in my mouth again, and I also wanted to fuck *him*, instead of him fucking me, like when we first had sex.

"Did you bring a lunch?" Jeremiah asked me. He looked a bit awkward, standing there with his hands behind his back, showing little expression.

"Not today," I said. "I figured we could get some food at a nearby restaurant. There's plenty of places to choose from around here."

Jeremiah revealed what he'd been hiding behind his back: a brown paper lunch bag. "This is just a little something," he said, before putting it behind his back again. "But we can still grab a bite to eat somewhere." After a pause, he added, "I actually brought the lunch for you."

My face lit up.

We went to Dunkin' Donuts, where we ordered hot chocolate and two donuts each, and sat at a table in the back. Jeremiah placed the lunch bag on the table.

"What do you have in there?" I asked him.

"I'll show you in a minute," he said, and took a bite of a French cruller.

"Did it take you long to get here?"

"Not really. The bus driver thought he was playing *Mario Kart* and gunned it. I'm surprised we didn't get into an accident. So…what have you been doing these past few days? Did you even tell your parents that you got suspended?"

I shook my head.

"Probably better that way," Jeremiah said. "So you've been, what, just going to the library? Is that it?"

"Yeah," I replied, and took a sip of my hot chocolate. "Mostly reading."

"What the hell else are you gonna do in a library, right?"

I nodded weakly and took another sip of my drink, then looked at Jeremiah's slicked-back hairdo. I still hadn't gotten used to seeing him without a headdress on. He looked great regardless, but Jeremiah with a keffiyeh and Jeremiah without a keffiyeh seemed like two different people, in both appearance and personality. Even though I'd known "Jeremiah without a keffiyeh" for only a short time, it became quite apparent that, after having discarded the hammer and sickle lapel pin and later his keffiyeh, as well as the Ho Chi Minh poster, Jeremiah was now a changed person, for better or worse.

"Why did Mr. Van Orton tell you that I got suspended?" I asked him.

"Because he thought I needed to know," Jeremiah said. "He also told me to tell *you* that he wants you to attend the Rais Frolic. It's going to be sometime in December. I'll be there, too. That should be pretty cool, huh? Staying in a mansion for the weekend, not having to worry about school or anything. Dr. Jeunet told me he's even got a personal chef who'll be there to cook all kinds of food for us. How fucking amazing is that?"

He smiled in delight and stuffed a half-eaten donut into his mouth, then took a swig of his hot chocolate as if it were alcohol and wiped his mouth. There was something about him that made me feel sorry for him, which was a feeling I thought I'd never experience with regard to Jeremiah, whom I still considered superior to me in every way imaginable. Perhaps it was the way he smiled at the thought of spending the weekend in a mansion, which would certainly be a first for him, and having a chef cook his food—things that "Jeremiah the Communist" would've found vulgar rather than enticing. I could only imagine, with a shudder, how much of his former Communist identity had deteriorated since we had last seen each other in Van Orton's classroom.

"You talked to Dr. Jeunet?" I said to Jeremiah, who nodded in response. "When was this?"

"Well…I've talked to him a bunch of times," he replied.

"Do you, uh, talk to him about *me*?"

"We've talked about you a few times, actually, including just yesterday when I went to the Todd House. Mr. Van Orton was there, too, obviously, since it's technically his house now."

I couldn't fathom Jeremiah being at the Todd House with both Van Orton and Jeunet. *What do they do there? What do they talk about?*—besides *me*, evidently, as difficult as that was for me to wrap my head around. But what I really wanted to know was, *Did Jeunet tell Jeremiah the same bullshit he told me in his office?*

"When Mr. Van Orton sent me to Dr. Jeunet's office that one day," I said, pausing to gather my thoughts, "Dr. Jeunet told me some crazy stuff that made no sense. I'm not even sure if I heard him correctly, or if my brain was just acting stupid, because some of the shit he told me was fucking *out there*."

Jeremiah, on the verge of laughter, nodded as if he knew exactly what I was talking about, then slid the lunch bag toward me and said, "Open it. Then I'll explain."

"I'm not hungry anymore, but I'll save it for later."

Jeremiah smiled. "Trust me, you'll be hungry for what's inside."

Nonplussed, I looked at him for a moment, then slowly opened the lunch bag and saw that there was a book inside, *Behold a Pale Horse*, with its surrealistic cover art of a winged horse and a figure donning a skull mask. My heart began to race as I stared at the book, too scared to take it out of the bag, fearing that simply touching the cursed book could possibly indoctrinate me in the same way that it had indoctrinated Jeremiah, and I didn't want to risk losing my newfound identity as a Communist. However, I desperately wanted to read the book and find out what was in those pages that had compelled Jeremiah to adopt a new identity.

"Why are you giving me this?" I asked Jeremiah, who finished his drink and set the empty cup aside.

"Because you need to read it," he said.

"*Why?*"

"Because Dr. Jeunet and Mr. Van Orton want you to read it so you can discuss it with them. Does that seem 'weird' to you or something?"

I scoffed and looked at Jeremiah as if to say, "It seems totally fucking weird!" Then again, I did tell him that I wanted to read the book, and now he was obliging me.

Jeremiah took the book out of the bag and placed it in the center of the table. "Everything you've ever wanted to know about the world is in this book," he told me, in a tone so earnest that I felt almost obligated to believe him. "This is the most-read book in American prisons, even more than the Bible. It's also the most shoplifted book in the country. Any bookstore that sells this book keeps it behind the cashier's counter to prevent people from stealing it. The author is a man named Milton William Cooper, and he published this book—his manifesto—in 1991. Here's where things take a weird-ass turn. Nobody knew what the fuck this book was until someone snuck a copy into Attica prison, right here in our own beloved New York, about a year after it was published. Soon, people from Harlem, Brooklyn, and other parts of the state started peddling the book on the streets, and that was when rappers began referencing Milton William Cooper and his book in their music, everyone from Mobb Deep to Tupac Shakur to the Wu-Tang Clan. Eventually, people from New York who were familiar with *Behold a Pale Horse* stopped calling it by its title. Instead, they just referred to it as 'The Book.' What's ironic, though, is that Cooper was a middle-aged white dude who lived in Arizona, and yet most of his readers today are Black folks from New York. But they like him because they believe he spoke truth to power."

Jeremiah's sales pitch, as it were, definitely piqued my interest, even if everything he had said sounded like a regurgitation of what Van Orton had told him, which I assumed was the case. But it didn't matter, since I was determined to take the book home with me and read it from cover to cover.

"If the book is sold in bookstores," I said, "does that mean I can just walk into a Barnes & Noble and buy a copy right now?"

Jeremiah lay his hand on the book as if he were being sworn into office and said, "Not *this* copy. You'd be buying a counterfeit. This is an original copy of the book, owned by Mr. Van Orton and given to him by Dr. Jeunet."

"And how did Dr. Jeunet get an original copy?"

"That's something I don't know, and neither does Mr. Van Orton."

"So—what exactly is this book about?" I asked.

Jeremiah put the book back in the bag and closed it, then told me, "It's about all the things you've been too afraid to ask. Read the book with an open mind, and think about this while you're reading it. In June 2001, Cooper predicted that there was going to be an attack on a large American city and that the U.S. government would blame Osama bin Laden for the attack. Just three months later, the Twin Towers fell. Then Cooper made another prediction—that he was going to be killed. Sure enough, less than two months after the 9/11 attacks, Cooper was killed by sheriff's deputies and died a martyr."

"And I thought David Lynch 'predicted' 9/11," I quipped.

Jeremiah snorted a laugh, then replied, "More than one person can prophesy the same thing, my Yankee friend."

"Does that make Milton William Cooper, like, a prophet?"

"Some might say that."

"And what do *you* think?" I asked.

"What I think isn't important," Jeremiah replied. "Just read the book. And after today, don't talk to me again until you do."

I kind of flinched and hoped that Jeremiah would say, "Gotcha!" But after several moments of silence, I finally said, "Why can't we talk until after I've read the book?"

"Because I don't want you to get distracted by anything."

"*You're* not a distraction."

Jeremiah, flashing a sly grin, nodded and said, "I have a feeling that my face has kept you up many nights. In fact—more than a feeling. I wonder how many times you've dry-humped your pillow thinking about me. I bet you come in globs when you jerk off to me. I'd be disappointed if you didn't."

It was such a pompous thing to say, all of it. But he was right. His face *did* oftentimes keep me up at night, almost to exhaustion. Jeremiah might've become a changed person, but he still had the same pleasant, cherubic features and almond-shaped eyes, and his body still emanated the same rich scent of cinnamon and clove that made me fall in love with him in the first place. Communist or not, Jeremiah remained my greatest obsession, the boy who had lit the lamp that required little to no oil. He was my Constantinople, my Taj Mahal, my Versailles, my *only* reason for wanting to remain an inhabitant of this world.

"How are things between you and Mallory?" I asked, almost as an afterthought.

Jeremiah feigned confusion and replied, "Who's Mallory?"

We both smiled.

After leaving Dunkin' Donuts, we went to the movies and watched the new Tarantino film, *Kill Bill*, in a mostly empty theater, then stayed and watched it again. While watching the movie a second time, Jeremiah placed a gentle hand on my cheek in a kind of motherly way. His hand felt so nice against my cheek that I almost wanted to cry. I cocked my head to the side, embracing his warm hand. He then stuck his middle finger in my mouth and began sliding it in and out repeatedly, as if to arouse me. He leaned over and licked the side of my neck, which sent a euphoric chill down my spine. I let out a moan, then turned to Jeremiah and said, "I love you." Then waited and waited for him to say it back to me.

Eventually, Jeremiah, gazing at me with pitiful eyes, said something that I'm sure I'll never forget: "You can't love a corpse. Besides, I don't have enough love in me to feed you."

He then put his hand on my crotch and began to caress it, then unzipped my pants and gave me a mechanical, loveless handjob—though I still came.

CHAPTER NINETEEN

I read *Behold a Pale Horse* by Milton William Cooper in four days, during which Jeremiah didn't utter a single word to me. When I saw him in our history class on the third day, which was the day I came back to school after my suspension, I went up to him and said, "Hey, uh…I'm still reading that book, but…it's messing with my head, though." Jeremiah gave me a slight nod, then looked away as if I weren't there. His indifference hurt me, but I tried not to show it.

On the fourth day, I spent hours in my room reading the book, and when I'd finally finished it close to midnight, feeling as if brain fluid were leaking out of my ears, I slumped on my bed and closed my eyes, trying to make sense of what was unquestionably the most unbelievable book I'd ever read in my life.

According to The Book, which runs a lengthy 640 pages, HIV/AIDS is a man-made disease used to decrease the population of three "undesirables" (Blacks, Hispanics, and homosexuals); the Bilderberg Group, originally established in 1954 to prevent future world wars, as well as to bolster free market capitalism, hopes to install a world government, with Adam Smith as its eternal God; the Illuminati, a secret international organization controlled by the Bilderberg Group, is conspiring with the Knights of Columbus, Freemasons, and Skull and Bones—i.e., "The Order," which itself controls the CIA—to establish a New World Order; President Dwight D. Eisenhower, an Illuminati member, negotiated a treaty with extraterrestrials in his second year of presidency, which allowed the aliens to abduct humans in exchange for technological assistance; the Illuminati have invented alien threats for their own personal gain, unbeknownst to their Bilderberg Group masters, and are actively conspiring with the aliens to take over the world, unaware that they themselves are being manipulated by the extraterrestrials, who rule the human race through religion and myth; President John F. Kennedy, who had intended to reveal the existence of extraterrestrial life to the public, was assassinated on orders from the Illuminati; pharmaceutical companies are encouraging physicians to prescribe psychoactive drugs like Prozac and Ritalin to children, with the realization that doing so will inevitably lead to more school shootings, which would enable the government to take away citizens' guns.

The book concludes with a reproduction of the anti-Semitic text *The Protocols of the Elders of Zion*, which Cooper claims to be an Illuminati work, instructing readers to substitute "Sion" for "Zion," "Illuminati" for "Jews," and "cattle" for "goyim."

Cooper, who believed that the Illuminati consisted primarily of Communists, states in the book's foreword that he had fought the Commies in Vietnam and was willing to fight them again, if necessary. He considered himself an American patriot and a devout Christian, which I interpreted to mean that Cooper was not only a nationalist but a religious zealot, and likely a capitalist. Thus, I made sure to take whatever he said with a grain of salt. It was only when Cooper made shockingly accurate predictions, like the Ruby Ridge standoff and the Columbine High School massacre, that I lowered my guard and wondered if maybe he wasn't crazy after all. Yet his conspiracy theories were too outrageous for me to take seriously, other than his belief that HIV/AIDS was a man-made disease created to eradicate certain "undesirables," which seemed at least plausible. After all, why would Cooper—a heterosexual, middle-aged white man and conservative Christian—make such a daring claim...unless it was true? It's no wonder, then, that his book has found an audience among America's most prominent skeptics, Black people, who have been hoodwinked so often throughout the country's history that it seems only appropriate that they would gravitate toward a book whose author, like themselves, had a deep distrust of the government.

I fell asleep with my clothes on that night and was besieged with bizarre dreams unlike any I'd experienced before. In one of the dreams, I found myself riding in a presidential limousine with the top down, sitting in the backseat beside my ex-girlfriend, Athena, who was donning a pink suit reminiscent of Jacqueline Kennedy. Sitting in the passenger seat was Raekwon, a member of the Wu-Tang Clan, donning a headdress similar to the one Jeremiah used to wear. The driver was Van Orton, dressed in drag and smoking a fat cigar. Raekwon turned to me, held up a battered copy of *Behold a Pale Horse*, and began speaking in French, although I couldn't understand a word he was saying. Athena placed a tender hand on my arm and, with terror in her voice, said, "Sean—please take the book." As I reached for the book, a single shot from what must've been a bolt-action rifle hit Raekwon in the jaw, splattering blood and teeth everywhere. Horrified, I froze and watched as Raekwon, bleeding profusely, tried to speak with a shattered jaw. Suddenly, another shot rang out and hit Raekwon in the head, killing him. Athena pointed toward a seven-floor building and cried, "Over there!" I looked and, despite being a great distance away, could see a smiling Wolfgang von Strudel in the window, gripping a rifle. Van Orton, driving in circles around a city park, turned to me, then started laughing. "You've got war paint on your face," he told me. I touched my face and realized that it was smeared with blood from the fatal shot that killed Raekwon.

"Mr. President," I suddenly heard a voice say. "We need to get you out of there before it's too late."

The voice seemed to be coming from above, as if God Himself were speaking to me. Yes, I was "Mr. President." There was no doubt about it.

I looked back at the seven-floor building, where Wolfgang von Strudel was readying to fire another shot, with me as the target. However, before the anthropomorphic duck could fire another shot, a blazing light came upon me, filling me with a sense of tranquility. With the light beckoning me, I ascended into a large, disc-shaped aircraft, whose interior consisted of nothing more than an all-white space, like an endless limbo. As I walked about the empty space, Jeunet, dressed in papal regalia, including the papal crown, suddenly materialized before me. Beside him was Simon, naked and on all fours, with a leash around his neck, which Jeunet held on to as if walking a dog.

More confused than shocked, I asked Jeunet, "Where am I?"

He smiled and replied, "Do you still consider me a 'traditionalist,' *Monsieur* Quell? What about *Monsieur* Van Orton? Are we to remain 'conservatives' in your eyes much longer? Do you even know what the word means?"

I looked at Simon, who was staring at me with lifeless eyes, then looked back at Jeunet. "I don't want to be here."

"Nobody does…at first," Jeunet said. "Then they learn to appreciate the beauty of this place and its devilish inhabitants, who so yearn for your company. Oh, *Monsieur* Quell, what devils we have here! And you'll get to know them all soon enough. But don't think of 'devils' as ugly beasts. In fact, the devils here are as lovely as embroidery on a Persian rug—and they emanate such sweet scents. Alas, those who detest us say that we drink from the cup of genocide, but I assure you, it's a most refreshing drink. And once you've had a taste, you'll never want to leave this place we call 'Chronovisor,' where the blood of the righteous mingles freely with that of Satan."

Fear coursed through my body at the utterance of the word "Chronovisor." Oddly enough, I felt no such terror at the mention of Satan, treating it as if it were any other word.

"Tell me about Chronovisor," I said to Jeunet, my voice trembling. "Not this place, but the *real* Chronovisor."

Jeunet studied my face for a brief moment, then said, "I believe we've discussed this matter before, haven't we? I won't tell you any more than I already have, but I will tell you this, *Monsieur* Quell. The Chronovisor has allowed me to see things that you wouldn't believe. I was there when Stanley Kubrick faked the Moon landing. I was there when Thomas Jefferson raped Sally Hemings and inadvertently invented biracial people. I was there when the Moors conquered Spain, Portugal, and Sicily. Most importantly, I was there when Lucifer whispered Satanic verses into Constantine the Great's ear the moment he saw the Christian cross in his dream. Oh, the things that I have seen would make you vomit up your mother's milk. Such horrors, such marvels."

"But what *is* Chronovisor?" I asked.

Jeunet shook his head as if frustrated, then replied, "What a silly question, especially since you already know the answer. If you haven't figured it out by now, then you never will. Perhaps I was wrong about you, *Monsieur* Quell. If there's one thing I cannot stand, it's people with shit for brains. Are you one of those people? I sure hope not, because if you are, I'll have no choice but to put you against the wall. Say the word and I'll have you riddled with more holes than a honeycomb. But I'd hate to lose someone like you. Remember in my office when I told you that I admired you? I meant it. I'd prefer to write lullabies on your inner thighs, rather than tear you apart vertebrae by vertebrae…"

As Jeunet continued to speak, his voice became a muffled mess, until eventually I couldn't hear anything. My vision suddenly became blurred, and I awoke with violent stomach pains, which took an hour to finally subside.

CHAPTER TWENTY

On Halloween, the school's biannual literary journal, *The 400 Blows* (named after François Truffaut's classic French New Wave film), published a poem written by Jeremiah, simply entitled "Sufi." I read the poem so many times in the span of an hour, as if under a spell, that I was able to recite it verbatim:

"A Rome invisible I rule, as fallen angels defecate on my head,
eluding a Sunday lynching in exchange for—
my (sealed) lips. I exhale locusts in honor of Emir Abdelkader,
then place a prickly crown of thorns upon the
Sufi's head, and we embark on a children's crusade to Lebanon.
Along the way, I allow my empathy to sink to the bottom of
the Atlantic Ocean, where the lost souls of America's
BLACK fathers float undisturbed,
still chained at the ankles / hoping in vain to catch a glimpse
of Heaven's cavity."

Van Orton congratulated Jeremiah on the poem during class, saying it was better than much of the "schlock" that passed for poetry in *The New Yorker* and *Harper's Magazine*, then asked the class to give Jeremiah a round of applause. Everyone clapped except me.

"Now then," Van Orton said, standing at the front of the class, "as you know, after chapel, there's going to be a Halloween party held in the gymnasium for all grades, as well as a procession honoring Christ, which will be held on campus grounds. The party will continue for the rest of the school day, and trust me, there will be plenty of food, drinks, and music to keep you all happy for hours. However, if you happen to find yourself bored with the festivities, Dr. Jeunet has given you free rein to walk about the campus. Just don't do anything reckless, gentlemen."

Some of the students chuckled. I turned around and looked at

Jeremiah, whom I hadn't told yet that I'd finished reading *Behold a Pale Horse*, since I needed more time to reflect on what I'd read. The thought that Jeremiah had loaned me the book as some kind of prank did cross my mind for a moment. But, although Jeremiah had a witty sense of humor, I didn't think he'd go so far as to have me read a 640-page book just as a gag, unless he'd gone totally bonkers.

When I turned back around, Van Orton was staring directly at me, his face expressing some displeasure. Then, in an instant, he smiled, as if suddenly pleased with me. "Mr. Quell," he said in a probing tone, "would you be so kind as to remind us what we've been discussing in class these past few days?"

I thought for a moment, then said, "We've been, uh…talking about New Spain, or the—"

"We've left Latin American history, Mr. Quell."

The boy sitting next to me raised his hand, but Van Orton curtly shook his head at him, as he clearly wanted *me* to answer.

"I'm sorry," I said, after a pause. "I've been scatterbrained these past few days. Honestly, the last thing I remember is the expulsion of the Moriscos from Catholic Spain."

"And oh, what a sad day it was," Van Orton said, somewhat sarcastically. "However, we've since moved on across continents to the East, where the Mongols have ravaged the once-beautiful city of Baghdad, bringing an end to the Islamic Golden Age. The Crusades, ignited by Pope Urban II, have come and gone, leaving Christians with nothing and Muslims with contempt in their hearts, paving the way for modern jihad. Which brings us to the Ottoman Empire—admired by few, hated by many. Although the Ottomans behaved no differently than other empires from that time, history is known to inflame emotions, thus distorting minds. For example, according to many conservative Americans, John Brown the abolitionist was a madman, even a terrorist. Yet those on the political left view him as a hero. So which side is right? Well, it depends on whom you ask."

"John Brown was definitely a hero!" Jeremiah hollered, which made Van Orton smile with approval.

"Yes, Mr. Kateb, I'm inclined to agree with you. But not everyone shares our sentiments."

"Then those people are *wrong*."

"Now you're beginning to sound like your former Communist heroes," Van Orton said. "I hope you haven't relapsed into Bolshevism since we last spoke, because that would just break my heart, Mr. Kateb. Please say it isn't so."

The way he said "former Communist heroes" hit me like a kick in the chest, especially the word "former," as if reminding Jeremiah that his Commie days were over—or rather, they should remain buried in the past.

"No, Mr. Van Orton," Jeremiah said with a disarming grin, "I haven't gone back to Trotsky, although at times he does whisper sweet melodies into my ear."

"Fortunately, mine are sweeter."

The room went silent as Van Orton and Jeremiah shared a moment of bonding. No, it was more than that. They were gazing at each other like a pair of lovebirds, right in front of the whole class! I couldn't believe it. I glared at Jeremiah, who eventually broke eye contact with Van Orton and looked at me. Not appreciating my chiding stare, he scoffed in a "Fuck you" kind of way, then turned his attention back to Van Orton. I just wanted to shake Jeremiah and shout, "What the hell has gotten into you? Snap out of it!" Strangely, although he owed me nothing, in my delusion, I still felt like he owed me something, namely his love. But how do you force someone to give you their heart?

Van Orton, hands in his pockets, began walking around the classroom as he spoke. "During its final years, the Ottoman Empire, perhaps sensing that the end was near, behaved like a butcher and committed its worst atrocities, from the Chios massacre during the Greek War of Independence to the Armenian genocide. Going back to what I said earlier with regard to history's penchant for distortion, although the crimes that the Ottomans committed were abhorrent, we must keep in mind that, in many cases, the worst atrocities inflicted upon a people are those inflicted by its very own people. As much as Christians bemoan the crimes committed against them by Muslims in general and the Ottomans in particular, the most gruesome crimes committed against Christians are those committed by Christians themselves. The Rwandan genocide was a massacre that pitted Christians against Christians, resulting in the deaths of over half a million people in just three months. Mind you, it was white Christian missionaries who had instigated the genocide with their Willie Lynch-inspired tactics. From the Fourth Crusade, which saw the sack of Constantinople, and thus hastened the collapse of Christendom in the East, to the French Wars of Religion, which birthed the bloody St. Bartholomew's Day massacre, Christians, like every other religious, political, racial, and ethnic group, have often been their own worst enemies. The so-called 'Eternal City' of Rome was sacked by the godless Germanics three times in the fifth century, and yet it was in 1527, when an army of mostly German Lutherans stormed the city and unleashed an orgy of mayhem, which included the destruction of churches, the killing of cardinals, and the raping of nuns, that Rome experienced its worst calamity."

By the end of his lecture, Van Orton was standing beside Jeremiah in the back of the class. He looked down at an amused Jeremiah and said, "Go ahead, Mr. Kateb, spit it out."

"I was just thinking, you went from the Ottoman Empire to the sack of Rome, but I'm still trying to figure out what it all amounts to. Is there a lesson?"

"The *lesson*, Mr. Kateb, is that it's Halloween, that most *benign* of holidays, and I wish to impart to my students horrific accounts of bloodshed so that you may better understand the nature of man. And if I happen to expose Christian hypocrisy along the way, all the better."

"Now who sounds like a Communist?" Jeremiah said.

Van Orton, smiling, pinched his cheek, then walked back to the front of the class and took out a piece of paper from his pocket. "I'm going to read to you now an excerpt from the prominent book *A Short Account of the Destruction of the Indies*, written by the Dominican friar Bartolomé de las Casas, which details the horrors committed by the Spaniards against the indigenous peoples of the Americas in the sixteenth century."

> *The Christians forced their way into Native settlements, slaughtering everyone they found there, including small children, old men, pregnant women, and even women who had just given birth. They hacked them to pieces, slicing open their bellies with their swords as though they were sheep herded into a pen. They even laid wagers on whether they could manage to slice a man in two at a stroke, or cut an individual's head from his body, or disembowel him with a*

single blow of their axes. They grabbed suckling infants by the feet and, ripping them from their mothers' breasts, dashed them head-long against the rocks. They spared no one, erecting especially wide gibbets on which they could string their victims up with their feet just off the ground and then burn them alive thirteen at a time, in honor of our Savior and the Twelve Apostles. Some they chose to keep alive and simply cut their wrists. Since all those who could do so took to the hills and mountains in order to escape the clutches of these merciless and inhuman butchers, the Christians trained dogs to track them down—wild dogs who would savage a Native to death as soon as look at him, tearing him to shreds and devour-ing his flesh as though he were a pig. And when, as happened on the odd occasion, the Natives did kill a Christian, which, given the enormity of the crimes committed against them, they were in all justice fully entitled to, the Christians came to an "unofficial agree-ment" that for every European killed, one hundred Natives would be executed.

After class, I grabbed my things and went to talk to Jeremiah at his desk. But, barely making eye contact with me, as if he were incapable of looking directly at me, Jeremiah grabbed his things and told me that he had to talk to Van Orton. Then he added, "We can talk at our 'rebel base' after chapel."

I'd only heard him refer to the school library as a "rebel base" once before, although, at the time, I wasn't sure if he was being entirely sin-cere. Apparently, he was.

Before leaving the class, I stood and watched as Jeremiah went over to Van Orton, and the two spoke in a hushed tone. Then, as he had done earlier in class, Van Orton pinched Jeremiah on the cheek, both of them smiling, and then put his arm around Jeremiah like a father comforting his son, which made me jealous. It wasn't so much that Van Orton had his arm around him. Rather, it was that the two had evidently devel-oped an intimate bond, perhaps stronger than the one Jeremiah and I had once shared.

———————

I sat next to Jeremiah at chapel. While Father Hawkins and his obedient group of altar boys were performing the introductory rites, I turned to Jeremiah and asked him if he was going to stay for the Halloween party.

"Yeah," he replied. "I'll stay for the rest of the day, and we can just hang out and talk about the *book*." He looked at me with a serious expression and asked, "You did finish it, right?"

I nodded.

"Good," Jeremiah said. "We might be able to go to the Todd House today, but Milo wants us to wait a while before going there because there are too many people on campus right now. I'm sure half the students will probably go home after spending less than an hour at the lame Halloween party."

Jeremiah snorted in mocking laughter when he said "party," as if the idea of boys attending a school Halloween party seemed absurd to him. But I was just thinking about how he had referred to Van Orton by his first name, Milo. I'd never heard Jeremiah utter Van Orton's first name before, so it came as somewhat of a surprise to me when he said it. In fact, I hadn't heard *anyone* call Van Orton by his first name before, and hearing it from a student seemed almost unnatural.

"Now you're calling him 'Milo'?" I said to Jeremiah.

He looked at me like I was crazy, then chuckled and replied, "Yeah, what a *game-changer*."

"By the way, am I even allowed at the Todd House?"

"You are now. Congratulations."

"Why *now*?"

"Because...Dr. Jeunet thinks you're finally ready to join us," Jeremiah told me.

"Ready to jo—" I started to say, but Jeremiah quickly put his finger to his lips as if to shush me, then gestured to Father Hawkins, who was now standing at the pulpit, facing the congregation and ready to begin his sermon.

"What are we to make of this century so far?" Father Hawkins asked rhetorically, his voice forlorn. "The new century has just begun, and yet we've already seen great disturbances, from the attacks on 9/11 to the launching of the Tenth Crusade in Afghanistan and Iraq, where the forces of good and evil battle for the soul of mankind. Unfortunately, Satan's little puppet, Saddam Hussein, remains at large, but I have faith in our army's ability to flush him out and send him to Hell where he belongs, along with all his minions, who are nothing more than fallen angels in human disguise. That's right, gentlemen, the fallen angels—their hearts drunk with blood—have come to Earth to wage war against Christians, and they are not leaving without a fight. But if it's a fight they want, then arm yourselves with Zyklon B, gentlemen, because we're going to give those demons a fight they'll wish they'd never started! Oh, yes…praise the Lord and pass the cyanide!"

Father Hawkins, pausing for a moment, took out a handkerchief and wiped his mouth with it, then resumed speaking.

"Gentlemen, I am not one for 'conspiracy theories,' but in the past few years, America, as well as the rest of the world, has turned topsy-turvy. That became all too clear to me when, earlier this year, a heretic by the name of Dan Brown published *The Da Vinci Code*, a work of blasphemy against the Roman Catholic Church that I'm sure some of you gentlemen have read. And for those of you who *have* read the nefarious book, I demand that you see me in the confessional after chapel, no exceptions! Dan Brown, like Martin Luther before him, wishes to see the Church burned to the ground and its ashes urinated on. But I'll cut the throats of every boy standing on this altar before I let that happen. Listen to me when I say—there is a conspiracy to undermine this holy institution of ours. The United States government talks of weather balloons and clouds and swamp gas when people claim to have seen flying saucers, and what does the government do to these people? They pump them full of drugs to keep them docile. And when people express knowledge of shapeshifting reptilian aliens roaming the Earth, they're immediately ridiculed and ostracized. I fear, gentlemen, that the same fate awaits us Christians when we begin spouting the truth about demons."

As Father Hawkins continued his sermon-turned-rant, becoming more aggressive, I noticed Jeunet standing near the Caravaggio painting depicting the crucifixion of Saint Peter. I didn't know how long he'd been standing there, but he appeared engrossed by what Father Hawkins was saying, as if the cleric were bringing to light shocking "revelations" about the world—revelations that only he knew about.

"If God loves ugly," Father Hawkins continued, "as some cynics claim, then oh God, there is much to 'love' in this sinful world we live in! I see unwed women wallowing in whoredom like pigs in filth. I see famished men eating violence in substitute of sex. I see children being devoured as if they were the offspring of the Roman god Saturn. But most troubling of all, I see the Christian cross being spat and trampled upon by demons whose evil hearts burn like ether. At times I wonder if God, having ordered the musical notes to be played, has bowed out, shirking His duties, and left us with untrained dancers as our spiritual guardians. But I must bury that notion in the deepest part of my brain, because dwelling on such vile thoughts causes me too much torment. Just remember, gentlemen, there are demons among us, perhaps in this very chapel. And if you happen to confront them, dislodge their spines, because I can assure you, violence is the only thing these devils seem to understand. That's why we must fight evil with greater evil!"

When I turned back to Jeunet, he no longer appeared enthralled by Father Hawkins' words, but rather agitated. Then, in an uncharacteristic move, Jeunet suddenly spat on the floor.

CHAPTER TWENTY-ONE

There wasn't much in the way of Halloween decorations on the school grounds, probably at the insistence of Father Hawkins, who detested the holiday for puritanical reasons, though there were some carved pumpkins scattered about the campus, mostly under trees. Many of the younger students were dressed in costumes, including a doleful Simon, whom I spotted among a throng of boys outside while Jeremiah and I were on our way to the library.

I told Jeremiah that I'd meet him in the library, then I approached Simon, who was dressed as a wizard and donned a hat reminiscent of the one Mickey Mouse wears in *Fantasia*. He looked a bit surprised to see me.

"I like your costume," I told Simon, forcing a smile. I hated forcing a smile, but seeing him again suddenly felt as if I were seeing an old friend.

"Thanks," he said.

There was an awkward pause.

"I just got out of chapel," I said. "You're probably happy about not having to go to chapel anymore, huh?"

Simon nodded, then lowered his gaze. I could tell he felt awkward, so I told him, "It's OK if you don't want to talk to me anymore. I know I flaked on you a lot, and I wasn't the best chapel partner. But let me tell you, this school year so far has been—Jesus Christ, a fucking roller-coaster for me. I'm not saying that as an excuse or anything. That's just how it is. And I'm not mad at you for narcing on me about the *thing* you saw in the auditorium that one day. I actually think it's cool that you didn't mention Jeremiah to anybody. Personally, I would've been an asshole and snitched on everybody."

I chuckled, but Simon didn't find it amusing. "Anyway," I continued, "are you still playing the guitar in your music class and all that?"

"No," he said. "We've moved on to the violin, but...it's a lot harder to play than the guitar because you have to practice way more. It's still fun to play, though."

"So are you, like, going to become a musician when you're older or something?"

"My dad wants me to become a pharmacist like him, but what I really want is to become a motocross racer. My mom says that I'll change my mind when I ride a motorcycle for the first time and break my neck. I guess neither of my parents want me to become a motocross racer."

"Well," I said, "they might change their minds in the future. If not, fuck it and just do what makes you happy, I guess."

I suddenly heard shrieking laughter and turned in the direction of the laughter. There were a group of young boys, aged eight or nine, out on the playground painting pictures, while their art teacher, a thirty-something woman, observed them. Each boy was standing in front of an easel and donning paint-spattered used shirts (backward) so as not to get any paint on their school uniforms. While looking at the boys, gloomy with unease, I thought about what might happen to them if they were to find themselves in the crosshairs of Van Orton.

"Listen," I said to Simon, turning to him, "if you're still going to Magnolia when you're in high school, stay away from Mr. Van Orton, the history teacher. He's not a good guy. In fact, stay away from Dr. Jeunet, too. This school is…so much weirder than you think."

Simon, puzzled, stared at me for a moment, then said, "Are you just playing a joke on me?"

"Definitely not," I told him. "But I wish I was."

I sat across from Jeremiah at the same study table (on the second floor of the library) where we'd had our first serious discussion about Communism. The bust of a Spartan soldier still rested on an elevated plinth off to the side, which I stared at, prompting Jeremiah to quip, "He's not going to blink or move his head."

I snorted a laugh, then said, "Congrats, by the way, on the poem. I really liked it. So Mallory wasn't kidding about the scholarship."

"No, sirree. I'm a real William Blake. He was a Satanist, you know."

"What about *you*?"

Jeremiah chuckled in response.

"I don't have the book with me," I told him. "But I did read all of it."

"Keep it."

"A—are you sure?"

Jeremiah nodded and said, "Dr. Jeunet thinks you should hold on to it for a while. You can give it back later."

I thought that was kind of strange, but I ignored it and asked Jeremiah, "Why did you bring up the 'Satanist' thing about William Blake? What does that have to do with anything, unless…is that why you had me read the book?"

Jeremiah chuckled again, then told me, "I like how we can just refer to it as 'the book,' and we both know which book we're talking about. That's the sign of a great fucking book." He flashed a smile of utter glee and said, "The book tripped you up, didn't it? Imagine how I felt when I first read it."

"Why did Mr. Van Orton tell you to read it?"

"What a goddamn head trip, that book," Jeremiah said, once again ignoring my questions. Now I knew he was doing it on purpose, which started to aggravate me.

"Jeremiah, what was the point of having me read that book? And why did Mr. Van Orton, or Dr. Jeunet—whoever the fuck, make *you* read it?"

Noticing how irritable I'd become, Jeremiah paused for a moment, then held up a finger as if gesturing to the heavens and said, "I didn't make you do shit. *You* wanted to read the book, so I loaned it to you, just like *I* wanted to read it when Milo told me about it at the Todd House a while back. Nobody was forced to do anything. I made my own choice, and so did you. Now stop asking me dumb-fuck questions that aren't even relevant, because you're too smart for that, unless you've suddenly turned into a retard like Lennie from *Of Mice and Men* since we last talked."

That was the first time he'd insulted me. It was one thing to call me a "queer" or a "homo," since those insults were made in jest, but to call me a "retard" was a sincere fuck you.

"Why do you have to talk to me like that?" I asked Jeremiah, sounding like a disappointed parent. "You've never talked to me like that before."

"You're so dramatic," he sneered. "And if you think the shit I said was disrespectful, you should listen to Paul Mooney."

"Fuck all that. Just don't be a dick to me. I'm your friend."

"I've honestly said a lot worse things to you, but sometimes you don't listen very well. Do you even know why I showed you that hollowed-out book with the razor inside? Or why Mallory and I aren't together anymore? Do you care enough to ask...or are you too busy fantasizing about us fucking?"

I remained silent.

"Mallory didn't break up with me, if that's what you're thinking," Jeremiah told me, resting his chin on his hand, his darting eyes expressing latent sorrow. "I was the one who decided to put an end to our 'relationship of convenience' because it was no longer convenient for either of us. It didn't seem right to keep it going when it became obvious that we had both stopped caring whether the other lived or died. What a depressing thought, going from holding hands to making out to not giving a fuck if your boyfriend or girlfriend drops dead. Don't you just love being a human? What a shame it would be to not have kids and deny them a chance to experience this life—being yelled at, getting sick, breakups, losing all hope, and the inevitable destruction of the soul."

I knew he was being sarcastic, but he didn't smile or laugh. Instead, he bit his lower lip the way one does when trying to suppress anger and shook his head, his face contorted. I could tell his mind was racing.

"Listen," Jeremiah continued, pausing to collect his thoughts, "I know every time I mention Mr. Van Orton, it feels like someone's poking you with a needle. You don't have to say anything because I can see it in your face how much he repulses you. Maybe you'll come around to him one day. Maybe not. It doesn't matter. But here's something I want you to know, since I doubt you can figure it out on your own." His tone abruptly changed when he uttered the next words: "You don't know what it's like growing up without a father to guide you. There's only so much my mom can do—and whatever she can't do...Mr. Van Orton does."

"What exactly does Mr. Van Orton *do* for you?" I asked timidly.

Jeremiah lay his right arm on the table and said, "Put your hand on my forearm." (I did as he told me.) "*That* is what Mr. Van Orton does for me."

He had a painfully honest look on his face, so I knew he wasn't being comical. I pulled my hand away, wearing an expression of dumb bewilderment while hiding my true feelings of disgust and fear.

"You're *not* Lennie," Jeremiah said, as a way of letting me know that he could see through my baffled façade. "Anyway, I don't expect you to understand what this means to me—having a father figure to look up to, someone to care for you, to guide you…"

"To fuck you," I interjected with vitriol.

Jeremiah looked hurt, and I immediately regretted my words.

"*You* fuck me," he said matter-of-factly.

"We're both fifteen. It's not the same thing, and you know it. Besides…you penetrated *me*, not the other way around. I just sucked you off."

"Then let's change that."

"Huh?" I said.

Jeremiah, visibly upset, got up and said, "Let's go. Right now." He started to walk toward the nearby restroom, then stopped and turned to me. "Come on," he insisted. "Let's go."

Reluctantly, I got up and followed Jeremiah into the restroom, where he checked under the stalls to make sure that nobody was using them. He then opened the door to the stall in the distant corner and went inside, while I hesitated, thinking how ridiculous this all seemed.

"Come the fuck on!" Jeremiah hollered from inside the stall. "Before somebody comes in here." The bitter tone of his voice made it clear that he wasn't happy with me, which made things seem all the more ridiculous, since he was trying to coerce me into having sex with him.

I walked to the stall and stopped at the door, looking at Jeremiah as he stood over the toilet, his pants unzipped. I entered the stall and closed the door.

"Lock it," Jeremiah told me.

As I turned to lock the door, Jeremiah pressed up against me with such force that it caused me to hit my forehead against the door. I yelped in pain while Jeremiah, indifferent to my painful cry, licked the back of my neck and reached around to grab my dick.

"Jeremiah—what the fuck?" I said with a grunt.

He continued to lick the back of my neck, even my hair, while dry-humping me. "Are you *really* this horny?" I asked him.

"I'm doing this for you," he said, almost defensively. "To get you hard, you fucking prick. This is the only reason you started talking to me, right?"

"What...?"

Jeremiah stepped back, and I turned around, surprised to see that his eyes were moist with tears. "Come on," he said, and forced my hand on his genitals. "This is what it's all about. Always has been with you."

I jerked my hand away and said, "That's not true. I love you."

Jeremiah scoffed. "Do you know how many fucking people have said that to me, both girls and boys? It doesn't mean a damn thing to me anymore. Even when my mom says it, I don't feel anything. Now come on," he said, pulling his pants and underwear down to his thighs. "I want you to fuck me so we can be even, and you can finally stop being fucking jealous of Milo just because he made the first move. And yeah, he's been inside me."

Instead of being appalled by what Jeremiah had told me, my adolescent brain bypassed the feeling of shock and went straight to resentment.

"He fucked you?" I said.

"You said it yourself earlier," Jeremiah replied, "so don't act surprised. I told you I've been with three other guys. Who do you think one of them was? Christ, if you had used your brain a bit more, I'm sure you would've figured it out. Now unzip yourself and do what Milo was able to do before *you*."

He was obviously trying to rile me up—and it worked. He turned around and bent over the toilet, while I pulled my pants and underwear down to my ankles. I was filled with mixed emotions: anger, regret, jealousy. What's more, despite being fully erect, I didn't feel particularly aroused or excited, and I was pretty certain Jeremiah didn't either. I felt ashamed for even following him into the restroom, but I wasn't going to let an opportunity like this slip away, not with Jeremiah freely offering himself to me.

I penetrated him from behind, both of us grunting like wild boars, unconcerned that at any moment someone could walk into the restroom and hear us fucking. My grunts grew louder, more animalistic. Jeremiah, however, went silent after a while. I thought about how he had given himself over to Van Orton, whose only interest in him, I was sure, was carnal. At that very moment, I hated Jeremiah more than

Van Orton, and I wanted to punish him. I pulled his hair and hurled obscenities at him: "You piece of shit, fucking cocksucker, goddamn retard!" Finally, I came inside him, then stepped back and pulled my pants up, feeling exhausted, pitiful.

Jeremiah, his back to me, pulled his pants up as if in slow motion, then turned around, with tears in his eyes. He sat down on the toilet, looking more miserable than I'd ever thought possible. I almost didn't want to believe that I was looking at the real Jeremiah, because the Jeremiah I knew would've never shown such naked vulnerability.

"Do you think anybody heard us?" I said in jest, trying to lighten the mood, then felt stupid when Jeremiah didn't respond.

I thought about leaving the stall, but when I saw Jeremiah wiping tears from his eyes, with the look of a broken soul, I decided to stay. Seeing a vulnerable Jeremiah was unsettling, like when a young boy sees his father, a real-life Superman, cry for the first time. Now I was witnessing the unraveling of my own personal Superman, and, for perhaps only the second time since I'd known him, I felt genuine pity toward Jeremiah. I was no longer looking at the great Moorish prince whom I'd known for months, but rather at a whimpering child, which devastated me.

"Hey…are you all right?" I asked Jeremiah, concerned.

There was a long silence.

Finally, Jeremiah, not making eye contact with me, began to speak in such an introspective manner that one would think he was reciting a Tennessee Williams monologue. "During my third year at Magnolia, when I was thirteen, I had English class with this Salvadoran boy named Ignacio, who had the most feminine features I'd ever seen in a boy. His hair was dark and short like mine, but wavy. I used to think he was a girl because of how delicate he looked, like a porcelain doll. It was hard not to stare at him, especially when he'd stare back with his warm amber eyes. Whenever he'd look at me, I would freeze. During silent reading, I'd stare at him and think about us becoming close friends. I also thought about fucking him, even though I was still a virgin. My obsession with him grew to the point where I couldn't go a day without thinking about him. Sometimes I'd think about him so much that I'd start to feel nauseous and convulse. One day, during a holiday break, I experienced a grueling case of 'withdrawal' because I hadn't seen

Ignacio in four days, and I threw up. My mom took me to the hospital, thinking that I'd swallowed pills, and I ended up getting my stomach pumped."

Jeremiah looked at me, smiling sadly. "I was able to convince my mom that I'd just gotten a stomach ache from eating too much sugar the day before. I didn't actually *talk* to Ignacio until a month later, when our English teacher took us on a field trip to the Museum of Modern Art. I tried sitting next to Ignacio on the bus, but a boy beat me to it, so I sat behind him, angry that someone else got to sit beside Ignacio. At the museum, all the students were divided into groups of five, and Ignacio was in my group. But he soon broke off from the rest of the group and went to explore the museum on his own, so I followed him. At one point, he suddenly stopped to look at a painting of a boy leading a horse. It took every ounce of courage I had to walk over and stand next to Ignacio—both of us staring at the painting. He then looked at me and smiled, and I smiled back. We started talking, and from that day on, we became inseparable. We sat next to each other in class, ate lunch together, went to chapel together, hung out at Blondie's, went to the movies, everything. We even lost our virginity to each other. Nobody knew that we were a 'couple,' though, because if anybody at school had found out, we definitely would've gotten our asses kicked… *multiple* times. Maybe even expelled."

Jeremiah, apparently having nothing more to say about Ignacio, fell silent. But I wanted to know more, so I asked him, "What happened between you guys?"

He looked stumped, as if he'd forgotten what he was talking about just a moment ago. Then he said, with sadness in his voice, "One day, Ignacio just disappeared. That was it."

"I don't understand. Where did he go?"

"I came back to school after a long winter break, but Ignacio wasn't there. It was like he'd never existed. No matter how hard I tried to rationalize his sudden disappearance, I couldn't come up with an answer that made any sense. I cried for days, weeks, and had to drag myself out of bed every morning to go to school, or do anything. You have no idea how badly I wanted to kill myself. But I didn't want to put my mom through *another* suicide. Her life was already depressing, and I didn't want to make it any worse with my shit. Anyway, I eventually got over it, you know…after the tears had dried. But I'll bet you a day doesn't go by that I don't think about Ignacio, however briefly."

I felt such empathy toward Jeremiah that I wanted to give him a hug, but I felt too awkward about embracing him after I'd penetrated him just minutes earlier and called him all kinds of vulgar names. Instead, I simply told him, "I'm sorry about what happened with Ignacio."

He nodded a little, then got up and looked at me with a solemn expression. "I want you to promise me something," he said, after a pause.

"Sure," I replied.

"Promise me you'll never say 'I love you' to me again."

Jeremiah might as well have punched me in the face, because it would've hurt just as much as what he had asked of me. In fact, I would've preferred it if he'd hit me instead.

"Why don't you want me to say 'I love you' anymore?" I asked him, trying to conceal the hurt on my face.

"Because it doesn't work on me," he said. "It's nothing personal."

"You mean *love* doesn't work on you?"

Jeremiah chuckled. "When you say it like that, it sounds silly, but… yeah."

He was smiling, but I didn't find any of this funny. In fact, it depressed the hell out of me and made me wonder if I'd just been wasting my time trying to get closer to Jeremiah, who, by his own account, was incapable of love.

If he's incapable of love, I thought, *then what are we even doing?*

CHAPTER TWENTY-TWO

We went to the gymnasium, where the Halloween party was being held, although I wasn't in a particularly festive mood, and, judging from the glum look on his face, neither was Jeremiah, whose demeanor had changed soon after we'd left the library. I didn't ask what was bothering him, as I was still reeling from our conversation earlier, though I imagined it had something to do with his painful recollection of Ignacio.

I looked around the large gymnasium, which was decorated with dozens of balloons, spider webs, bats, crows, and skeletons, as well as a giant spider suspended above the center of the gym. There appeared to be over a hundred students, mostly elementary and middle school-aged students, and about three or four chaperones, all secretaries, none of whom seemed thrilled to be there. One of the secretaries, the youngest of the bunch, was being hit on by two high school boys. I nudged Jeremiah, who was standing beside me, and gestured to the audacious high school boys.

He snorted a laugh as he watched the two boys flirt with the young secretary, who rebuffed their advances with a chuckle, then waved them off. Jeremiah turned to me and said, "Only seniors have the balls to do something like that. Good effort, though."

"You sound like Mr. Van Orton," I said, to which he replied with a shrug. After an awkward pause, I asked him, "Are you feeling better?"

"I guess," he said. "Why?"

"You've been kinda quiet since we left the library…and you didn't look too happy earlier. Were you thinking about Ignacio?"

"Not exactly." Jeremiah looked around as if admiring the festivities and decorations. Then, staring out at the sea of students, he said, "I'm gonna miss this."

"Miss what?"

"Being here, alive."

That seemed like such an odd thing to say that, for a moment, I

155

wasn't sure how to respond, until finally, I said, "You know you can tell me anything, right?"

Jeremiah looked at me. "That's what I'm doing." He then shook his head in disappointment and said, "You really *don't* listen, do you? You're so smart…but only when you want to be."

I paused. "Did you love him—Ignacio?"

Jeremiah chuckled sadly. "Are you jealous now? Jealous of someone who may not even be alive?" (I didn't respond.) "Anyway," he said, "what difference does it make if I loved him or not? He's a ghost now."

The music, which I hadn't paid much attention to, despite blaring from speakers, suddenly shifted from spooky to menacing, as intense death metal music roared throughout the gymnasium. The chaperones, realizing that something was amiss, looked at one another in trepidation, while a small group of high school boys, dressed as the "droogs" from *A Clockwork Orange* and standing off to the side near the audio rack, were laughing and playing air guitar, with one of them shouting "Cryptopsy!" at the top of his lungs. Meanwhile, the two audacious high school boys from earlier made a beeline for the young secretary who had previously rejected them and began accosting her. She responded by slapping one of them across the face and, removing her high heels, chasing the other one out of the gymnasium, threatening to hit him with her shoes. Jeremiah and I laughed as we watched the chaperones get into a heated argument with the droogs, who were undoubtedly the saboteurs, while the younger students, seemingly unbothered, danced to the uproarious music like Pentecostals.

In the midst of the chaos, Jeremiah walked to the buffet, where an assortment of fried foods and sugary drinks were laid out, and returned with a paper plate of chicken tenders and fries, with a cinnamon roll on the side and a Coke in hand. He then handed me the drink and said, "Don't say I never gave you anything. But I'll appreciate a sip later."

I smiled and watched as Jeremiah attacked his plate of food like a ravenous carnivore, then, as my smile faded, thought about how pitiful he looked after I'd fucked him in the stall.

He suddenly looked at me and said, rather sadly, "River Phoenix died on Halloween exactly ten years ago. I didn't even think about that till now. Fuck…what a bummer."

"Yeah," I replied.

The procession honoring Christ, led by Father Hawkins, was in full swing as Jeremiah and I walked across a grassy, open quadrangle—on our way to the Todd House. We stopped to observe the pompous ceremony, which featured a wooden statue of the Messiah, adorned with paper money and a golden crown atop his head, being carried around the school grounds by a group of students, accompanied by a brass band that played what sounded like a funeral march. Father Hawkins, with his altar boys behind him, all of them carrying banners that bore images of Christ, walked solemnly ahead of the others. It was such a gross display of religious vanity that one couldn't help but recoil in disgust.

Jeremiah turned to me and said, "This looks like a circus." He then spat on the ground just as Father Hawkins walked past us. The cleric paused and glared at Jeremiah, who blew him a kiss like John Travolta did to Uma Thurman in *Pulp Fiction*, though without the sincerity. An outraged Father Hawkins grumbled and shook his head, then resumed with the procession.

I looked around and noticed that there weren't many students walking the campus, perhaps less than twenty, not including those taking part in the ceremony. I presumed many of the middle school and high school students went home after chapel, particularly the latter, since they weren't required to stay for the full day.

As we continued our walk to the Todd House, I asked Jeremiah if he'd had any unusual or recurring dreams lately. "I always have 'unusual' dreams," he told me. "Those are pretty much the only kinds of dreams I have. As for recurring…there is this one dream I keep having. I'm in an old manor house somewhere in Europe during the eighteenth century, and I'm the only one there, but I can't leave. There's someone or something preventing me from leaving the house, like an unseen force field. I'm not scared at all, just confused. I eat and drink, but because I'm the only one there, I feel lonely and wonder when, if ever, I'm going to leave this place. The thought of killing myself never enters my mind, even though in real life I'd definitely think about doing it."

"Are you dressed in eighteenth-century clothes?" I asked.

"That's the funny thing," Jeremiah said. "I'm totally naked, except for a crown of flowers on my head."

"Maybe it's the afterlife."

Jeremiah scoffed. "Then it must be Hell."

CHAPTER TWENTY-THREE

I couldn't believe that I was about to step foot in the Todd House, evidently only the second student to do so, after Jeremiah. The house, which featured an elevated terrace, looked bigger than I'd remembered. It was completely white, and the curtains were drawn, so it was impossible to see who, if anybody, was inside the glass house.

Jeremiah, walking ahead of me, approached the house and knocked on the sliding door, as I stood a few feet behind him, curious to see if anybody would actually open the door. A moment later, the door opened and we were greeted by a beaming Van Orton, donning his usual black pants and white linen dress shirt (with the sleeves rolled up), his platinum blond hair striking as ever. I stood closer to Jeremiah and narrowed my eyes at Van Orton, as if readying for a duel.

"It's good to see you, boys," Van Orton said. "Come on in."

We entered the house, and Van Orton, drink in hand, closed the door, all the while his eyes fixed on Jeremiah. The expansive living room, which appeared to be the largest room in the house, featured immaculate white walls and hardwood floors, with an upholstered couch and chairs, white coffee table, a huge flat-screen TV (on which an old black-and-white film was being shown), and a reel-to-reel tape deck in the corner of the room. There was no carpeting, save for a small Versace rug, featuring the company's "Medusa" logo.

Jeunet, clutching his walking stick, was sitting in an armchair, smiling, watching Jeremiah and me.

We'll make her one of us, a dwarf on TV announces.

The dwarf, one of many carnival sideshow performers featured in the black-and-white film, stands atop a formally laid dinner table, set with food and drinks, and initiates a chant:

We accept her, one of us! We accept her, one of us!

Gooble gobble, gooble gobble! We accept her, we accept her! Gooble gobble!

One of us, one of us! Gooble gobble…

"*Monsieur* Van Orton, please turn that down a bit," Jeunet said. "I don't think I can handle any more 'gooble gobbles' today, I'm afraid."

Van Orton grabbed the remote control and turned the volume down to a whisper, then, eyes fixed back on Jeremiah, approached him and held his drink up to Jeremiah's lips, as if daring him to take a sip. Jeremiah, putting up no resistance, took a sip, and almost immediately made a bitter face. Van Orton laughed and gave him a pat on the back, saying, "White Russian isn't your drink after all."

"Have a seat, gentlemen," Jeunet said to Jeremiah and me, pointing at the couch with his walking stick. "And please forgive your teacher for his lack of decorum," he added, glaring at Van Orton as if to say, "Don't be foolish."

Jeremiah and I sat on the couch. On the wall above the couch hung a large oil painting that depicted five shirtless men in blue jeans, sitting on motorbikes in the woods. The men, all of them donning eerie tribal masks, had their arms stretched out, with their fingers curled into claws.

Van Orton, having finished his drink, went into the adjacent kitchen and placed his whiskey glass on the counter, then returned to the living room and sat down in a chair. He suddenly looked at me as if analyzing me and asked, "What did you think of *the book*, Mr. Quell?"

I thought briefly about playing dumb, but I decided against it and replied, "It was a hell of a trip. Milton William Cooper must've been high on something when he wrote it."

"I don't know about narcotics, but Cooper might've been a little paranoid, perhaps rightly so, when he penned the book. Then again, how does one maintain one's sanity in a world designed to drive one mad? It's a miracle that Cooper was actually able to publish the book without receiving a bullet to the head first."

"Oh, he received a bullet, all right," Jeunet interjected. "But it came later."

"Is any part of the book true?" I asked.

Jeunet, barely hiding a grin, stared at me and said, "*Monsieur* Quell, would you be surprised if I told you that every so-called 'conspiracy theory' you have ever heard, from Roswell to Bigfoot, has a basis in truth?" (I remained silent.) "I know, I know. We live in a world of half-truths, so you don't know what to believe anymore. Did intelligent extraterrestrial beings, or 'ancient astronauts,' visit Earth and make contact with humans in prehistoric times? Are black helicopters an indication of a military takeover of the United States, as the American militia movement would have people believe? Is Bohemian Grove really a front for a secret worldwide elite organization, or just another gentlemen's club? Today, there are people who claim that the Earth is flat, and others who continue to believe that 'Paul is dead.' What are we to make of all this?"

I wasn't sure if Jeunet expected me to answer him, but I let out a weak chuckle, then turned to Jeremiah, who looked at me like he was waiting for me to respond to Jeunet's inquiry. I glanced at Van Orton, whose face wore a scowl, as if my very presence irked him. Realizing that all eyes were on me and that I needed to say something, I told Jeunet, "I think maybe people believe in all that stuff because…I guess they're bored, and maybe believing in things like secret societies makes them feel better."

"Better how?" he asked.

"Like their lives have meaning," I replied.

"So I presume you weren't taken with *Monsieur* Cooper's book, then?"

"Well…he mentioned something called a 'One World Totalitarian Socialist Government,' and that's when he lost me. I don't like it when people use the word 'socialist' that way."

"In *what* way?" Van Orton asked.

I turned to him. "Like it's the bogeyman," I said, sneering.

"He's a Communist," Jeremiah interjected. He said it with such contempt that it was almost like he was calling me a dunce for believing in the ideology. I glared at him as if confronting him, but he cocked his head and looked away. I wanted to call him a traitor, spit on him, punch him in the face. Instead, I just sat there, seething. The compassion that I'd felt toward him earlier was all but gone.

"Karl Marx has you by the balls, huh?" Van Orton said to me. "I assume you've read *1984* by George Orwell, although it didn't seem to have much of an effect on you, now did it?"

"Orwell was a socialist and an anti-Stalinist leftist," I replied. "Just like Albert Camus and Malcolm X and John Steinbeck and Nina Simone and H. P. Lovecraft and James Baldwin. As you can see, Mr. Van Orton,

I've done my research. Do you want me to continue? I can add a few more names to the list."

"Oh, I'm sure you could, Mr. Quell. You're a well-trained seal. Tell me, do you know how many people have perished under Communism?"

"I don't know. Fifty billion, trillion, quadrillion! Your heart breaks for all those Cambodian and Chinese and Russian peasants whose names you don't even know, and if you did, you wouldn't be able to pronounce any of them if your life depended on it. Give me *one* name— not just bullshit statistics."

An aggravated Van Orton rolled his eyes, then turned to Jeunet while gesturing to me as if to say, "Are you hearing this?" Jeunet, disappointed in his apprentice, shook his head, causing Van Orton to recoil in embarrassment. He then shot me a nasty look, the kind a schoolyard bully would give to a third-grader at recess.

"I'm so glad you can make jokes about the suffering of others," Van Orton said to me, his face reddening. "But what else can a child do when—"

"Enough!" Jeunet barked, and gave Van Orton a piercing look, shaking his head again. He then turned to me and, having mellowed, said, "It seems that you're playing chess, *Monsieur* Quell, while your teacher is playing mere checkers. That's what happens when you underestimate a recent convert. I bet you've got enough fire in you to torch this place to the ground. How much richer life seems when you've embraced a new ideology. You must feel like the most powerful being on the planet right now, strutting around with a newfound weapon at your side as if it were Thor's mighty hammer. And oh, what an impressive weapon it is, capable of inciting both joy and torment. How I envy youth. At your age, you soak up everything like a sponge, without any regard for what came before you crawled out of your mother's vagina, because who cares what happened when dinosaurs roamed the Earth? To remain a child is the ultimate goal in life. In fact, I would argue that life after childhood ceases to be legitimate life."

"That's all well and good when you're still young, dumb, and full of cum," Van Orton said, looking at Jeunet. He then turned to me and added, "But life doesn't end at puberty."

"Sadly, it does for some," Jeunet said candidly.

He and Van Orton suddenly turned to each other, with the latter looking slightly indignant about Jeunet's remark, as if the headmaster had taken a personal dig at him. Jeremiah, noticing the evident discomfort between Van Orton and Jeunet, cleared his throat, then turned to me and, lifting his voice, said, "There must've been *something* in the book that resonated with you."

It was embarrassing how obvious he was in his desperate attempt to shift the conversation back to Cooper's book. The Jeremiah I knew (or thought I knew) wouldn't have degraded himself like that.

"The part about HIV/AIDS being a man-made disease created to kill Black, Hispanic, and gay people was interesting," I said. "More 'believable' than the other stuff."

Jeunet bellowed a laugh. "Yes, well…you can certainly understand why those in the Black community have developed such a strong affinity for the book—that is, the mutilated version sold in bookstores. I have great respect for the Negro, always have. Are you familiar, by the way, with the African-American religious organization known as the Nation of Islam?"

"Um…I know it *exists*," I said.

"The Nation was founded in Detroit in 1930 by Wallace Fard Muhammad, a man claiming to have come from Mecca with the goal to awaken the slumbering Negroes of America. He taught that God was Black, and so was the first human that God had created…some trillions of years ago. He also taught that, at one point, the world was run by twenty-four imams, or 'scientists,' one of whom, Yakub, went rogue and created the white race—a race of wicked devils—over 6,600 years ago. This mad scientist was able to achieve this through a unique form of selective breeding called 'grafting,' in which he separated the dominant black gene from the recessive brown gene, and then, after a six-hundred-year procedure, he succeeded in creating the white race. Yakub performed this eugenics experiment while living on the Greek island of Patmos, where, thousands of years later, John the Apostle would author the Book of Revelation." Jeunet smiled at me. "I imagine this must all sound absurd to you."

I chuckled and turned to Jeremiah, thinking that he was going to find what Jeunet had said equally as amusing as I did. However, he kept a solemn face, his eyes cast downward as if deep in thought. Befuddled, I looked at Van Orton, who, like Jeremiah, appeared to be in a similar state of contemplative detachment. I then turned to Jeunet, who was no longer smiling.

"Now that you've had your laugh, *Monsieur* Quell, allow me to add one more thing about Yakub and his eugenics experiment. A few years ago, there was an article published in *The New York Times* discussing a remarkable discovery made by researchers at the University of Chicago. The researchers found five skin genes selected some thousands of years ago, which suggested that white Europeans had acquired their pale skin much more recently than was previously thought. In fact, the lead researcher at the university had a rough estimate of when the genes of the Asian and European populations were altered under the pressure from natural selection. Can you guess what that estimate is?"

I slowly shook my head.

"6,600 years ago," Jeunet said, then rose to his feet, walking stick in hand. He stared at me for a moment before continuing to speak. "*Behold a Pale Horse*, the Nation of Islam, Lucifer, the Rais Frolic, Chandler Faust, the supposed 'Magnolia Academy' book that you claim to have read. They all lead back to the Chronovisor. I can only imagine the dreams you've been having lately. Perhaps I've made a few cameo appearances." Jeunet smiled. "As for *Monsieur* Faust"—his smile suddenly dropped—"that's something I'll discuss at a later time."

He walked to the couch and stood opposite Jeremiah and me. "Next week," he said, looking at me, "we're going to take a day trip into the city, where I'll introduce you to some special people. I want you to meet them before the Rais Frolic in December." Jeunet turned to Jeremiah. "You'll be joining us, *Monsieur* Kateb, because you, more so than *Monsieur* Quell, deserve to meet these people, to speak with them, so you may better understand why you were chosen to make the final sacrifice."

I looked at Jeremiah, who seemed to accept everything that Jeunet was saying. Meanwhile, I was trying in vain to make sense of "*the* Chronovisor" and its connection to everything.

Jeunet gestured for me to get up, which I did. He then placed a gentle hand on my shoulder and told me, "I want you to go to the back room where my nieces, Ayn and Rand, are playing their games, and bring them back here for a little show."

I hesitated, prompting Jeunet to give me an assuring pat on the back. "Don't worry, they're sweet girls. You'll see. Go on now."

I turned to Jeremiah, who gave me a nod as if to say, "It's fine." I started to leave the room, then paused to look at the TV, where the old black-and-white film was still playing, although the dialogue was inaudible. I suddenly heard a voice in my head say, "Turn around," and so I did. Van Orton was sneering at me, like he couldn't wait for me to leave his sight, while Jeunet and Jeremiah were watching the movie. I finally exited the room, then stopped and leaned against the wall in the hallway. I waited for a while, and then I heard the following exchange:

VAN ORTON: If that was a test, master, then he certainly failed. He's a liability.

JEUNET: You don't get to decide that. *I* do.

VAN ORTON: Why are you so invested in this boy? It's utter madness, I swear!

JEUNET: Keep your voice down. (*Pause*) I see potential in him.

VAN ORTON: No, you just see a plaything.

JEUNET: He reminds me of what I've lost. I don't want to lose it again. I can't...

VAN ORTON: Chandler Faust is dead, master. Please, find comfort elsewhere. I beg you.

JEREMIAH: Whatever happens, please don't hurt Sean.

VAN ORTON: Are you in love with him?

JEREMIAH: I want to see him again in the hereafter. He's worth it.

VAN ORTON: You *too* now? Does he have you both bewitched or something? Incredible!

JEUNET: That's enough. Naberius, guide us in these times, O Lord.

I waited for a while longer, but nothing else was said between them. I had mixed feelings about their conversation. While part of me was troubled, even downright frightened, by the covert nature of their exchange, I also took comfort in knowing that Jeremiah still cared for me and wished to see me again in the "hereafter," the meaning of which I understood to mean "I need him by my side always."

As I continued down the wide hallway, I noticed several photographs and paintings on the wall, only a few of which I recognized: Teddy Roosevelt, Dimebag Darrell of Pantera, a Salvador Dalí painting depicting a pomegranate hallucinatory dream, a Norman Rockwell illustration, and a picture of Mobb Deep's Prodigy, showing the rapper brandishing a large revolver, masked with an American flag like a Taliban.

I reached the back room, one of three rooms in the hallway, and the only one with its door open. I looked inside and saw twin blonde girls, aged eleven or twelve, both of them donning light blue, sleeveless mini dresses, sitting on the hardwood floor, with a partially-eaten white cake and a bucket of fried chicken laid out in front of them, as well as bottles of Nesquik vanilla milk. One of the girls was reading a magazine, while the other was playing a shooter video game—equipped with a pink gun-shaped controller—on a Super Nintendo. I entered the pristine, sparsely-furnished room, which contained a queen-sized bed, a small bookshelf, and a twenty-inch TV, on which the one girl was killing digitized enemies. The girl who was reading a magazine suddenly noticed me and smiled nervously, then nudged her sister and said, "Ayn, look."

The girl, Ayn, glanced at me, unfazed, and went back to playing her game. Her sister shook her head in mild frustration, still smiling, then looked at me and said, "I'm Rand. Are you the other boy?"

If Jeremiah was *one* of the boys, I rationalized, then that meant I had to be the "other boy."

"Y—yeah," I said. "I'm Sean."

Rand gestured for me to sit down and said, "Come and join us. We're having a mini-party in here. You like cake? We've got vanilla milk, too. Uncle Marc says vanilla is the Light-Bringer's favorite scent. But fried chicken is *Ayn's* favorite," she added with a giggle.

It took me a moment to remember that Marc was Jeunet's first name. He was the only other person I'd heard utter the cryptic name or title "Light-Bringer," which sounded like a nickname in ancient Greek or Roman folklore. I sat down next to Rand, who put the magazine that she had been reading on the floor. The magazine, *Omni*, featured a futuristic cover of a feminine robot riding a zebra on a desolate beach, with Egyptian pyramids hovering over the water.

"We're playing *Lethal Enforcers*," Rand told me. "Well…Ayn is, anyway. But after she's done, you can take a turn."

"That's OK," I said. "You guys can play. But, um, Dr. Jeunet—I mean, your uncle, wants you guys to come to the living room for some kinda show."

Rand sighed in annoyance. "Ah, not again. We already did it earlier today. How many more times does he want us to do it? I bet he just wants us to do it again for *you*."

I paused. "So what is it that he makes you guys do?"

"Fucking dance," Ayn said, eyes glued to the screen, shooting digitized enemies with gusto.

"Dance?" I said.

"It's like a ceremonial dance," Rand replied. "Uncle Marc loves it. He makes us do it every time we come here. He gave us this tattoo last month as a reward for all the times Ayn and I danced for him," she said, holding up her left hand to reveal a tattoo of an inverted cross on her wrist. She then turned to her sister. "Show him, Ayn." Her sister put the controller down and showed me the same tattoo on her wrist.

I couldn't tell if the tattoos were real or not, though they looked authentic. "What did your parents have to say?" I asked them.

"About what?" Rand said, confused.

Van Orton suddenly appeared at the door. "Girls, your uncle wants to see you in the living room."

Ayn sighed and said, "We know, we know. Gotta do the dance."

We all made our way to the living room, where Jeremiah and Jeunet were seated. The twins walked to the Versace rug and moved it aside, revealing a painted sigil that I knew to be associated with Satanism: a goat's head inside an inverted pentagram flanked by Hebrew letters. I went over to Jeremiah and sat beside him on the couch, waiting for him to tell me that this was just a practical joke. And if it wasn't a hoax, then it had to be a fever dream, because I couldn't possibly be seeing what I thought I was seeing.

Jeunet gestured to Van Orton, who then went to the reel-to-reel tape deck and turned it on, filling the room with Celtic music featuring loud bagpipes.

The twins stood opposite each other outside the Satanic sigil, their hands on their hips, and bowed in allegiance before dancing around the sigil in the style of the Irish stepdance, then raised their arms over their heads. Jeunet and Van Orton were grinning, with the former cheering on the twins. I turned to Jeremiah, who appeared jubilant. After a while, the strangest thing happened: I found myself beguiled by the scene before me, as a faint smile formed across my face.

CHAPTER TWENTY-FOUR

Jeremiah insisted that we play hooky and take the bus to the Art Mill after lunch hour, since he no longer wanted to attend chapel. When I reminded him that we were required to attend chapel, he told me that, so long as Jeunet was the headmaster, we didn't have to do anything if we didn't want to. He said it with conviction, so I knew he wasn't just talking nonsense.

During the bus ride, I tried to talk to Jeremiah about what we'd experienced on Halloween at the Todd House, but he kept shushing me, saying things like, "Wait till later" and "Not in front of the animals."

That last remark struck me as particularly uncharacteristic of him, since a true Communist would never say such a thing about passengers on a transit bus. I decided to call him out on it, and he scoffed before responding: "That's funny coming from you."

"What's that supposed to mean?" I said.

He didn't say anything.

"Tell me," I demanded.

Jeremiah looked at me and said, "I called your house three days ago, and do you know who answered? Your *maid*. This whole time I thought you didn't invite me over to your house because you were too insecure to ask. But no, it was actually because you didn't want me to know that you owned a slave."

"That's not fair. You act like I'm the one who hired her. And don't say 'slave.' You're just trying to make me feel guilty for something I have no control over."

"Have you thought about telling your parents to let her go?"

"What good would that do?" I asked.

Jeremiah shrugged and replied, "Maybe give her back her fucking dignity."

"We *pay* her...very well."

"How much?"

I began to stammer, then soon realized that I had no idea how much my parents paid Stana, though I'd always assumed that it was a "fair" amount.

"You don't even know, do you?" Jeremiah said. "Maybe you don't care." He looked at me with weary eyes for a moment, shoulders stooped. "Let me tell you something. During these past few months, Mr. Van Orton and Dr. Jeunet have provided me with all the food and drinks I could ever want. Sometimes I bring leftovers home, and guess what? My mom doesn't ask where it came from, because she knows not to ask questions when there's free food involved. They also give me money—a couple of twenties and fifties here and there, some of which I slip into my mom's purse. At times I wonder if she notices. Even if she did, though, I don't think she'd say anything about it. In about a month, after the Rais Frolic…my mom is expected to receive the kind of money people definitely notice. That should make life a lot easier for her."

"What's the money for?" I asked.

Jeremiah shook his head dismissively, making me feel like an idiot for even asking such a question. Then he said, "The point I'm trying to make is, for the first time in a long time, probably since I came to America, I'm getting a taste of paradise. You've been living in paradise since you were born, so it means nothing to you. You've become accustomed to it. But to me, this is like a whole new world. Even Mallory didn't have it this good, and that girl was spoiled rotten—upstate New York's very own Marie Antoinette. Let's hope she meets the same fate as the queen."

I snorted a laugh. "You never lose your sense of humor."

"Who's joking?" Jeremiah said.

I had no clue what movie we were going to watch until we took our seats in the theater (as before, it was mostly deserted) and saw the title of the film appear on the screen: *Pinocchio*.

I turned to Jeremiah. "We're watching a Disney movie?"

"Don't tell me you're too old for Disney."

We watched the movie in silence. I'd seen it at least five times before, as it was a childhood favorite of mine, so I knew it almost by heart.

After the movie was over, I started to get up just as the lights came on, but Jeremiah put his hand on my arm and, looking at me, shook his head. I sat back down, thinking that he wanted to wait until everyone else had left the theater before exiting, despite there being less than ten people in the theater, including us. Finally, after the last moviegoer had left the theater, Jeremiah scanned the auditorium to make sure that we were alone, then turned to me.

"What do you know about Walt Disney?" he asked.

The serious tone of his voice suggested that he wasn't just being cute with me. "Not much," I told him. "I know there's a crazy rumor that he was cryogenically frozen."

Jeremiah waved it off as if to say, "Never mind that." Then he said to me, "Did you know that Disney was a 33rd degree Mason?"

"A Freemason?"

Jeremiah nodded. "I'm sure you've seen *Pinocchio* many times before, but I bet you never thought much about the song 'When You Wish Upon a Star.' It's heard twice in the movie—once in the beginning and again in the end. You ever thought to yourself what 'star' Jiminy Cricket was wishing upon? Probably not. When Jiminy Cricket sings 'When You Wish Upon a Star,' the 'star' that he's wishing upon is the 'morning star,' or the Light-Bringer. In other words, Lucifer. I know when most people hear the name 'Lucifer' or 'Satan,' they imagine horns and pitchforks. But that's not the real image of Lucifer. The *real* Lucifer is beautiful, every bit as beautiful as…well…River Phoenix. And he's incredibly smart. You know, it was Lucifer who discovered the meaning behind the word 'Bible.' It's actually an acronym, or rather a 'backronym.' B-I-B-L-E—Basic Instructions Before Leaving Earth. You can imagine how dumbfounded God was when Lucifer, before anyone else, had uncovered the real meaning of 'Bible.' The truth is, being a 'Satanist' just means revering knowledge, wisdom, and understanding. God wanted to keep Adam and Eve dumb, deaf, and blind by discouraging them from eating from the Tree of the Knowledge of Good and Evil. Rather than being a paradise, the Garden of Eden was a prison, a loony bin, where a spiteful, paranoid, jealous, and ruthless creator lorded over his creations like a tyrant. God is no different than Stalin, whereas Lucifer is an intellectual who only wishes to set us free and help us become gods."

Everything Jeremiah said seemed "reasonable," despite sounding somewhat rehearsed. He waited for me to respond, but I wasn't sure what to say. *How do I respond to something like that?* I thought. Ever since the sixth grade, when I first heard the story of Lucifer and the War in Heaven, I'd been fascinated by Lucifer, and Jeremiah was tapping into that fascination. I figured Jeunet or Van Orton had instructed him to tell me about the "real" Lucifer in hopes of persuading me to join their what I imagined was a Luciferian cult.

Finally, I said to Jeremiah, "I don't know if what you've told me is true or not, but hearing it from you makes me want to believe every word of it, because I know how smart you are. To be totally honest, you're so smart that it scares me. You could tell me that Venus or some other planet is inhabited by killer clowns, and I'd believe you. Jeremiah, you have no idea how much I fucking respect you. I don't revere anyone but *you*. I've spent the past five years looking for my own River Phoenix, and you're it."

Jeremiah smiled a little and said, "I don't need you to revere me. Believe me, if you'd seen me taking a shit earlier this morning, you wouldn't think I was so special. I know you're not going to believe me, since your dick tingles every time you look at me now, but I swear what you think of me *today* won't last forever. In about ten or fifteen years, maybe less, you'll forget I ever existed. I know—you don't believe me. But just give it time. Everyone's special, until they aren't anymore. Remember that. And just so you know, I got excited the first time I saw *you* in class."

My eyes widened. "Are you serious?"

Jeremiah nodded.

"I don't fucking believe you," I said. "Why would seeing me get you excited?"

"Hey, don't sell yourself short. You're a good-looking dude. Even Mallory thought so. But she thought every guy with a functioning dick was cute, so whatever."

I chuckled.

"Listen," Jeremiah said, "I want you to think about everything I've told you today." He got up. "I know Communism has a tight grip on you right now. That's my fault for teaching it to you in such a way that it's now become a part of your DNA. That's the way it was taught to me, which is why I had such a hard time letting go of it. I was going through a 'transitional period,' as Samuel L. Jackson says in *Pulp Fiction*, when you first met me, and I still had Communist residue on my fingertips. That's why I kept relapsing. Also," he added with a solemn grin, "I really did think that we could become like the modern-day Lenin and Sverdlov. But then reality hit me in the face, and I came down from that fantasy. I hope one day you'll come down too, sooner than later, because I don't see us reuniting any other way. Sean, if you love me like you say you do, make the necessary leap. Otherwise, stay as far away from me as possible and erase my name from your memory bank. I don't mean to sound dramatic, but that's the way it's gotta be. And I'd really like to keep you as a friend. You're the only friend I have who's my age. Everyone else left me."

Jeremiah held out his hand to me. I took it, then kissed it and held it against my cheek. The warmth of his hand made me feel safe. He suddenly stuck his index finger in my mouth as if daring me to suck it, which I did. He then gave me a playful slap on the cheek and said, "Let's get some food, Capote."

———————————

We sat in a booth at the Denny's down the street from the movie theater, both of us having ordered the same thing: burgers, fries, and vanilla milkshakes. I kept staring at Jeremiah, who sat across from me, devouring his food and drink. Although I'd previously noticed that Jeremiah often attacked his food like a hungry canine, I hadn't thought much of it until now. *Is he always hungry?* I wondered. The thought that he had little to eat at home was difficult for me to imagine, what with his mother (presumably) cooking him delicious Algerian cuisine.

Jeremiah, noticing that I was staring at him, smiled and said, "Considering how often you stare at me, I'm surprised you haven't asked me for a picture yet. I've got one if you need it."

"Really?" I said.

Jeremiah laughed. "I'm only teasing, you fucking dope. How conceited do you think I am?"

I forced a laugh, then asked him, "How do you do that, by the way?"

"What do you mean?" he replied.

"How do you find the humor in everything?"

"Easy. I don't take life so seriously. Whether I'm eating, fucking, or in pain, I know not to take anything to heart. You should try it sometime. It'll help you sleep better, I promise."

"But…I remember when you used to talk about humans being primates and apes, and now you're telling me about Lucifer, like you believe in the afterlife."

"Two things can be simultaneously true. Humans are part of the animal kingdom, as every biology book tells us. We're also mammals, primates, and great apes. That's life science. But when I talk about Lucifer or God or the afterlife, that's something entirely different, almost like a parallel universe. But you don't give a shit about that, and I understand. You just want to know whether or not I actually believe in Heaven, Hell, and all that good stuff, right? Well, let me put it to you this way." Jeremiah paused momentarily, as if mulling over what to say. "I don't know what I believe, but I do know what I *don't* believe—and that's in myself. You know, I used to think that the only reason people believed in God was because they were afraid of death and wanted to see their loved ones again, supposedly in Heaven. I still think that's a huge part of it…but there's also something more primal at work. Now I think the main reason people believe in God is because they want to believe in something bigger than themselves."

"Sounds like an inferiority complex," I interjected, then winced when I realized how smug I sounded.

Jeremiah shrugged and said, "Maybe. But what I'm getting at is, since I don't really believe in myself, then I need *something* to believe in. Communism was that something for a while, but it wasn't enough. I wish it was. Thoughts of Kerala made me happy, even though I knew deep down that it was just a pipe dream. Kerala isn't some magical utopia. Sure, it's better than a lot of places in the world, and I hope it continues to thrive, but that's only temporary. Everything is, except one thing: the hereafter. Is it real? I have my doubts…but if that's where my dad is, then that's where I'm going. And if it *is* real, then I'm pretty sure that my dad isn't in some paradise, because people who kill themselves don't get that luxury. Not according to God's laws. That's why I'm following in my dad's footsteps. I'm willing to risk my life for something that may not even be real, and you know why? Because my dad is worth it. And also to ensure that my mom never has to clean other people's shit again." He suddenly looked at me with a penetrating stare. "Do you remember when you asked me about my dad a while back, and I told you that I only remembered him in fragments? I was lying through my teeth. The truth is, I remember every wrinkle on his face, every vein on his rugged hands—and if I saw him right now, I'd revert to a sniveling little kid."

Jeremiah, his face softening, looked like he was about to cry. However, as if suddenly void of any emotion, he shook his head and went back to eating. It was a rapid shift in feeling, or rather a lack thereof, that one would expect from an android.

I took a sip of my drink, then, after a moment of silence, said to Jeremiah, "We still haven't talked about the Todd House."

"What's there to talk about?" he replied, then chuckled and nodded. "Oh—right, the ritual dance. I had a feeling that would shake you up a bit. I even told Dr. Jeunet. But don't think I didn't notice the smile on your face."

"That wasn't a smile. That was…something else." (Jeremiah looked at me as if waiting for me to elaborate.) "I got caught up in the moment, you know? With the music and the dancing…and *you* sitting beside me—with your scent. It was all too much. I felt like my heart was going to cave in, but in a good way. In that moment, with everything going on, I felt like I was a part of something special."

"You mean something bigger than yourself?"

I didn't want to admit it, but Jeremiah was right. That was exactly how I felt at that moment, like I was a part of something bigger than myself, something unique. And that "something" had a name: Satanism—or, more accurately, Luciferianism.

"Jeremiah," I said, almost whispering, "aren't you tired of all this?"

It was a genuine question, one that I felt obligated to ask him, for both our sakes. However, he remained silent.

"Don't you feel drained?" I asked him. "Be upfront with me now. With everything that you and I have experienced, *especially* you, don't you just want to say 'fuck it' and go back to living a normal life? Is that even an option for you anymore?" (No response.) "Jeremiah, please talk to me. Tell me to go fuck myself, anything."

"Tomorrow," he finally replied, pausing to clear his throat, "when we go into the city with Dr. Jeunet and meet others like him—like *us*—that feeling you had at the Todd House will return, maybe even stronger this time. Remember what I told you a while back? Human beings are social creatures. We thrive on collectivism."

I stared at him, realizing, with sadness, how enraptured he had become with his newfound philosophy, and that if I wanted to remain in his life, I had to climb through the same looking glass as him.

CHAPTER TWENTY-FIVE

Before the start of class, Van Orton called Jeremiah and me to his desk and told us to report to Dr. Jeunet's office. He then added, looking at Jeremiah, "I won't be able to join you on the trip, unfortunately." Jeremiah, visibly disappointed, nodded. Van Orton turned to me and, thinking that he was going to say something, instead shook his head as if fed up with me and let out a begrudging sigh. Jeremiah looked at me and gestured to the door with a nod. *Time to go.*

When we got to Jeunet's office, the headmaster was just locking up, then turned and, upon seeing Jeremiah and me standing before him, smiled brightly.

"I thought I was going to have to fetch you two myself," he said. "Our car's waiting for us at the main quadrangle."

Outside, a white luxury sedan was parked a few feet away from the Christopher Columbus statue. The chauffeur, an aging Black man dressed in a neatly pressed tuxedo and a hat, was holding the passenger door open.

"*Merci beaucoup*," Jeunet said to the chauffeur as he entered the car.

The chauffeur then opened the back door for Jeremiah and me, and we thanked him as we got in. There was an assortment of candy bars, everything from Butterfinger to PayDay to Turkish Taffy, laid out in the backseat. Jeremiah grabbed a candy bar and offered it to me, but I shook my head.

"Try not to make a mess back there," Jeunet said, presumably to both of us. He then turned to the chauffeur and told him, "Take us to the Frick."

I looked out the car window, lost in thought, as we began the hour-and-a-half-long drive to the city. I'd been to the city at least a dozen times before; however, I hadn't gone back there since 9/11. While gazing out the window, watching the landscape change from rural to urban, I thought about my last trip to the city, when my father took my mother

176

and me to see a revival of *One Flew Over the Cuckoo's Nest* on Broadway. I didn't think I'd enjoy watching a two-hour-plus play, but to my surprise, I found myself easily enthralled by the production, what with the lighting and sets, and also because the lead character was portrayed by Gary Sinise, whom I remembered as Lt. Dan from *Forrest Gump*.

After the play, we went to an old-fashioned soda shop and ate hot fudge sundaes. My father had planned for us to go to Central Park afterward, but I ended up getting sick from the ice cream, so we cut the trip short. "This is what happens when I try to do something nice for you," my father scolded me during the car ride home. I hadn't seen or even thought about the Twin Towers during the short trip, but never in a million years would I have thought that the next time I went to the city the towers would be gone. Now it seemed like they were never there to begin with.

My thoughts eventually turned to the "special people" that Jeunet was keen on introducing me to. Based on the many horror movies I'd seen, I imagined a coven of devil-worshippers, mostly nobles, kneeling in a circle around an altar dedicated to Satan. I also imagined the coven's leader, dressed in a red hooded cloak, performing a Black Mass in a dingy dungeon surrounded by naked women. At times I imagined the coven's leader being Jeunet; in other moments it was Van Orton, or even Jeremiah. The locale would also change, from a dungeon to an abandoned church to, oddly enough, the basement of a pizzeria. None of this frightened me, however, because I had Jeremiah by my side, and if he was willing to go along for the ride, then so was I. With enough time, maybe I, too, would come to accept Luciferianism. After all, I'd embraced Communism easily enough. I could do it again.

I had no idea that when Jeunet told his chauffeur to "take us to the Frick," he was referring to a posh art museum on the Upper East Side called the Frick Collection, which features Old Master paintings and various decorative arts, including antique French furniture, Oriental rugs, and works of porcelain. As we walked around the museum, which seemed eerily devoid of patrons, a spirited Jeunet informed Jeremiah and me that the building—once a Gilded Age mansion—was turned into an art museum after the death of its owner, the American industrialist Henry Clay Frick, who had bequeathed his immense art collection, as well as his residence, to the public.

"They say art is subjective," Jeunet spoke with aplomb, clutching his trusted walking stick as he strolled, "but they don't elaborate on just how 'subjective' art truly is. If Vladimir Nabokov's *Lolita* is the greatest work of art of the twentieth century, which I personally believe to be the case, then the greatest work of art of the twenty-first century, so far, has to be the September 11 attacks. Whereas Michelangelo, with the aid of scaffolds and multiple assistants, spent four laborious years completing the Sistine Chapel, the September 11 attacks were accomplished in less than two hours on a crisp autumn morning—and all it took was nineteen men with box cutters. With that in mind, who's to say what's *art*? String quartets played beautiful music at Nazi death camps while victims were being marched to the gas chambers. Is that art or murder? That brings up another interesting question: Does genocide constitute 'art'? Or is art simply that which we find pleasing to the eye? But then we must ask, *whose* eye? Just because I find something to be beautiful doesn't mean that everyone else shares my sentiments. For example, I think Mozart's 'Requiem' is the most exquisite piece of music ever written. My wife, on the other hand, compares Mozart's Requiem Mass to the braying of a donkey. Now, does that mean my wife is an uncultured philistine? Perhaps. But it can also mean that she simply finds the music to be dreadful."

Jeunet suddenly stopped to look at a portrait of a man dressed in military regalia from what I presumed was the Renaissance period. The man stares at the viewer with a fierce gaze, hands on his hips, with a sword at his side and a steel helmet at his feet. Jeremiah and I looked at the painting as if instructed to do so.

"Boys," Jeunet said, still looking at the painting, "I'd like you to meet Vincenzo Anastagi, courtesy of El Greco. *Monsieur* Anastagi was a Knight of Malta who heroically defended the island during the massive Ottoman siege of 1565, in which barely 9,000 defenders withstood an onslaught against 40,000 Ottomans...many of whom were slain by Anastagi himself." He smiled and added, "There was an infamous moment during the battle when the Ottoman commander, having captured hundreds of Christian knights, ordered their decapitation, with their bodies sent floating across the bay on mock crucifixes. In return, the Grand Master of the Knights Hospitaller beheaded all of his Ottoman prisoners, loaded their heads into cannons, and fired them into the Turkish camp." Jeunet let out a hearty laugh. "Indeed, that's the kind of brotherly love expressed between Christians and Muslims that makes God smile with pride."

"So what makes Anastagi so special?" Jeremiah asked brazenly. "He sounds like a typical European military man."

"Upon first glance," Jeunet replied, "he certainly comes off that way. But what the history books don't tell you is that, just two years prior to joining the Knights of Malta, *Monsieur* Anastagi had seen a vision of Lucifer while on the battlefield, asking him to join the Light-Bringer's growing army. Anastagi, overwhelmed by the vision, fell to his knees and pledged to follow the fallen angel into battle against God in the 'Second War in Heaven,' a looming battle that receives no mention whatsoever in either the Bible or the Quran. But rest assured that it's coming, and oh when it does, the army of Lucifer will prevail against the unjust creator known as 'God,' who will ultimately be thrown into a lake of boiling hot semen. Christians and Muslims both believe that God will come out victorious. But what they don't know is that Lucifer plans to ignite the Second War in Heaven just before the Second Coming, thus giving the Light-Bringer free rein over Earth's inhabitants. I can hardly contain my excitement at the thought of that wretched, unholy creator finally receiving His comeuppance."

I looked at Jeremiah to see if he was buying any of what Jeunet was saying, believing that he might finally come to his senses about this whole Luciferian situation, and perhaps I would too. To my surprise, however, Jeremiah appeared genuinely intrigued by what the zealous headmaster had to say. I was a little disappointed, but at the same time, against my better judgment, I thought there might be some truth to what Jeunet was saying. After all, I reasoned, there was absolutely no way that Jeunet, the headmaster of one of the most distinguished boys' private schools in the state, would go to such extraordinary lengths to deceive two sophomore students, all for his own personal amusement. I couldn't imagine anyone, except maybe a lunatic, attempting such a prank. Neither I nor Jeremiah was worth the effort of such an elaborate hoax, especially me. Considering all that, there just *had* to be some truth to what Jeunet was saying, because the alternative—that Jeremiah and I were simply being duped by a deranged headmaster—seemed beyond far-fetched.

"What makes you think Lucifer will win?" I asked Jeunet.

"My boy," he said with a smile, "if I were to tell you just how unevenly matched the armies of God and Lucifer are, you would laugh to the point of tears. All the tens of thousands of soldiers who died in the Great Siege of Malta went to Hell. Not a single Turk or Christian reached the gates of Heaven. In fact, no one who has ever died fighting in the name of the God of Abraham, neither the Crusaders nor the militant jihadists, has stepped foot in God's corrupt paradise. Rather, every single one of those poor souls ended up in Hell, where Lucifer, being the benevolent ruler that he is, assured them that no harm would come to them, so long as they joined his army. One might say that Heaven is nearly empty, because most souls reside in Hell. But don't think of 'Hell' as a place of fiery torment. That's utter propaganda. If you want to know what Hell really looks like, imagine the Library of Alexandria infused with the spirit of Al-Andalus, or 'Muslim Spain.' That, my dear boy, is the *real* Hell, and no one there is punished except those who oppose Lucifer."

I was struck by how convincing Jeunet's argument was, so much so that I felt myself being swayed to the "dark side," as it were. However, the headmaster made it quite clear that Hell wasn't a place of darkness, but rather a sanctuary. Although I wasn't entirely converted, I could certainly see the appeal of Luciferianism, which wasn't a particularly big leap for me, since the Luciferian seeds had already been planted years ago thanks to Father Hawkins and his insistence on telling a bunch of sixth-grade boys a most remarkable story.

As we continued our walk around the museum, we made our way to the building's opulent, glass-domed garden, featuring a sunken pool and fountain in the center.

"You know," Jeunet said, taking in the garden's beauty, "as pigheaded and insufferable as many Americans are, I do have to give the Yankees credit for their ingenuity, as well as their rare moments of elegance, like this garden. In fact, this museum is a testament to the splendid work the United States is capable of, despite its national motto being 'In Ignorance We Trust,' which many Americans have taken to heart."

Jeunet sat down on a stone bench, holding his walking stick with both hands, on which he rested his chin. "Without meaning to sound like an alarmist," he continued, gazing thoughtfully at the fountain, "I firmly believe that Asia is rising against the United States, and I must admit that I look forward to America being demoted to an inferior class. Many people around the world have gotten fed up with Americans pretending like they're still living in the Wild West, convinced that their actions have zero consequences. Take the infamous 'music festival' that occurred in our very own upstate New York just four years ago—Woodstock '99. Instead of promoting peace and love, the Yankees, mimicking the Barbarians who had sacked Rome, decided to tarnish the last shred of nobility they had left by engaging in an orgy of unmitigated destruction and sexual depravity. What a sad sight. I just hope that when America is finally brought down to its knees by a greater power, possibly China—I sincerely hope that the Yankees, like the Moors of Spain, will have the decency to exit the world stage with some dignity." Jeunet suddenly looked at me and, smiling, said, "Your Communism might prevail after all, *Monsieur* Quell. That must make you happy."

I glanced at Jeremiah, who was standing on the other side of the fountain, looking on almost absent-mindedly, like he was there in body but not in spirit. I then turned to the seated Jeunet, who was staring at me with pensive eyes, and simply said, "Sure."

CHAPTER TWENTY-SIX

After leaving the art museum, we walked about five blocks to a large Renaissance Revival apartment building, while Jeunet's chauffeur waited in the car outside the Frick Collection. When Jeremiah asked Jeunet why didn't we just drive to the apartment, the headmaster replied, "I find it critical that my chauffeur remain in the dark about some things, like this apartment."

We took the elevator up to the seventh floor of the building, whose walls were sporadically covered with Impressionist paintings. Jeunet knocked on the door to Room 237, located at the far end of the long hallway, Jeremiah and I standing on opposite sides of him as if we were his personal bodyguards. I should've been nervous, since I wasn't sure what to expect. But I was surprisingly calm.

The apartment door opened, revealing a thirtysomething man in a white bathrobe, wearing black silk pajama bottoms, with a dress shirt and tie underneath. I looked down at his feet and saw that he was wearing socks—but no shoes. The man, smiling, checked to make sure that his cotton bathrobe (designed with a sash that was tied in a bow) was fastened securely, then folded his hands over his stomach and eyed Jeremiah and me.

"Which one is the 'offering'?" he asked, eyes darting back and forth between Jeremiah and me, still smiling.

"The Algerian, of course," Jeunet replied, placing a hand on Jeremiah's shoulder. "Do you even have to ask?"

"I suppose not. Come on in, gentlemen."

We entered the apartment, with Jeunet leading the way, and the bathrobe man, who hadn't bothered to introduce himself, trailing us. The spacious apartment featured high ceilings and pine wood paneling, as well as lavish furniture and chandeliers that looked like they were pulled straight from seventeenth-century France. As we made our way to the living room, which featured Rococo-inspired tapestries and ceramics, I saw a group of four men and one woman—mostly white, with one Asian man, ranging in age from thirty to seventy—lounging around, some with drinks in their hands. It wasn't until Jeunet went to greet one of the men that I noticed a Hispanic-looking boy of about twelve sitting on the floor, cross-legged, playing a Game Boy. He suddenly looked at me as if noticing that I was gawking at him, and I could see that his lips were smeared with what looked like pink lipstick and Cheetos residue, which struck me as not only odd but startling.

Jeremiah and I exchanged looks. But whereas I was put off, Jeremiah, who had also noticed the young boy, seemed rather amused, as if he'd seen similarly bizarre things before, and was thus no longer unsettled by such sights.

"Is that the man of the hour?" an old man, the oldest person in the room, bellowed. He was standing by the Gothic-style fireplace with a bright smile on his face.

"That's him," Jeunet said proudly, standing beside the old man. "Jeremiah, come and meet *Monsieur* Perot. He owns this lovely apartment."

"And half of Manhattan!" the bathrobe man interjected, eliciting a big laugh.

Jeremiah walked over to the old man, who, after giving him a once-over as if examining a new car, placed his hands on Jeremiah's shoulders and looked directly into his eyes. "Mr. Kateb, you will be rewarded beyond your dreams. Although no one on Earth will know of your immense sacrifice, I tell you with all sincerity—your name will carry more weight in the hereafter than that of Napoleon Bonaparte. Remember, this senseless journey we call 'life' is only temporary, but the hereafter is forever, and it's there where you will leave your mark. Some will curse your name for what you've become, while many others will revere you. If you're as special as Dr. Jeunet claims you are, and I believe you *are*, then I swear to you that God will gnash His teeth in rage for having failed to obtain you. And what a blessing it is that you've decided to join the righteous side, instead of kowtowing to a tyrannical creator. You are a treasure trove of vengeance."

Perot gently grabbed Jeremiah's left hand and kissed the back of it, then gave him a pat on the cheek, smiling. Jeremiah walked back over to me, his face showing no expression. I was about to ask him if he was feeling all right, when suddenly Perot's bellowing voice cut through the room: "Where's that son of a gun Milo? I haven't seen him in months!" He turned to Jeunet. "Marc, what have you done with him?"

"It seems that *Monsieur* Van Orton has, uh…" Jeunet, rather afflicted, glanced at Jeremiah before continuing to speak. "He's become a little overprotective of our golden boy and needs time to clear his head. But I'm sure he'll come to see things more clearly when the Rais Frolic arrives, or so I hope. The event will still take place in the first week of December, shortly after our students have returned from their Thanksgiving break. Should be fun."

The sole woman in the room, rising from a seated position, held up her drink toward Jeunet and said, "To the House of Montmorency!"

"May their reign continue for another thousand years!" Perot cheered.

"And to Naberius, the Lord of Lords!" the Asian man cried, gazing heavenward. "We serve you unconditionally, now and for all time!"

"Hail Lord Naberius!" they all cheered in unison—all except Jeremiah, the young boy, and me. It was a profoundly surreal moment, one that would've caused me to feel unnerved under most circumstances. But at that moment, all I could think was, *Who's Naberius?* I'd heard the esoteric name once before—at the Todd House. However, much like "Chronovisor," the name remained a mystery to me.

After a long silence (it almost seemed as if the adult occupants were in a state of prayer or meditation), I gathered up the courage to ask, "W—who exactly is Naberius?"

Everyone, except the young boy, turned to me.

"I don't believe you've had the pleasure of meeting *Monsieur* Quell," Jeunet said to Perot, smiling. "Sean," he called to me.

I walked over to Jeunet, who caressed my head as if I were an obedient canine, or a hospice patient. "Although he may not look like it, this boy here is a destroying angel. Boxing trainer Cus D'Amato had once said of his most prominent protégé Mike Tyson, 'I am going to do everything to coddle him, to protect him, to develop him, because he is my revenge on the world.' That's how I feel about Sean here. Mark my words, *Monsieur* Perot, this boy will accomplish what few in our circle have achieved, namely, to make God anguish over having created the human race."

Perot, his interest sparked, stared at me with curiosity, then took a step toward me and said, rather sneeringly, "A destroying angel, huh? You look like a pussycat to me."

"A pussycat who fucks hard," Jeremiah interjected, to the amusement of (almost) everyone in the room, especially Perot, who chuckled in delight.

I glared at Jeremiah from across the room, but he just shrugged as if to say, "You know it's true."

I suddenly felt a hand on my shoulder and turned to see Perot looking at me with a honeyed smile. "Perhaps Dr. Jeunet is right about you. I guess we'll just have to wait and see. Now…as for your inquiry about Naberius, I must say, young man, I'm a little surprised that you haven't already been informed of our valiant Lord." He turned to Jeunet. "Tsk, tsk, tsk. You haven't been shirking your duties, have you, Marc? If this boy is truly special, then you must cultivate him."

Before Jeunet could respond, the bathrobe man made a beeline toward me, almost bumping into Jeunet in the process.

"I'll speak to the boy," the bathrobe man said to Perot, and took me by the wrist. "We can talk privately in the Lord's room next door," he told me.

An uncomfortable Jeunet grabbed the bathrobe man's arm and, shaking his head, said, in a grave tone, "Marvin—no."

"It's all right, Marc," Perot assured him. "Let them speak in private." He then turned to the bathrobe man (Marvin) and said, "Just *speak* to the boy."

Marvin nodded, and off we went to the adjacent room, or "the Lord's room," which was a bedroom decorated in the style of an old opium den, not unlike the one seen in the film *Once Upon a Time in America*. On the wall opposite the bed hung an ink drawing of an anthropomorphic three-headed dog with the legs of a raven, dressed in the garb of an Enlightenment-era aristocrat. Marvin, closing the door behind him, walked over and stood next to me, looking at the drawing. I glanced at him, then turned back to the drawing.

"Well," Marvin said, still looking at the drawing, "you wanted to know who Naberius was. That's him right there. Are you satisfied with our Lord?"

I examined the bizarre portrait. But the more I looked at it, the more confounded I became.

I turned to Marvin and said, "Who is he? I mean, like…*what* is he?"

"According to *The Lesser Key of Solomon*, an anonymously authored book on demonology from the mid-seventeenth century, Naberius is one of the marquises of Hell, with nineteen legions of demons under his command. He is believed to be the most majestic of all the marquises, with a specialty in the arts, in particular rhetoric. Lord Naberius possesses the ability to restore lost honors and dignities, and teaches the art of gracious living. He began life as an angel and shared a special bond with Lucifer, soon becoming one of his most ardent followers. When Lucifer was cast out of Heaven for his so-called 'arrogance,' his followers, including Lord Naberius, were also banished. Lucifer's supreme followers are each classified as either a King, Duke, Prince, Marquis, President, Count, or Knight. Now then…let's see if you've been paying attention. Which classification does Lord Naberius fall under?"

I thought briefly, then said, "Marquis…right?"

"That's correct," Marvin replied with a smile. "And don't be alarmed by the word 'demon.' It's just another word for 'intellectual,' which is exactly what Lord Naberius is."

"But does he actually exist?"

Marvin chuckled a bit. "You'd break Dr. Jeunet's heart if he heard you talking like that. I used to be his apprentice, you know, before Milo usurped me. He was younger and better-looking than me, so it was only a matter of time. But now it looks like *you* might be the one to usurp *him*. Let me guess, you have no idea what the hell I'm talking about. Don't worry, you will soon enough. The good headmaster has his claws dug into you, and he won't let go until he gets what he wants. I know from experience. I used to be his little 'fuck-boy' back when I attended Magnolia." Marvin caressed my cheek, then said, "Have you two done the mambo yet?"

He tried to caress my cheek again, but I jerked my head away in disgust and told him, "No. I don't do that stuff—not with him."

"But you *have* done it before, yes? Maybe with the golden boy out there."

"That's…different."

"Of course it is—because you, what, 'love' him?" Marvin cackled. "To be young and naïve again. I stopped believing in love when Dr. Jeunet took me to the Todd House one night and fucked me so hard that

I blacked out and woke up with a broken pelvis. I had blood in my stool for a week after that. I was thirteen, by the way, the age at which Lucifer rebelled against God…supposedly. Take it from me, don't put too much stock in 'love.' No other word in the entire English language, not even 'sex,' has endured the abuse that 'love' has. The four-letter word drifts from one's mouth to God's ears and directly to my anus. Women parade the word as if they have ownership over it, although why anyone would want to lay claim to such a repugnant word is beyond me. If this thing we call 'love' truly exists, I'm quite certain that it is now buried somewhere deep within the bowels of the Atlantic Ocean, alongside Atlantis, where it rightly belongs. I fucking pray it never rises to the surface."

His words echoed in my head: love, blacked out, broken pelvis, Lucifer, the Atlantic Ocean. But the two words that stuck out the most to me were "Todd House."

"Students aren't allowed at the Todd House," I said, rather awkwardly, as if unsure of what I was saying.

"Come now. I'm sure you've been there. And I definitely know the golden boy has, because the good headmaster told me so. It's an awful privilege to be allowed inside the Todd House—and I do mean 'awful.' What kind of shenanigans have you and Dr. Jeunet been up to over there? Has Milo been at the house with you?"

I paused. "I've only been there once. And I already told you, I don't do shit with Dr. Jeunet, or *any* adult."

Marvin, hiding a smile, nodded, clearly not believing me (not that I cared). He then walked to the bedside cabinet, opened it, and took out a porcelain music box, then sat on the bed and patted the bed to join him. I hesitated, thinking it'd be best to simply leave the room. But I couldn't bring myself to just walk out. Not because it seemed "rude," but rather because I was genuinely curious about the music box. I walked to the bed and sat down beside Marvin, who was holding the music box with both hands, staring at it as if it were the Holy Grail, and caressing it lovingly.

"What's in the box?" I asked. It was a silly question, since I figured there was an automatic musical instrument in the box. But I felt obligated to ask anyway.

"A sweet melody," Marvin replied, smiling sadly. "Has Dr. Jeunet mentioned a boy named Chandler Faust to you, by any chance?"

I was taken aback by the question, as I didn't think he knew about Chandler Faust. After a moment, I said, "Yeah. Well…sort of."

"Chandler and I went to Magnolia together back in the Eighties. He was smart, but kind of a troublemaker. Sadly, he came from a broken home."

"A broken home?"

"Yeah. His dad left the family when he was only seven, and his mom was a junkie. But the good headmaster gave him a scholarship. He'd seen Chandler at an arcade one afternoon and talked to him for a while and decided to give him a scholarship right then and there." Marvin, shaking his head, let out a solemn laugh. "He was obviously smitten with the boy. The good headmaster would often go to local arcades to 'fish for boys,' as he described it. And Jeunet caught himself a big fish when he met Chandler Faust. The fact that he came from a broken home was perfect, because that meant if anything should happen to poor Chandler, nobody would care—not the police, least of all his junkie mom." Marvin turned to me. "Let me ask you something: Does the golden boy out there come from a broken home?" (I didn't respond.) "Then again, it doesn't matter, since he's a Brown kid."

"What does that mean?" I asked.

Marvin chuckled incredulously, then said, "When poor people and non-whites go missing, nobody cares. Thousands of Black children go missing every year, and nobody bats an eye."

"Was Chandler Black?"

"No, but he was poor, and that was enough. Being poor, especially in America, is a death sentence."

I paused. "Why are you telling me all this? I mean…why did you bring up Chandler Faust?"

"Don't you want to meet him?"

"You mean Chandler?"

Marvin looked at the music box, then, after a moment, carefully opened it. I looked inside the box and, instead of a musical instrument, saw what looked like ashes. There was also a black-and-white photograph attached to the hinged lid. Marvin removed the picture and handed it to me. The picture showed a teenage boy, thirteen or fourteen, smoking a cigarette while gazing into the camera. He had a soft face and dark blond hair, with a small hoop earring in his left ear. In a way, he looked like a young James Dean, but with a snarl. Although I'd never seen him before, I knew who the boy in the picture was. It was none other than Chandler Faust.

I handed the photograph back to Marvin, who put it back in the box, and examined what I could only assume—though I hoped to be mistaken—were the remains of Chandler Faust. Marvin, as if reading my mind, said suddenly, "These are the ashes of, to paraphrase the great Christopher Marlowe, the boy who launched a thousand ships…and, for a brief time, my chapel partner, whom I loved just as you 'love' the golden boy." He looked at me. "I imagine you believe that Mr. Kateb is special, a god among plebeians. I felt the same way about Chandler Faust. Until I didn't."

Marvin stared at Chandler's ashes for a while, then closed the music box that produced no music. It was essentially an urn; however, by placing Chandler's remains in a music box, Marvin was able to make believe, for his own peace of mind, that the spirit of his deceased friend, or rather lover, had transferred into a decorative art piece. It was better than building a shrine.

After what seemed like hours of silence, I got up and headed toward the door. Suddenly, I heard Marvin say, "Hold on a sec." I turned around and saw Marvin, now standing, reaching under the bed, as if scavenging for something he'd misplaced. To my shock, he retrieved a handgun, then started to walk toward me. My brain was telling me to get the hell out of there, but I couldn't move, as my feet seemed cemented to the floor. Marvin stood inches from my face and held up the gun, like he wanted me to inspect it. It was a small, white-framed handgun that I'd seen in movies many times before.

"This is a Glock," Marvin told me. "It holds six rounds, 9mm. Most Glocks can hold up to seventeen rounds, but this is a pocket-sized Glock, making it easily concealable. It's a nice pocket rocket." He handed me the gun. "It doesn't have a traditional on-off safety lever, so if you tuck it into your pants, try not to sneeze, or you'll blow your balls off."

I'd never held a gun before, but I liked the feeling it gave me, like I had power—the power to persuade, to take a life, including my own.

Marvin, as if sensing the authoritative feeling the weapon gave me, smirked and said, "You must feel like Billy the Kid with that gun in your hand, huh? Don't let it go to your head, though. It's only a tool. How you decide to *use* that tool is entirely up to you. The Rais Frolic is just around the corner, and who knows what can happen in a weekend at Dr. Jeunet's secluded country house on Long Island." He paused briefly, then added, "The gun has three rounds in it, and if you decide to use it—and I have no doubt that you will—do so with extreme prejudice."

CHAPTER TWENTY-SEVEN

Although it wasn't my initial intention, I spent the next month—a month I've since dubbed the "Great Leap Forward"—living a kind of hermetic life, as if suddenly compelled to imitate the life of Saint Anthony. Instead of seeking refuge in the Egyptian desert, however, I retreated to the Adriance Memorial Library, just as I had done during my week-long mock suspension.

The reason for this self-exile was twofold. Firstly, Jeremiah, evidently under pressure from Van Orton, had distanced himself from me, and to such an extent that I wasn't sure anymore if we were still friends. The second reason was that the school's Thanksgiving break had been extended from five to ten days, thus cutting me off from the one place where I had some remnants of a social life.

As before, for the sake of brevity, though with less precision (due to a lack of memory and not for the purpose of deception), I will chronicle my "Great Leap Forward" in epistolary form. It was a month of immense learning and intellectual curiosity.

November 10, 2003

Jeremiah wanted nothing to do with me in class. I stopped him in the hallway during lunch hour, and he told me that it would be "easier for both of us" if we didn't speak again—that is, not until the Rais Frolic.

"What do you mean?" I asked him.

"Just trust me," he replied.

I looked at him with a mixture of hurt and disappointment. He must've thought I was trying to guilt-trip him, because he rolled his eyes in exasperation, then told me, "Listen, there's nothing left for us to talk about. You've already been to the Todd House and talked to Dr. Jeunet and went to the city to meet the others. I've honestly told you everything you need to know, so if you're *still* confused, then you're either lying to yourself, or you're just too dense to get it."

I wanted to tell him about the gun that Marvin had given me, which I'd hidden in my closet under a pile of clothes. But something told me that Jeremiah wasn't meant to know about it. I was also afraid that if I told Jeremiah about the gun, he'd possibly tell Jeunet or Van Orton. *His loyalties lie with them now*, I thought wistfully, *not with me.*

"Did Mr. Van Orton tell you to stay away from me?" I asked Jeremiah, who didn't respond. "Can you at least tell me…what is 'Chronovisor'?"

Jeremiah remained silent.

"Come on," I said. "You *know* what it is, so just tell me."

"The only thing I'm going to tell you," Jeremiah said, "is that the Chronovisor is the reason why it was so fucking easy for them to convert me."

I didn't bother to ask who "them" was, since it was obvious to whom he was referring, and I didn't want to hear their names.

November 15, 2003

While browsing through the religion section of the Adriance Memorial Library, which I'd been going to almost every day for the past week, I came across a book on the correlation between Communism and religion, in particular Christianity. It was through this book that I discovered the League of the Just, a Christian Communist organization founded in 1836 (twelve years before the publication of *The Communist Manifesto*) and headquartered in Paris, later London. The religious and political organization, which consisted mostly of German emigrant artisans, aimed to establish the Kingdom of God, or the "New Jerusalem," here on Earth, based on the ideals of love of one's neighbor, equality, and justice.

Members of the group—who described themselves as "Utopian Communists"—denounced private property and money as sources of exploitation and corruption. They argued that evidence from the Bible suggests that the early Christians, including the Twelve Apostles (as described in the Acts), had established a Communist society in the years following Jesus' death. The teachings of Jesus, they argued, compel Christians to support Communism as the ideal social system.

The book also spoke of Franklin Spencer Spalding (1865-1914), an

Episcopal bishop from Utah, who advocated Christian socialism as the true teachings of the Bible and Christ, and had this to say:

> *The Christian Church exists for the sole purpose of saving the human race. So far, she has failed. But I think socialism shows her how she may succeed. It insists that men cannot be made right until the material conditions be made right. Therefore, the Church must destroy a system of society which inevitably creates and perpetuates unequal and unfair conditions of life, no doubt created by competition, or rather capitalism.*

Spalding argued that socialist principles and Christian values were one and the same, going so far as to say, "Christianity would get along better under socialism than under this individualistic form of government." He spent his life fighting against the gap between the wealthy and the poor, believing, like many Christian socialists, that capitalism was a form of idolatry rooted in the sin of greed.

About halfway through the book, I came to the blunt realization that social class, above all else, is what "defines" an individual—that is, according to society. Jeremiah knew that long before I did.

November 20, 2003

Van Orton bid the class a temporary farewell on the last day of school before Thanksgiving break. I approached Jeremiah in the hallway after class, but it was obvious that he didn't feel like talking to me. After asking him what he'd been up to and receiving no response, he finally said to me, rather desperately, "D—do you want me to suck you off in—in the bathroom?"

Rather than being aroused, I just felt sorry for him. The way his voice cracked and his lips quivered when he offered to give me a blowjob pained me. It almost made me want to cry, seeing how far Jeremiah had fallen in recent months. He might as well have been a drug addict asking me for coke. The fact that this was the same boy from whom, at one time, a mere glance would've left me paralyzed with fear seemed unimaginable.

I went to the Adriance Memorial Library after school, hoping to continue my self-education in political science, history, and religion. However, because of my disheartening interaction with Jeremiah earlier that day, which kept nagging at me for the duration of the bus ride to the library, I forwent what now seemed like trite subjects and instead grabbed a poetry book written by a man named Wilfred Owen. As profiled in the book's introduction, Owen was a British poet and soldier who wrote war poetry on the horrors of trench and gas warfare of the First World War. The notion of "war as poetry" seemed perverse to me. After all, how does one turn carnage into poetry? I was curious to find out.

Gas! GAS! Quick, boys!—An ecstasy of fumbling
Fitting the clumsy helmets just in time,
But someone still was yelling out and stumbling—
And flound'ring like a man in fire or lime.
Dim through the misty panes and thick green light,
As under a green sea, I saw him drowning.
In all my dreams before my helpless sight,
He plunges at me, guttering, choking, drowning.
If in some smothering dreams, you too could pace
Behind the wagon that we flung him in,
And watch the white eyes writhing in his face,
His hanging face, like a devil's sick of sin;
If you could hear, at every jolt, the blood
Come gargling from the froth-corrupted lungs,
Obscene as cancer, bitter as the cud
Of vile, incurable sores on innocent tongues...

November 23, 2003

My mother took my father and me to a small non-denominational church that we had never been to before. It was a "minimalist church," as my mother described it, whose stark white interior consisted of little more than plain wooden pews, a simple cross above the altar, and a single, large clear glass window, through which light streamed in, slicing across the lone cross.

As soon as the minister, a middle-aged white woman donning an outfit that resembled linen pajamas, walked to the pulpit, I heard my father say, "The fuck is this?" My mother responded by elbowing him, and I almost laughed.

I hadn't thought about Jeremiah at all that day, or the day before—until the minister began her sermon.

"With the recent death of Miss Katharine Hepburn, who embodied the human spirit, I find myself thinking a lot about the afterlife. Then again, don't we all? *Is* there a physical Heaven and Hell that await us? Is Purgatory in any of our futures, as our Catholic brethren believe? And if so, how can we be sure that God will make the right decision in His judgment of our souls? We'd hate to be someplace where we don't belong, especially for all eternity. It's a terrifying word, isn't it? *Eternity.* But…is it any more terrifying than the belief in reincarnation, which is a central tenet of the Indian religions? I know some people find the concept of reincarnation to be 'cute.' Personally, however, I find it more frightening than the idea of spending an eternity in a Bosch-like hellscape. Perhaps reincarnation is *my* version of Hell, hence why I find it so disturbing. And what about the nonbelievers? Are they correct in their assumption that death is simply an uninterrupted dreamless sleep? We all love getting into our cozy beds at night and falling into a peaceful slumber. Just not forever, maybe. In the late nineteenth century, French artist Paul Gauguin created his masterpiece, 'a philosophical work comparable to the themes of the Gospels,' in the artist's own words. *Where Do We Come From? What Are We? Where Are We Going?* Believers in the Abrahamic God claim to know the answers to the first two questions. But that last question, 'Where are we going?' That question, like Charles Darwin's 'human eye' conundrum, gives me a cold shudder."

As the minister, pausing briefly as if to recompose herself, went on with her sermon, images of Jeremiah filled my mind's eye, and soon the minister's voice faded into the void.

I imagined a crucified Jeremiah above the altar wearing a crown of thorns, his face a bloody mess. He was staring directly at me with pleading eyes.

"Sean, help me…"

Was that a voice I heard?

"Don't leave me to the wolves. You have to save me."

But how? What can I do?

"Come and lick my wounds. Quick—they're coming!"

Who? Jeremiah, tell me...

"Now, now!"

I love you—

"I told you never to say that to me again, goddamn it!"

But it's true...

"You disgust me! I should've never let you fuck me! Now I'm gonna die because of you!"

Jeremiah—no. I love you...

"Fuck you!"

No, don't say that, please...

"Fuck you! Fuck you! Fuck you! You fucking queer!"

Please, no...

My father suddenly nudged me. "What the hell's gotten into you?" he said, looking at me as if I'd struck him.

"N—nothing," I said, then looked around the church and realized that all eyes were on me. Fortunately, it was a small congregation.

Was that a voice I heard?

November 28, 2003

I spent the day after Thanksgiving at the library, burying myself in books. When my mother asked me one day why I'd been spending so much time at the library, I told her, "Because I trust books more than people." It was an off-the-cuff response, but the more I thought about it, the more reasonable it sounded.

In one of the religion books I'd read, there was a famous quote by the French Marxist writer and philosopher Jean-Paul Sartre, who wrote: "Hell is other people." I was certain Jeremiah would agree with that statement, as everyone who had ever hurt him was "other people." It was the same for me—for *everyone*. There's no greater Hell than other people. Not literature, not art, not music, not animals (though humans *are* animals), not food, not machines, not buildings. The only culprit is other people. With that, I unquestionably trust books more than people.

December 2, 2003

I hardly recognized Jeremiah when I saw him in class for the first time in almost two weeks since returning from Thanksgiving break. His eyes were sunken and his cheeks a purple hue, as if he were severely ill. His movements were slow, like he was walking underwater, and he appeared to have lost about twenty pounds. To say he was "a shell of his former self" would've been a gross understatement.

I approached Jeremiah at his desk before the start of class and asked him if he was all right. He just nodded, eyes closed, then mumbled something.

"What?" I said.

Jeremiah looked at me, smiling awkwardly, and drawled, "Fuck… they have made worms' meat of me." He let out a drunken laugh, then shooed me away with a waft of his hand.

"Jeremiah, please talk to me."

"Fetch my goat!" he shouted.

"Mr. Quell," Van Orton said suddenly, sitting behind his desk. (I turned to him.) "Have a seat."

"*Now*, my boy," Jeremiah intoned whimsically.

I sat down at my desk and wondered what the hell had happened to Jeremiah since I'd last seen him. I wasn't sure anymore if I could even call him "Jeremiah." His alluring scent remained, but everything else about him was different, including his hairdo, as he now donned a buzz cut. I didn't know how to feel about him anymore. I still loved him, I suppose, but it was all so confusing. I was grateful to him for having introduced me (in a way) to Communism, though if I'd been forced to choose between Jeremiah and Communism, I would've chosen the latter.

December 5, 2003

Jeunet had made an announcement over the PA system the day before about the Rais Frolic that was to commence on Friday, though for only "six lucky students." Besides Jeremiah and me, there were two seniors, a junior, and a freshman, none of whom I'd ever met before until that early winter day.

We boarded a Greyhound bus to Jeunet's country house in Old

Westbury, which, according to Jeunet, was an hour-and-a-half drive, depending on the traffic. All the students brought luggage, except for Jeremiah. I had Marvin's gun tucked into the back of my tweed suit-case—a thought that never left my mind, not even for a moment, during the bus ride. Although I hoped I wouldn't have to use the gun, I felt a kind of thrill knowing that I had a weapon at my disposal. I'd made sure to familiarize myself with the weapon days before by handling it in front of my bedroom mirror, like Robert De Niro in *Taxi Driver*. "You talkin' to me?"

Jeremiah and Van Orton sat next to each other at the front of the bus, with Jeremiah resting his head on the teacher's shoulder. Jeunet, accompanied by his twin nieces, sat directly behind the stocky, mid-dle-aged bus driver. Meanwhile, I sat by myself at the back of the bus, looking out the window as if deep in thought, although the only sober thought in my head (besides Marvin's gun) was Jeremiah and whether or not he would survive the weekend getaway, which was beginning to seem more like a honey trap the closer we got to our destination.

CHAPTER TWENTY-EIGHT

Jeunet's country house was a grand, all-white modernist mansion that sat on a five-acre lot in an isolated part of Old Westbury, on Long Island, with a nearby lily pond. According to Jeunet, the house, which was built in 1952, had once been the home of Salvador Dalí, who had painted his major work, *The Discovery of America by Christopher Columbus*, in that very house. The mansion, with its polished, wooden siding and horizontal windows, surrounded by towering trees, resembled an alien spacecraft that had landed in the middle of a forest.

The interior of the mansion, echoing the Todd House, featured immaculate white walls and hardwood floors, with nearly every room displaying sculptures, paintings, and drawings depicting biblical and demonic figures, like King David and Naberius, as well as historical scenes of carnage, like the sack of Rome by the Barbarians and grisly martyrdoms. The two-story house consisted of six bedrooms, four bathrooms, living room, kitchen, dining room, sunroom, recreation room, and an indoor swimming pool.

Aside from Jeunet, his nieces, Van Orton, and the students, there was another person in the house: Jeunet's personal chef, Alexander, an aging Hungarian man who spoke with a heavy accent. Alexander had arrived at the house by himself long before us, driving there in his old Yugo.

Jeunet, his nieces, and Van Orton had their own rooms, while the rest of us—that is, except for Alexander, who was told that he would have to sleep in his car—had to share a room in groups of two. Although we weren't exactly on speaking terms, Jeremiah and I, through pantomime, had decided to share a room. The bedroom, like all the bedrooms, was located on the second floor. The furnished room—equipped with a rocking chair, dresser, and cheval mirror—consisted of a single bed, so it was apparent that one of us would have to sleep on the floor.

———————

We all changed into our bathing suits and went to the swimming pool, which resembled an indoor water park, featuring two elaborate water slides, with a soaring ceiling and domed skylight above. Jeunet, his nieces, and Van Orton donned what looked like swimwear from the nineteenth century, with the men wearing a striped one-piece and the twins in bathing gowns, as if transported from the Victorian era.

Jeunet and Van Orton lounged on deck chairs, the former reading *The Paris Review*, while the twins swam with the boys in the pool. Jeremiah, donning thermal pajama bottoms cuffed at the ankles (most likely borrowed from Van Orton), was sitting at the edge of the pool, staring blankly ahead. Rather than swimming, I was simply wading in the pool, occasionally glancing at Jeremiah. I eventually approached him, but remained in the water, as I felt too awkward to get out of the pool and sit beside him—then waited for him to acknowledge me. When he didn't say anything or look in my direction, I quipped, "Nice beach shorts." He finally turned to me, expressionless, and said nothing.

I looked over at Van Orton, who was staring at Jeremiah and me, as if curious to see how our interaction would go. He eventually looked away.

I turned back to Jeremiah, who, despite not wanting to speak to me, looked like he was at least willing to *listen* to me. "You know, I went to this small church with my mom and dad during Thanksgiving break. It wasn't Catholic, though. It was one of those non-denominational churches that's super progressive—not like those corny megachurches that rob you blind. Anyway...it was probably the first time I ever actually enjoyed being in church, because the minister wasn't a total fraud. It reminded me just how positive religion can be when it *wants* to be."

Jeremiah looked at me and, after a moment, said, "Fuck, are you a religious zealot now or something?"

"No. It's nothing like that. I'm just saying...not every religious leader is Father Hawkins, you know? You just gotta wade through the mud."

"I did...and all I found was more mud, more deceit, more hypocrisy."

"I probably would've said the exact same thing until about two weeks ago," I told Jeremiah.

He scoffed. "And I thought *I* had changed."

"Didn't you go to a mosque when you lived in Algeria?" (No response.) "Well, if you did, was the, um, *imam* anything like Father Hawkins?"

Jeremiah shook his head and said, "No…we had an honorable imam. But he spent way too much time talking about the Second Coming. His sermons about the Second Coming and Judgment Day were definitely entertaining, though. Muslims believe that Jesus will return at the end of time to defeat the Antichrist and his followers, as well as to rid the world of injustice and evildoing. He will usher in a brave new world, a world of peace and justice, with himself as the leader. Jesus will rule over the world for forty years, then die a natural death and be buried in the holy city of Medina next to the Prophet Muhammad. In fact, there's an empty grave in Medina that's reserved for Jesus. However, there will be no such 'Second Coming,' I'm sad to say." He looked at me with a crooked smile. "Both Christians and Muslims will be sorely disappointed."

"You seem happy about it," I said.

"I am," Jeremiah replied.

———————————

I kept glancing at a blown-up picture that hung prominently on the wall as we all sat around the dining table, eating a savory meal (creamy pasta with grilled chicken) prepared by Alexander, who ate alone in the adjacent kitchen. The picture showed all three Culkin brothers, with Macaulay in the center, lounging in a luxury hotel room in their pajamas. It was such an unusual picture that I thought it might be a gag.

"That photograph was taken two years ago," Jeunet said, smiling at me. "And no, I wasn't the one who took the picture, but ah—I do wish I'd been in that room."

"W—why is it up there, though?" I asked. "Is it…a *statement*?"

Jeunet bellowed a laugh. "No, *Monsieur* Quell, it's not a 'statement.' I simply enjoy having art to look at while I'm eating. I find it helps with digestion. And that picture, unremarkable though it may seem, *is* an artwork." He looked at Van Orton, who was sitting across from him. "What do you think, *Monsieur* Van Orton? Do you enjoy the picture?"

Van Orton glanced at the picture, then turned to Jeunet and said, "It's shit, if you ask me."

Some of the students, as well as the twins, snickered.

"I suppose you'd prefer a more 'sophisticated' photograph," Jeunet said to Van Orton, "like a crucifix submerged in a glass tank of urine. Or perhaps Marcel Duchamp's parody of the *Mona Lisa*." He shook his head in indignation. "You know, when Duchamp drew a mustache and goatee onto a cheap postcard reproduction of the *Mona Lisa* in 1919 and called it 'art', the imbecile hadn't the faintest inkling of the irreparable damage that he was about to inflict upon Western civilization. He single-handedly invented postmodernism and, in the process, ruined Western culture, debasing all that was once held sacred. Now nothing is sacred...not even death."

I looked at Jeremiah, who was sitting beside Van Orton as if the two were joined at the hip. He hadn't touched his food, which Van Orton noticed and gave him an "encouraging" nudge, then leaned over and whispered something into his ear. Jeremiah, looking jaded, responded by shaking his head, and then planted an awkward kiss on the side of Van Orton's mouth. The teacher gently brushed him off with a pat on the hand, then looked around the table to see if anyone had witnessed the discreet kiss. I looked away so as not to suffer Van Orton's glare.

"Did you girls like the swimming pool?" Jeunet asked his nieces, who sat beside each other.

The twins smiled and nodded.

"I knew you would," Jeunet said, then turned to Van Orton. "I told the contractor I wanted the swimming pool to look like North Korea's indoor water parks. Say what you want about North Koreans, but they sure know how to build swimming pools. I visited the country just last year and was taken with its many water parks. Kim Il Sung University has an especially wonderful indoor swimming pool."

Van Orton turned in my direction, seemingly eager to pick a fight. "Yes, well...the fascist 'hermit kingdom' may be the mecca of water parks," he said, "but the country is a perfect example of everything that's wrong with Communism. While their South Korean counterparts continue to flourish, North Koreans can barely feed themselves."

"North Korea *isn't* a Communist country anymore," I interjected, taking the bait. "I thought a history teacher would know that North Korea hasn't been Communist since the mid-1970s, when they replaced Marxist-Leninist ideology with their current *Juche* ideology. And in case you didn't know, North Korea had a higher GDP than South Korea for decades after the Korean War...until they abandoned socialism for *Juche*."

Jeunet, visibly frustrated, glared at Van Orton and said, "I guess an Ivy League degree isn't worth what it used to be."

"Dr. Jeunet," Van Orton said, desperate to redeem himself, "the boy is simply regurgitating what he's read in books."

"Indeed, he is, *Monsieur* Van Orton. And might I add, he's doing a smashing job of it. Now hold your tongue for the rest of the dinner so that I may eat my meal in peace."

Van Orton stared me down from across the table, almost daring me to look away, but I held my ground and stared right back. He then leaned over to Jeremiah, though his eyes remained locked onto mine, and whispered something into his ear. Van Orton finally looked away, then rose to his feet, as did Jeremiah, and they exited the room together.

Jeunet, pretending as if Van Orton and Jeremiah hadn't just left the dining table, looked at the remaining seven people sitting around the table: the twins, four students, and me. He gave me a nod, the meaning of which was unclear, then turned to the other students, none of whom seemed particularly excited about being at Jeunet's lavish country house, despite having had a pretty good time earlier in the swimming pool. After a while, Jeunet wiped his mouth with a napkin, then got up.

"*Monsieur* Quell," he said, clutching his walking stick, "when you have finished with your meal, please join me in the sunroom. As for the rest of you, the recreation room is your playground, so have at it, though be sure to meet us in the living room in about half an hour for some after-dark entertainment and treats."

CHAPTER TWENTY-NINE

Jeunet and I sat across from each other amid the chiaroscuro of the sun-room, which seemed a lot darker than I thought it would be, although it might've only appeared that way because it was nightfall. The room was lit by a single oil lamp that sat on a rustic coffee table between Jeunet and me. If it weren't for this one light source, the room would've fallen into total darkness.

There was a round silver-plated tray on the table, upon which a big yellow envelope lay. I looked at the envelope, wondering if Jeunet had placed it there on purpose, and then examined the room with squinted eyes, though I couldn't see much because it was so dark.

"Just windows, my boy," Jeunet said suddenly to me. "And beyond that, nature. That's all there is."

"Why did you want to see me?" I asked him, after a pause.

"I really do love this house," he said, evading my question. "Many young boys have passed through here. You wouldn't believe how many. Of all the boys who have ever stepped foot in this house, my absolute favorite has to be an enchanting Salvadoran boy whose name I'd rather not say for fear that he might be listening in, the little sneak."

The only "Salvadoran boy" who came to mind was Ignacio—Jeremiah's former lover who had mysteriously vanished. I wasn't sure if Jeunet was talking about the same boy, though it made my stomach churn, nevertheless.

"He had the most charming amber eyes that I had ever seen," Jeunet continued. "Oh, those eyes could've pierced through the hardest of souls. I brought him here once, and we had quite the time together. He told me that he had lost his virginity just days prior, which, I regret to say, drove me into a jealous rage, causing me to penetrate the young boy with such unabated ferocity that one would've thought that I was trying to kill the poor boy."

Before I could respond—not that I had a response in mind for something so vulgar—Jeunet added, with a smile, "Hard to believe, right? You look at my small frame and wonder, 'How in the world can someone so feeble perform at such a high level? It's just not possible!' Well, believe it or not, I'm quite well-endowed."

Still smiling, he reached into his vest pocket and took out some Polaroid photographs, then tossed them onto the table. "Go ahead," he said, "take a look. I want you to."

Reluctantly, I grabbed the pictures and looked at them. My hands began to tremble as I saw images of boys, ranging in age from ten to sixteen, many of them naked, being subjected to sexual bondage. Some were bound, others gagged, and a few mummified with plastic wrap. Perhaps the most disturbing of all was an image of an emaciated teenage boy who was hogtied and ball-gagged, with his nipples clamped. There were over a dozen pictures, each featuring a lone boy; some white, though most were either Brown or Black. The pained looks on their faces disturbed me more than the bondage itself. The pictures fell from my hands, as I could no longer bear to look at the hideous images.

Jeunet chuckled and, after a moment, said to me, "This may be difficult for you to believe right now, but in time such images will be as commonplace to you as those of dogs and cats."

"No," I replied, shaking my head. "I'll never get used to something like that. And why did you show me those sick pictures, anyway?"

"*Monsieur* Quell, I was merely showing you your future." Jeunet swiftly held up a hand as if to offer an apology. "Don't worry…I don't mean you'll be one of the subjects in the photographs. Rather, you'll be the one inflicting pain. Perhaps the idea sickens you at the moment, but with time and guidance, you'll learn to love it. In fact, there will come a time when the idea of *not* inflicting pain will repulse you far more than those silly Polaroid pictures."

I looked down at the scattered pictures on the floor, some of which (I wasn't aware of this until that very moment) I'd crumpled before allowing them to fall from my hands. I wondered who the boys in those pictures were. Marvin? Ignacio? Chandler Faust? I didn't see Jeremiah, which I was relieved about. In fact, had I seen Jeremiah in one of those pictures, I would've had no choice but to grab Marvin's gun from my suitcase and shoot Jeunet in cold blood, then and there.

"What exactly happened to the Salvadoran boy?" I asked.

Jeunet scoffed in amusement, then replied, "I'm afraid there are some things that you will never know, *Monsieur* Quell, like the Salvadoran boy's fate, as well as the existence of that book of yours detailing Magnolia's secrets."

"It *does* exist."

"Oh? Please tell me, then, where exactly is it? I imagine you went back to the library where you first came across the elusive book."

I nodded.

"And?" Jeunet said, toying with me. "Did you find the book?" (I didn't respond.) "So…the book wasn't there, huh? I suppose that means the book never existed to begin with. Perhaps it was all just a figment of your imagination, and we know what an extraordinary imagination boys your age possess, don't we? Oh, yes, indeed."

I remained silent.

Jeunet, looking rather remorseful, let out a deep sigh, then said, "I don't want us to become enemies. Far from it. I want us to work together. You already know that I admire you, even more so than *Monsieur* Van Orton, with whom, I'm sure you've noticed, my bond has weakened thanks to the Moor's intrusion."

"The Moor?" I said, puzzled. "You mean…?"

"*Monsieur* Kateb, yes. Don't get me wrong, he's a fine boy, smart as a whip, not to mention wise beyond his years. But he's as good as secured, and tomorrow he will fulfill his duty, much to the chagrin of *Monsieur* Van Orton, who has fallen madly in love with the Moor."

"He's not the only one, you know."

Jeunet nodded and said, "I'm acutely aware that the Moor has cast a spell on both you and *Monsieur* Van Orton. But that will all become trivial in the hereafter, where, I assure you, Lucifer will be the only being you'll revere. The love that he'll show you will be worth a thousand Jeremiah Katebs, so don't give any more thought to the Moor. Just take comfort in knowing that, should you decide to spit on the cross, you will undoubtedly see *Monsieur* Kateb again, as often as you'd like, in a setting far greater than anything you can imagine. I sincerely hope that you'll join us, *Monsieur* Quell, because you would make an advantageous addition to our ever-growing family. I swear on the souls of my nieces, Heaven is made up of servants, while the kings reside in Hell.

Please, make the right decision, and all your wishes, no matter how extravagant, will come true."

I stared at Jeunet, his face a mask of trepidation and curiosity, as I thought about everything that he had just told me. However, my mind kept going back to Van Orton and how he was "madly in love" with Jeremiah, which, despite not being as devoted to him as I once was, upset me more than anything else. I knew that Van Orton (and possibly Jeunet as well) had fucked Jeremiah, the thought of which made me want to kill him, not only for desecrating Jeremiah but for brainwashing him beyond repair. Van Orton had wounded him so deeply that he was better off dead than living as an invalid, even if being dead meant possibly suffering eternal damnation.

"What does Mr. Van Orton want with Jeremiah?" I asked Jeunet. "And don't give me that 'madly in love' bullshit, because a grown man can't love a boy."

"You'd be surprised," he said with a scowl. "In any case, *Monsieur* Van Orton suffers from the delusion that he can live an unencumbered life with the Moor in the countryside, as if inhabiting a Monet painting. But that's all in his head, as he will have to hand over the Moor to Lord Naberius, who craves young flesh. I know how much the lovesick Van Orton is hurting right now, because I went through the same painful ordeal many years ago with *Monsieur* Faust."

I paused. "I've seen his ashes."

"Whose ashes?"

"Chandler Faust's," I said, thinking that Jeunet would react in shock to the revelation, but he displayed no emotion whatsoever. "Marvin showed me his ashes when you took Jeremiah and me into the city that one day. It was in a music box…"

I stopped suddenly when I saw that Jeunet, rather than looking surprised, was smiling and appeared to be on the verge of laughter.

"I apologize," he said, then put his hand over his mouth to keep himself from laughing. "I don't mean to be callous…but whatever Marvin showed you, I assure you that it wasn't *Monsieur* Faust's ashes."

I hesitated for a moment, then said, "W—why would Marvin make up something like that? It doesn't make any sense."

"Not unless you know how much Marvin resents me for taking *Monsieur* Faust away from him. Envy is definitely my favorite of the seven deadly sins, and both Marvin and I have swum in it to the point of exhaustion. You see, we both wanted Chandler Faust to ourselves, but in the end, as always, Lord Naberius was there to seize the boy while Marvin and I scuffled."

Jeunet, glaring at me as if I'd suddenly offended him, shook his head solemnly. "You think a grown man can't love a boy? Call it perverse, deranged, immoral, whatever you like. But let me tell you, the love that *Monsieur* Faust and I shared was as real and pure as any love you have ever known or read about. Jane Austen would've slashed her wrists in shame had she seen how madly in love we were. Yes, 'madly in love'— those three words that cause you to wince. Go on, wince! But don't you ever tell me that a man and a boy, two *humans*, two souls, can't fall in love, because it's been happening since the dawn of man!"

"Then *man* is broken," I said, glaring back at Jeunet.

After a reflective pause, he said, "I'm glad we finally agree on something."

Thinking that we had nothing more to discuss, I got to my feet to leave the room, but Jeunet shook his head as if to say, "Sit back down," which I did, and waited for him to speak. He glanced at the yellow envelope on the table, then looked at me with a distant, benign expression for a long moment.

"When *Monsieur* Faust was here many years ago," Jeunet spoke with discretion, "he came upon something that he shouldn't have, something very few people know about." He paused, as if conflicted. "Do you recall when I told you the story of my visit to the island of Nias?" (I nodded.) "Well, I wasn't being entirely truthful with you. The black-and-white photograph I showed you *is* authentic, and it *was* taken in the year 1915...by *me*. However, I wasn't *physically* there. That, I'm afraid, is just a tall tale I recite to amuse myself. I can't help it," he said with a soft chuckle, raising his hands as if surrendering to police. "But what I'm going to tell you now is one hundred percent factual."

I stared at him with intrigue, my heart pounding, waiting for him to tell me whatever it was that he was so discreet about divulging. There was a small part of me that didn't want to know for fear that he might tell me something that would incriminate me in some way—or would cause me to become indoctrinated like Jeremiah. But my curiosity was screaming, *Tell me!*

"Last year," Jeunet said, before briefly pausing to clear his throat, "a Vatican priest by the name of François Brune published a book detailing an incredible story involving a time machine, or, more accurately, a 'time viewer.' In his book, *Monsieur* Brune claims that a Benedictine monk named Pellegrino Ernetti had invented a device that allows one to see through time and photograph the past. Think of it as a time-traveling television, if you will, but without sound. *Monsieur* Ernetti built the complex device in the 1950s, with the help of twelve renowned scientists, including Nobel Prize-winning physicist Enrico Fermi and former Nazi aerospace engineer Wernher von Braun—names that mean little to most people, but are highly revered by those in the scientific community. The device is made of cathode rays, antennas, and mysterious metals that receive and absorb light signals on all wavelengths. Along with a massive screen and a recording apparatus that takes black-and-white pictures, the device is also equipped with a direction finder for tuning to a specific time and place. Upon its completion, *Monsieur* Ernetti and his team of scientists crowded around their creation and watched scenes from ancient times, including the assassination of Julius Caesar at the Curia of Pompey on the Ides of March, as well as a performance of *Thyestes*, a lost tragedy by the ancient Greek dramatist Euripides. *Monsieur* Ernetti claimed to have used the device to photograph Jesus as he died on the cross and kept the picture as a souvenir. The Benedictine monk called this astonishing device the *Chronovisor*, which, in his own words, 'catches echoes from days long gone that are floating in space.'" Jeunet leaned in a bit and asked me, "Would you like to see the picture of the crucified Jesus?"

I was too frightened to speak, so I simply nodded. I didn't know if what Jeunet had told me was true or not, but at that moment, I was willing to believe just about anything.

Jeunet gestured to the envelope with a nod and said, "It's right there on the table, *Monsieur* Quell. Look inside the envelope and see for yourself."

I hesitated. "I—I thought you said that Ernetti kept the picture for himself...as a souvenir."

"He did. Then he died in 1994, and now the picture is in *my* possession."

I looked at the envelope, trying to work up the courage to grab it.

I felt like Indiana Jones in the opening sequence of *Raiders of the Lost Ark*, as he attempts to retrieve the Golden Idol from a booby-trapped Peruvian temple. Finally, I reached out, ever so slowly, and grabbed the envelope. Afraid to open it, I stared at the envelope as if I possessed X-ray vision and could see its contents without needing to open it.

"Go on, *Monsieur* Quell," Jeunet said.

My hands sweaty, I opened the envelope and, with my eyes closed, reached inside and took out the photograph. I kept my eyes closed for a while, then finally opened them and found myself staring at the face of a dark-skinned man with a broad face, crudely-shaved head, and a short beard. A look of anguish streaks his face, and his eyes almost seem to be rolling back into his head, as if from sheer pain.

"This incredible story, as told by *Monsieur* Brune in his book, is in fact a *true* story," Jeunet told me as I continued to stare at the photograph. "I have seen and operated the Chronovisor myself on two occasions, the last time being in 1983—the year *Monsieur* Faust was taken away from me. The device is now buried deep within the catacombs of the Vatican City to safeguard it from falling into the wrong hands. In 1988, five years after I had last seen the Chronovisor, the Vatican decreed that 'anyone using an instrument of such characteristics would be excommunicated.' The Vatican believed that I was a 'faithful Roman Catholic,' hence why they allowed me to see and operate the Chronovisor years ago. However, after the unfortunate mishap with *Monsieur* Faust, which I won't go into, as it doesn't concern you, the Vatican had lost trust in me. Woe is me." Jeunet, bearing a sly grin, snorted bitterly and said, "Fuck them with a horse's cock anyway. I'd already gotten what I needed from them, having used the Chronovisor to witness Lucifer expose God for what He truly is—a savage."

I finally looked at Jeunet, my head aching uncontrollably, and paused for a moment before speaking. "Does everyone in the Vatican know about the Chronovisor?"

Jeunet shook his head and replied, "Absolutely not. Only a select few higher-ups are aware of its existence. Pope Pius XII was the first pope to be informed about the Chronovisor—and after witnessing the device's capabilities firsthand, forbade *Monsieur* Ernetti and his team of scientists to disclose any details about the device."

"So, then...how do *you* know so much about it?"

"I'd met and befriended *Monsieur* Ernetti in Venice in the late Seventies, and it was during a boat ride across the Grand Canal that he first told me about the Chronovisor, believing me to be trustworthy. How easily men of the cloth are deceived when you whisper the name of their whorish god into their ears. Feigning the role of a 'pious believer' is an art form, and I excel in it with such ease that I sometimes forget that I'm simply playing a role. I imagine God curses my name almost as often as he does Satan. Good—because I revel in playing His followers for the dim-witted fools that they are."

Jeunet spat on the floor as if spitting on God. I wanted to leave the room, but when I tried to get up, my legs wouldn't move. I took it to mean that I should ask Jeunet something else—but what? Then it came to me.

"Does Father Hawkins know about any of this?" I asked.

This elicited a loud cackle from Jeunet, who covered his face with his hands as if in shame. He then looked at me and said, "The old goat is a useful idiot, and nothing more."

"But he *is* a little off, right?"

"If by 'a little off' you mean he has a fondness for his altar boys that goes beyond religious worship, then you're absolutely correct. However, the fact still remains that Father Hawkins is not, nor has ever been, a member of our circle. You see, the old goat is a slave to his pig-fuck god and his mischievous ways, so attempting to convert the cleric would be a fool's errand. But here's what tickles me to no end. Father Hawkins believes that his future lies in Heaven with his God, when in fact, being the chicken plucker that he is, the old goat is destined to pass through the gates of Hell, where he will be forced to make a choice—bend the knee to Lucifer or be punished for all eternity. But just between you and me, I hope the cleric chooses the latter so that I may personally strangle him with his rosary, again and again."

Jeunet smiled and mimicked strangling Father Hawkins, then let out a roaring laugh, nearly falling off his chair. I got up and left the room, with the headmaster still laughing.

CHAPTER THIRTY

I walked around the house in a strange daze, digesting my conversation with Jeunet, which seemed almost otherworldly. However, unlike my previous conversations with him, especially the one we had in his office prior to my mock suspension, I didn't feel overwhelmed afterward, or that he had gotten into my head, even if some of what he said *did* send chills down my spine. Whatever deceptive tricks he had used to bamboozle Jeremiah weren't going to work on me. I was confident of that, now more than ever. The pictures that Jeunet had shown me were merely props, I assured myself, and I would use them to fuel my hatred toward Jeunet and Van Orton for having corrupted Jeremiah.

I made my way to the living room, where the twins and four students were watching a rock concert film featuring Talking Heads. The film was being projected onto a large screen at the front of the dimmed room. Jeremiah and Van Orton were nowhere to be seen. I stood off to the side, not wanting to be noticed, and watched the rollicking concert film for a while.

When I have nothing to say, my lips are sealed
Say something once, why say it again?
Psycho killer, qu'est-ce que c'est?
Fa-fa-fa-fa, fa-fa-fa-fa-fa, fa, better run, run...

I looked at the twins and noticed that they seemed more preoccupied with the four boys in the room than with the film. They glanced at them, then giggled and whispered to each other when one of the boys (the junior) reciprocated their glances and stuck his tongue out at them, mimicking the act of cunnilingus.

Disgusted, I left the room and went to the kitchen, where Alexander was making hot fudge sundaes and ice cream floats. He looked at me and smiled. "Hello, young man."

"Hi," I replied, and just stood there, watching him.

"These are for you and the others," Alexander said, after a moment.

"Which do you prefer, the hot fudge sundae or ice cream float?"

I sat on a stool at the counter and looked at the various desserts Alexander had made, which looked so good that I momentarily forgot about my unsettling conversation with Jeunet, as well as the creepy incident in the living room. "I like both," I told Alexander, eyeing the desserts, "but I'll take the float."

He slid a strawberry ice cream float toward me. "Thanks," I said, and took a sip. Alexander looked at me, awaiting my verdict. "It's very good." He beamed a smile, then placed the remaining desserts onto a serving tray, excused himself, and took the tray into the living room. The music of Talking Heads could faintly be heard, which I treated as ambient noise.

Alexander returned moments later, holding the tray, upon which a single hot fudge sundae rested. He looked at me and said, "I don't want to impose, but would you mind taking this dessert to Mr. Van Orton's young companion upstairs? I don't know the boy's name, but I imagine you're familiar with him, yes?"

Hearing someone refer to Jeremiah as Van Orton's "companion" made me feel sick, though Alexander was right, in a morbid way, as Jeremiah was now Van Orton's devoted companion—or *concubine*, to be precise.

"I can take it to him," I told Alexander, putting my ice cream float down, then grabbed the hot fudge sundae from the tray.

Holding the sundae with both hands (one would think the dessert held special powers from the way I was holding it), I slowly made my way upstairs, where the bedrooms were, and walked down the long, ornate hallway, whose walls were crimson red. Just as I was about to turn a corner, I heard what sounded like painful groans coming from one of the rooms. I stopped, placed a hand on the doorknob, and held it there for a moment, debating whether to open the door or simply walk away. My curiosity got the better of me, however, so I opened the door about halfway and peered inside. It took a while for my brain to register what I was seeing, but once it became clear, I wanted to pluck out my eyes. I saw a naked Jeremiah being penetrated from behind by someone donning a red cloak and Venetian carnival mask. The groans, I now realized, belonged to Jeremiah.

I stood there in a catatonic state, watching the grotesque scene, though not really believing it. The figure in the red cloak, who I pre-sumed to be Van Orton, looked like something one would see in a Gothic horror movie. No longer able to bear it, I moved away from the door as if in a deep trance and went to my room, holding the melted hot fudge sundae. I put the sundae on the dresser and crawled into bed, desperately wanting to forget what I'd seen.

I dozed off for a few minutes, or so it felt like, then opened my eyes to find a blurry figure hovering over me—and suddenly realized that the figure had jabbed a syringe into my arm. I could scarcely make out a face, though I noticed a monocle over the hazy figure's right eye, which made me believe that the figure was Jeunet. I felt an intense rush of euphoria the moment the figure had removed the syringe from my arm, then, amid the feeling of tranquility, a burning sensation surged through my body as if I were on fire. I clawed at my chest like a beast, then heard the figure, whom I was now certain was Jeunet, as I could definitively make out his prune-like face, say to me, in a gentle voice, "Don't fight it, my boy." My vision, briefly restored, went blurry again, then, as if in an instant, I fell into a hypnotic state and experienced what I can only describe as a drug-induced hallucination.

Where Do We Come From? What Are We? Where Are We Going?
Nowhere.

There was darkness, and I was free-falling into what seemed like a bottomless pit. I heard an Orthodox liturgy resembling demonic chants, but where was it coming from? I wasn't meant to know. "I don't want to be here…"

Where Do We Come From? What Are We? Where Are We Going?
Nowhere.

I found myself in a white void, naked. I was surrounded by jackals, baring their sharp teeth and growling at me. A paintbrush dipped in red paint suddenly appeared in my hand and a soothing voice told me to draw a circle on the floor around me. I did, and the jackals quickly ran off.

Where Do We Come From? What Are We? Where Are We Going?
Nowhere.

On the floor, inside the Todd House, lay the corpse of Jeremiah, with his throat slashed and a straight razor clutched in his hand. Seeing his dead body, I felt the same excruciating pain that River Phoenix must've felt when his head hit the pavement outside the Viper Room on that fateful night that took his life. I held Jeremiah in my arms and caressed his head, then kissed him on the lips and began to weep.

Where Do We Come From? What Are We? Where Are We Going?
Darkness.

"Sean," I heard Jeunet say. "Time to wake up."

CHAPTER THIRTY-ONE

I was roused from sleep by the morning light, which bathed the room in a celestial orange glow, and uncurled myself from the fetal position as if born anew. I didn't know how long I'd been asleep, though it felt like weeks, even months. I licked the roof of my mouth because it was so dry, and it almost made me gag. Sitting up in bed, I looked around the room and saw that it was empty. I was hoping to see Jeremiah sleeping on the floor, as I didn't want to believe that he was actually dead. I tried to block out the grisly image of Jeremiah with his throat slashed from ear to ear, to no avail.

I got out of bed and walked to the dresser. The hot fudge sundae was still there, albeit now completely melted into soup. I exited the room and walked down the hallway. It was eerily quiet, and I got the strange feeling that I was the only person in the house. When I got downstairs, I went from room to room, but there was no sign of life. The kitchen, sunroom, recreation room, even the swimming pool, were all uninhabited. Finally, I went to the living room, where I saw a naked man bound to a chair, with a burlap sack over his head. Sitting on the couch across the room was Jeunet, who looked at me and nodded with a soft smile, as if he were expecting me. Befuddled, I wondered if I was still hallucinating, as I was having trouble differentiating between fantasy and reality. For a moment, I truly did believe that I had lost my mind.

I started to walk toward the bound man, then stopped suddenly when I noticed a gun on the coffee table. Upon closer inspection, I realized that it was Marvin's gun, and I nearly shit my pants because I figured the gun was meant to be used against me. I had no idea how Jeunet—or anyone else—could have discovered Marvin's gun, unless he had rummaged through my suitcase while I was asleep.

I thought about running out of the house; however, because I was closer to the gun than the dwarfish Jeunet, I was confident that I could reach the weapon before him.

After a few tense moments, which seemed like hours, likely due to how oppressively silent it was, Jeunet, in a wistful tone, said to me, "You know, when the Visigoths lost Spain to the Moors in the early eighth century, a Visigoth historian lamented, 'Even if all my limbs developed tongues, I still would not be able to accurately express my grief.' I felt the same way when I lost *Monsieur* Faust, although his sacrifice served a purpose that went far beyond my carnal delights. So my loss is the world's gain. However, it will take some time before the world realizes the precious jewel it has gained."

Ignoring Jeunet's words, I turned to the bound man, who had yet to move, or make a noise, and wondered if he was dead. It certainly appeared that way.

"Never mind him," Jeunet said.

"Is—is he alive?" I asked, turning to the headmaster.

"For now," he replied. "And don't ask me who it is, because someone with your perception should already know, so don't play the fool. You can't afford it. Now focus."

I looked around the room. "But where is everyone?"

An annoyed Jeunet sighed, then said, "Gone, *Monsieur* Quell. They've all gone back home. It's Sunday, you see, which means the Rais Frolic has officially concluded…"

"Sunday?" I interjected.

"You slept through an entire day and a half, more or less. So, yes, today is Sunday. Don't be alarmed, though. I put you under for your own good, believe me."

"W—where's Jeremiah?"

Jeunet said nothing, as if he didn't hear me.

"Where's Jeremiah?" I asked again.

"I'm not sure to whom you're referring," Jeunet said, baffled.

The way he said it was so sincere that I almost believed him. "Jeremiah Kateb," I said, my voice rising. "The so-called 'Moor.' You know him, Dr. Jeunet. You've seen him, you've spoken to him. Where is he?"

Jeunet, feigning concern, shook his head in sadness and said, "*Ça alors!* The poor boy has lost his senses. Perhaps I injected him with too much. *Pauvre garçon*, what's happened?"

I paused, taken aback. "Why are you doing this?"

"Me?" Jeunet said, his expression suddenly bitter. "I'm not the one concocting stories about imaginary people. I recall you telling me about a book you'd read, or *thought* you'd read, and yet no such book exists. Now here you go again with this 'Jeremiah' person that you've concocted for reasons that are unclear to me." He sighed in distress. "I worry about you, *Monsieur* Quell. I really do. But I want to help you because I think you're worth the trouble."

"What do you mean...*help* me?" I said.

"You have a sickness in you, my boy. A sickness of the mind, ten times more deadly than any physical malady. And this sickness is called 'Communism.' There's a reason why the Spanish dictator Francisco Franco aerial bombed Guernica and initiated the White Terror, killing hundreds of thousands of Communists, socialists, liberals, intellectuals, homosexuals, Jews, and other such undesirables. It's the same reason why, from 1965 to 1966, the Indonesian government wiped out over a million Communists, leftist sympathizers, and labor unionists. The exact same reason why the United States funded death squads in Latin America to eradicate any and all Communists. Do you know the reason why, *Monsieur* Quell? It's because the right-wing monkeys, like Luciferians, know all too well just how destructive the Communist ideology can be. It's perhaps the one thing we share—a severe hatred against an ideology that draws potential followers away from us. There are no Communists in Hell, you see, except for a few impostors."

Jeunet, walking stick in hand, rose to his feet. "There are some who believe that Jesus, who had notably expelled the money changers from Herod's Temple, was in fact the first 'Communist,' and that Communism, in its purest form, is simply Christianity in practice—though only as it was practiced by the early Christians, before Constantine the Great seized the cross. Islamic socialists view the teachings of the Quran and Muhammad, in particular the *zakat*, which is a religious duty for all Muslims to give alms to the poor, as being supportive of socialism. Be that as it may, most Christians and Muslims today detest Communism and its many variants, for they have convinced themselves that the ideology is much too 'radical,' and therefore incompatible with their respective faiths." Jeunet smiled and said, "Lucifer is indebted to these pious Christians and Muslims for their backward thinking, because they have provided him with more souls than there are grains of sand on Bondi Beach."

He laughed boisterously, then walked toward me and stopped when he got close enough to feel my breath. After staring at me for a moment, biting his lower lip, he continued to speak. "The American writer Kurt Vonnegut is a big admirer of Jesus' Sermon on the Mount, believing that it sounds 'socialistic.' *Monsieur* Vonnegut has even expressed disappointment that Communism and socialism seem to be such unsavory topics for many Americans, as he believes that the ideologies offer 'beneficial substitutes to contemporary social and economic systems.' Is he right? He might very well be. But what's 'right' and what's 'necessary' are two different things. Communism is a relic of the nineteenth century. It has no place in modern society. The ideology seeks to disrupt the status quo, and that's unacceptable. Not only is it unacceptable to me, but it's also unacceptable to every man, woman, and child who aspires to one day live a life of luxury. Granted, few will obtain wealth. But no matter, because those who fail to obtain wealth were never meant to obtain it in the first place. I believe *Monsieur* Darwin's law—'survival of the fittest'—tells us as much."

Suddenly, behind me, I heard the bound man groan as if in pain. I spun around and saw the man jerking his head from side to side, trying to get the burlap sack off his head.

"He is risen," Jeunet quipped. "Go on, *Monsieur* Quell. Remove the sack from our savior's head."

I hesitated for a moment, then walked slowly over to the bound man and removed the sack from his head, revealing a shaken Van Orton, who had snot coming out of his nose. I stared at him in disbelief. The fact that he was naked only added to the surrealism of the scene, and I almost felt sorry for him, given how pathetic he looked.

"Jeunet!" he cried. "What...*is* this? Have you lost your goddamn mind?"

"This, my dear companion," Jeunet replied, "is the passing of the torch. You see, much like in the *Star Wars* universe, in which the Dark Lords of the Sith must adhere to the so-called 'Rule of Two'—that is, there can be only two Sith in existence at one time, a master and an apprentice—the same applies to Luciferianism. I never told you that before, did I, *Monsieur* Van Orton? Well, now you know. Lord Naberius himself demands that we respect this age-old decree." He suddenly looked at me and said, "*Monsieur* Quell, please grab the weapon from the table."

I remained motionless, wondering if I'd somehow been transported into an episode of *The Twilight Zone*. Jeunet sighed as if frustrated with me, then walked to the coffee table and grabbed Marvin's gun. He then walked over to me and held out the weapon, waiting for me to take it. After a few moments, realizing that I wasn't going to take the gun, Jeunet lowered the weapon, his face contorted in a pained smile, as if he weren't sure whether to laugh or scream.

"Let me explain something to you, *Monsieur* Quell," he said. "When I lock eyes on a boy I want, I *get* that boy, one way or another. And right now, regardless of how you feel about it, *you* are that boy. I assure you, it's a great privilege, even though it may not seem like it at the moment. As for *Monsieur* Van Orton, my one-time confidant who has sadly outlived his usefulness, he must perish."

"Fuck you!" Van Orton shrieked. "This isn't what we di—" He stopped suddenly, his eyes dilating as if suffering a panic attack. Then, after a paralyzing moment, he began to drift in and out of consciousness, until finally, he went unconscious, with his head slumped over. I didn't know if he was dead or alive, but he looked like a corpse.

Rattled, I looked at Jeunet and said, "I don't know what kind of game you're playing, but I don't want any part of this, OK?"

"Do not fret," he replied. "Our savior will rise once more. It's just the injection working its magic."

"I mean *all* of this. I don't want it. Please, Dr. Jeunet…"

He looked genuinely moved and gazed into my eyes with affection. "Oh, my dear boy. Say 'please' again and I will surely die."

"Dr. Jeunet, I'm *not* your apprentice, or whatever you think I am. I'm just a fucked-up kid who's still learning."

"Still learning indeed. And from here on, I'm the one who's going to teach you everything you need to know about life, the world, the entire universe. *Monsieur* Quell, are you aware that by the time you reach adulthood, our solar system will comprise of not nine but *eight* planets? Do you realize what that means? The world as we know it is changing, and you'll need my help to navigate through it." Jeunet held out the gun and said, "Now take the weapon and use it against our common adversary. Unless, of course, you'd rather wait until he comes to before killing him."

I felt like I was caught in a nightmare and had difficulty believing that what was happening at the moment was in fact *happening*.

"You want me to kill Mr. Van Orton?" I said, then shook my head in dismay.

"Don't act like you haven't thought about it, *Monsieur* Quell. You despise the good teacher just as much as I do, albeit for different reasons. I know you believe that *Monsieur* Van Orton has taken something from you. Perhaps he was the one who made the 'Jeremiah' character that you've invented go away for good. If so, it would be a terrible shame to allow the good teacher to breathe another breath."

I paused. "Why don't *you* like him anymore?"

"Because he failed to keep his promise of remaining faithful to me and our cause. Someone like that doesn't deserve to exist. I'm sure you agree."

I looked at the gun, which Jeunet was still holding out for me to take. After a while, I finally grabbed the weapon, and a jolt of anticipation ran through me, as if using the weapon against Van Orton was in some way my destiny. As much as I loathed Jeunet for his purported depravity (I had yet to witness the headmaster commit heinous acts against children, photographs notwithstanding), I despised Van Orton even more, as his crimes were indisputable. He was actively responsible for having planted seeds of corruption into Jeremiah's head. And where was Jeremiah now? Possibly dead—because of *him*.

I turned to Van Orton, who was still unconscious, and aimed the weapon at him, but didn't pull the trigger.

"There's no point in stopping now," Jeunet told me. "We both know the good teacher must die—for all he's done…to me…to *you*." After a pause, he added, "I apologize for bringing this up, but do you remember your former chapel partner, Simon Calloway? It pains me to say this, but it seems that *Monsieur* Van Orton has, on more than one occasion, taken advantage of the young boy while at the Todd House—against my wishes, of course."

Enraged, I fired at Van Orton, hitting him in the stomach. The bullet apparently acted as a kind of defibrillator, as the teacher suddenly came to with a violent rush, inhaling deeply, as if his lungs were on the verge of collapsing, then started wheezing and panting. He cried in agony when the shot to the stomach became evident.

"You have to finish him off," Jeunet said to me. "It would be cruel not to."

I took a step forward and aimed the weapon at Van Orton again.

"Go on, my dear boy. Aim for the head this time."

Hand trembling, I fired at Van Orton, hitting him in the right ear, which caused him to cry out in pain. *Fuck*, I thought, watching my once-proud teacher bleeding profusely from his stomach and mangled ear.

"Again, *Monsieur* Quell. You alone can end his suffering."

I aimed the weapon at Van Orton for a third time, though this time I pressed the gun firmly against his forehead. I squeezed the trigger and watched as his head jerked back as if experiencing a whiplash collision. I stared at his lifeless body, stunned, as blood trickled from a hole in his head the size of a grape. After a moment, I turned to Jeunet, who looked rather pleased, and then pointed the gun at him. Instead of reacting in terror like I thought he would, the headmaster simply grinned and glanced at the gun as if it were a toy.

"I'm not sure what you hope to achieve, *Monsieur* Quell," he said, looking at me, "but the weapon contained only three rounds, all of which you've fired into the good teacher. But then, you already knew that."

I lowered the gun. "So…what now?" I asked, after a pause.

"*Now*, my dear boy," Jeunet replied, placing a hand on my shoulder, "you have a decision to make, an important decision that will determine the next five to twenty years of your life. In just a moment, I'm going to pick up the telephone and call the police. When they arrive, you can either tell them that you killed *Monsieur* Van Orton in self-defense—after we've untied him, of course—or…you can tell them that the good teacher, who happened to be a 'Satanist,' along with Magnolia Academy's headmaster, had raped and killed a nonexistent student named 'Jeremiah Kateb.' And while you're at it, you can also tell the police about a time-traveling device called a 'Chronovisor' that is currently in the Vatican's possession. Oh, I'm sure the authorities would love to hear about that. So, my dear boy, which will it be? Do you want to spend five years in prison for involuntary manslaughter, or would you rather spend a minimum of fifteen to twenty years in a mental hospital for the cold-blooded murder of a beloved private school teacher?"

My first thought was to pistol-whip Jeunet for deceiving me, but I was afraid that he might have a weapon on him. I suddenly felt like crying—not out of sadness or regret but out of trembling fear. I dropped the gun and looked hard at Jeunet, refusing to allow myself to cry. I didn't want to give the bastard the satisfaction of seeing me in such a pitiful state.

"So how many years do you think I would get if I killed you, too?" I said to Jeunet, putting on my best Humphrey Bogart impression.

The headmaster chuckled. "This is why I've chosen you as my apprentice. And you can be certain that after your release from prison, or the madhouse, I'll be waiting for you at the front gate with arms wide open, ready to take you under my wing. That's right, *Monsieur* Quell. You and I are destined to be together." Jeunet took a step back and said, "Now, if you'll excuse me, I have a phone call to make."

He turned and started to walk away, then stopped suddenly and turned to face me. "Should you choose prison over the mental hospital, you might want to untie the good teacher."

Jeunet exited the room, leaving me alone with Van Orton's bullet-riddled corpse. Although I was glad, even delighted, that my former teacher was dead, I was fearful that years down the road I'd become stricken with overpowering guilt about having killed someone in cold blood. Granted, I could argue that Van Orton was a monster who "deserved" to die. But who endowed me with the godlike power to decide who lives and who dies...?

EPILOGUE

For the past seventeen and a half years, I've been an involuntary resident of Autumn Creek Hospital, a psychiatric facility for the morally destitute and criminally insane. My fate was sealed the moment I'd told the police that Jeunet and Van Orton were part of a Satanic coven and that I'd killed the latter for having sexually assaulted a friend of mine, Jeremiah Kateb, who, according to school records, never attended Magnolia Academy. Jeremiah had, in the words of Orwell, become an *unperson.*

When the police searched my bedroom and discovered a copy of Milton William Cooper's *Behold a Pale Horse*, they instantly branded me a "lunatic." I was unaware that simply owning a copy of Cooper's book was the same as owning a copy of *Mein Kampf*—at least as far as the police and, particularly, psychologists were concerned.

Dr. Marc Jeunet, I'm happy to announce, died nine years ago at the hands of a former pupil named Marvin Oppenheimer II, the same Marvin who had given me the Glock, presumably with which to kill Jeunet. According to the *Poughkeepsie Journal*, Marvin, armed with half a dozen or so Molotov cocktails, drove to the Todd House one night and hurled the incendiary weapons at the modernist glass house, where Jeunet and his twin nieces were currently residing. They were asleep at the time of the attack, and all three perished in the flames. Marvin was immediately arrested and charged with three counts of murder. He was sentenced to life in prison without parole.

I've spent much of my time here at the hospital—"12 Monkeys," as it's called by many of its residents, in reference to the 1995 science-fiction film—reading, writing, and simply reflecting on my life. My parents, who have since divorced, rarely enter my mind, least of all my father, who disowned me the moment I was admitted to Autumn Creek Hospital. I do feel sorry for my mother, however, as I'm sure she never expected that her son would end up in the madhouse.

While in the hospital, I joined a historically African-American philosophical organization known as the Five Percent Nation, or the Nation
of Gods and Earths, which, in a sense, is a more liberal offshoot of the
Nation of Islam. Founded in 1964 in Harlem by Clarence 13X, or Allah
the Father, a former minister in the Nation of Islam, members of the
Five Percent Nation (both Black and non-Black) refer to themselves as
the Five Percenters. This reflects the organization's concept that eighty-
five percent of the world's people are "dumb, deaf, and blind and ignorant of the truth," while ten percent of the people in the world are elites,
or bloodsuckers, who, despite knowing the truth of existence, choose to
keep the eighty-five percent of the world in ignorance and under their
control. The remaining five percent, known as "poor righteous teachers," are those who know the truth and are determined to enlighten the
eighty-five percent.

The Five Percent Nation teaches that Black people are the original
people of Earth, which is scientifically accurate, with regard to *Homo
sapiens* originating in Africa, and are therefore the fathers ("Gods")
and mothers ("Earths") of civilization. Allah the Father created a set
of principles known as the Supreme Mathematics and the Supreme
Alphabet as a way of helping us understand our relationship with the
universe. The Supreme Mathematics, a unique system of numerology,
is as follows:

1. Knowledge
2. Wisdom
3. Understanding
4. Culture/Freedom
5. Power
6. Equality
7. God
8. Build or Destroy
9. Born
0. Cipher

"What's today's Mathematics?" is a common question a Five
Percenter would be asked by a fellow Five Percenter. Being that today
is April 17, the response would naturally be, "Knowledge God," as we
know numeral 1 represents Knowledge and numeral 7 represents God.
If one were to say "1 + 2 = 3," an informed Five Percenter would interpret

that to mean "Knowledge plus Wisdom equals Understanding."

The Supreme Alphabet, which assigns meanings to the letters of the Latin script, is a more complex system than the Supreme Mathematics. It took me months to master it, as I not only had to learn what each letter stood for, but I also had to expound on each word. For example, the fourth letter, D, stands for Divine, which, when expounded on, means "Divine is knowledge and wisdom being understood, showing its completion and manifesting a perfect state of existence." The eighth letter, H, meaning "He or Her is the man or woman who has Knowledge of Self and is building a strong foundation." The tenth letter, J, meaning "Justice is the star (that is, your reward), regardless of whether it is one of happiness or sorrow." That's my personal favorite letter.

I was introduced to the Five Percent Nation, which defines itself as a way of life and not a religion, by an older Black man named Fard, who was admitted to the hospital for having shot and killed his mother's abusive boyfriend. In return, I reintroduced Fard, a one-time Communist in his youth, to Communism, as I've remained a devoted Communist and will remain so until my dying breath. To abandon Communism would be to submit to imperialism, racism, fascism, and Nazism and admit that Ronald Reagan and Margaret Thatcher—the most abominable union of two people since Smith & Wesson—"were right." I'd just as soon cut my own throat than give the far-right a victory lap. The way I see it, Communism *must* prevail over its far-right adversaries, if for no other reason than hubris.

"What if a country implements Communism, but then it fails?" Fard asked me during one of our many late-night conversations, which often stretched into the early morning hours.

"In that case," I replied, "the country would implement Communism again, then again and again and again, until it finally gets it right, like the people of Kerala."

"What if it takes decades?" he asked.

"It makes no difference how long it takes," I said. "Don't expect immediate perfection from a sociopolitical system...especially one as audacious as Communism."

It is only recently, however, that I've come to regard Communism as less of a sociopolitical system and more of a cultural movement. After all, I revere Pablo Picasso, Jean-Luc Godard, Diego Rivera, Frida Kahlo,

Dashiell Hammett, Tupac Shakur, and Pier Paolo Pasolini far more than I do Karl Marx or Vladimir Lenin. Politicians come and go, but artists are eternal. Which brings me to the composition of *this* book.

I began writing this book three years ago, as I felt it necessary to preserve Jeremiah Kateb's memory. The world can no longer afford to remain ignorant of this marvelous Algerian boy, whose life was tragically cut short at the tender age of fifteen. Had Jeremiah lived to adulthood, I have no doubt that he would've moved mountains and conquered cities, from Milan to Timbuktu.

With the publication of this book, I will baptize the world with the name "Jeremiah Kateb." This, dear reader, is literature as shock therapy, with a dose of Wisdom.

Spineless *puritans* need not apply.

www.ingramcontent.com/pod-product-compliance
Lightning Source LLC
Chambersburg PA
CBHW020326200626

46814CB00006BB/2436